OF

EROTIC DOMINATION

If you like one you will probably like the rest

A NEW TITLE EVERY MONTH
NOW INCLUDING EXTRA BONUS PAGES

Silver Moon Books Ltd
PO Box CR25 Leeds LS7 3TN

Silver Moon Books Inc
PO Box 1614 New York NY 10156

*Distributed to the trade throughout North America by
LPC Group, 1436 West Randolph Street, Chicago, IL 60607
(800) 826-4330*

If you like one of our books you will probably
like them all!

Write for our free 20 page booklet of extracts from
early books - surely the most erotic feebie yet - and,
if you wish to be on our confidential mailing list,
from forthcoming monthly titles as they are published:-

Silver Moon Reader Services
PO BOX CR 25 LEEDS LS7 3TN
or
PO Box 1614 NEW YORK NY 1016

or leave details on our 24hr UK answerphone
0113 287 6255

<u>New authors welcome</u>

www.silvermoon.co.uk
www.silvermoonbooks.com

<u>CONTENTS</u>

I CONFESS!
your full length new novel
by Dr Gerald Rochelle

BONUS PAGES

All this is is fiction: in real life practice safe sex

I CONFESS! by DR GERALD ROCHELLE.

CHAPTER 1

Maria looked up at the ornate ceiling of the entrance to the church to see the carving again. The woman was naked and suspended by a rope around her waist. Her long hair hung in swirls over her face and her arms reached down at full stretch as she clung desperately to her ankles. Behind her, a naked masked man wielded a cane and was bringing it down hard onto the woman's taut buttocks.

There was also a carving of another woman, blindfolded and tied by her wrists to a post, being beaten by three naked men: one with a chain, one a rope and another with a long knotted whip. Yet another depicted a woman, spread-eagled on her back and manacled to the floor by her wrists and ankles. She was being fucked while two other men forced their cocks deep into her mouth. The last woman in the series, the most realistic and therefore her favourite, clothing in tatters, hung suspended by a rope around her neck, and was being beaten across her buttocks and breasts as dogs snarled menacingly around her feet.

Maria had gazed up at these same carvings as a young girl. She had wondered what it would be like to be whipped and chained, and how it would feel to be beaten, fucked and humiliated. Often she had leant against the wall of the entrance, gazing up as she lifted her school skirt and slid her fingers down the front of her white panties. She had dribbled from the corner of her mouth as she slowly inserted her fingers between the pink folds of her young

5

cunt, and gasped with anxiety and joy as strange shivers of excitement coursed jerkily through her limbs.

Maria had been brought up a strict Catholic, and had been used to confessing as a young girl, but it had been years since she had come here to pour out her sins.

She stopped just inside the heavy oak doors, and for a few moments stood in the silence. She stared down towards the dimly lit altar. Candles flickered on the white cloth that draped it and the gold candlesticks stood up glistening with darkly etched veins mysteriously entwined around them.

She jumped as the door closed behind her with a low thud. She must be even more tensed up than she had expected.

The metal-capped heels of her shiny black shoes clicked on the stone floor as she walked over to the small wooden confession box that was built into the wall behind some towering grey columns. She paused at the closed door and peered through the lattice-work front; she could just make out the dark figure that crouched like retribution inside. Without hesitation, and falling into the old habit, she reached up and drew back the heavy red curtain that hung in velvety folds from a brass rail fixed between the side of the box and the wall.

She paused for a few seconds, just to let her eyes get used to the dim light inside, then, bending slightly, she pushed behind the dark shroud of the smooth curtain.

There was a narrow seat fixed to the side of the booth and below that, raised only a few inches from the floor, an even narrower shelf for penitents to kneel on. She knelt down as she had always done before, but the hard wood hurt her knees so she got up again and slithered onto the little seat. It was cold and she shivered. She turned her shoulders towards the grill in the side of the confession box and, as if sensitive to her presence, it slid back.

She looked through the open grill and saw the white teeth of Father Thomas, it was as if no time at all had passed since she had last crouched trembling there.

He waited in silence. She felt sure that he recognised her even after all this time and a wave of embarrassment swept over her as she wondered where to start. She squirmed her bottom around on the narrow wooden seat, tightening the muscles of her buttocks and lifting the soft flesh inside her panties away from the cold wood. But it was no good, it only felt worse, so she eased the tension in her buttocks and felt her panties press down against the smooth surface of the seat.

Maria's thick black hair was cut to shoulder length and lay tousled around her pale face. She had full lips, bright blue eyes with long lashes, and was slim and very attractive, although, as people sometimes told her, she looked too vulnerable and could have made more of herself.

She had a small delicate frame and was not very tall, but she had shapely hips which curved out from her narrow waist. She had firm thighs and her compact calves led down to slender ankles. Her feet were narrow and her carefully filed toenails were painted with the same bright red varnish as her fingernails.

She had to wear a black suit for work and her skirt was quite short. The cold wood of the seat was pressed against the bare flesh of her smoothly curved thighs as they peeped out between the flattering tops of her fine, sheer stockings and the plain edge of her white panties. She wriggled her bottom again and nervously pulled her skirt down as far as she could, but she could only get the hem halfway down her slender thighs. She wore a white shirt which was open at the neck and her jacket was buttoned up tightly around her slim waist. Her small, firm breasts were se-

7

cured snugly in the cups of a flimsy, embroidered bra. A small sewn flower just poked from the open neck of her well-ironed shirt as it nuzzled snugly between the curves of her cleavage.

Now she was sure that he recognised her, but still she could say nothing...

She had not felt tongue-tied when she was a child; then there had been so many things she seemed to do wrong that she could hardly wait to pour them out. She would wait anxiously all week to do her confession on Friday. She would write down all her sins in a little notebook then read them out carefully, one by one, to the thoughtful, shadowy figure behind the fretwork panel.

"Oh Father, what must I do to put these things right?" she would beg as she sat forward eagerly on this same hard seat with her hands clasped tightly between her legs. "I feel so dirty, so sinful, so horrible! What must I do? Oh Father, how can I be punished?"

Father Thomas would listen quietly, occasionally drawing his long fingers down his thin moustache and tugging at his pointed beard. Every now and again, when she looked through the grill, she would catch sight of his flashing white teeth and staring eyes and imagine that he was a wolf. Sometimes, she pretended that she was Red Riding Hood and that he was going to eat her and that she did not care if he did, as long as she could tell him how bad she was before he sank his pointed teeth into her neck. She tingled all over at the thought of that first bite and tingled more as she felt herself wanting to bleed for him and be sucked dry as he gnawed and slobbered at her throat.

Sometimes, as she leant forward to pour out her secrets, she thought she saw him staring at her budding breasts. It caused a dark terror to well up inside her and she trembled with fear. But it was not a fear that she wanted to run away from; it was a fear that seemed to delight and beguile her, it was a fear that she wanted more of and it forced her to lean even closer to the lattice-work grill.

In a way, she sincerely believed that she tried not to be sinful. But how could she confess if she did nothing wrong? The two things went hand-in-hand, she did not so much want to be sinful but she could not bear the idea of having nothing to confess. She wanted to be purified but she did not want to be pure, for if she was pure she would never be able to confess again. Her life was driven by this perverted desire to confess; driven by a need to be forgiven for being so sinful. Her badness was the means of acquiring purification, and as the act of purification was what she needed more than anything, she always needed to be bad.

Wrongdoing stalked her everywhere. By the time she was thirteen, her lists grew so long that sometimes, when she came out of the shadowy booth, she was sweating and exhausted.

Sometimes she felt a tingling deep in her stomach as she told Father Thomas every detail of her sinful behaviour. She would squeeze her hands tightly together and move them higher up her thighs, feigning to ease the delightful pain that the confession bestowed on her. He knew everything about her yet still she wanted him to know more. He knew all her sins and always forgave them, but still she wanted to be more sinful and suffer the pain of confession and forgiveness.

Then the problem got even worse.

One summer, there had been some men working on the road outside her convent school. There were three of them, all dark haired and swarthy. She saw them from a distance as she approached one warm morning. She was

9

wearing her new white panties and a light cotton dress. Even before she got close to them she felt an excited fear prickling across her skin as she sensed their rough masculinity. Their torsos were naked in the warm sunny morning and they leant lazily on shiny steel shovels with hard-skinned hands. They flexed their glistening muscles and looked up eagerly as she approached; then they leered at her and instantly she felt a sting of shame and fear run through her ripening young body.

Their hole was right across the gates to her school. It was deep and contained a heavy iron railing against one of its sides; it looked like the entrance to a subterranean cavern. The three men stood around its rim, pushing each other and laughing as she approached nervously. There was no way around them; she hung her head, drew her brown leather school bag up onto her shoulder and scurried towards them, hoping to get past as quickly as possible. As she drew alongside them she could smell their sweat; it was sweet and sticky and hung heavily in the air like steam rising from overrun horses.

The one nearest her said something, she did not know what, or could not understand. Then, as the others chimed in, she gripped tightly to the leather strap of her satchel and ran past them shaking with fear. When she got inside the school gates she looked back at them and they laughed and jeered at her. They leant back on their shovel handles and as they stretched their bodies backwards she could see how their stomach muscles ribbed up hard and shiny with the tension of their laughter. She turned and ran inside, shaking and gasping for breath.

The next day it was the same, but this time she did not hang her head so low. As she came up alongside them the first one shouted something. Again she could not really make it out, only the word 'panties'. It frightened her as it had done the day before, but this time she also felt something that thrilled her. When she got inside the gates she turned and looked back at them and this time she noticed the way the material of their trousers mounded up at their crotches.

For the next few days, though she dreaded running the gauntlet of the workmen, she also found herself looking forward to it. One night she woke up sweating with her fingers probing high between her thighs and she lay awake for quite a while before she moved her hands outside the bedclothes. The next morning she felt so guilty she cried as she wrote down what had happened in the little notebook.

Every day they were causing her to be sinful and providing her with everything she needed. On the Thursday morning of that week, as she excitedly pulled up her satchel and ran towards the hole in the road, her heart sank when the men were not there. She stood at the rim of the gaping excavation and looked down into it.

There were two girls from the school down in the bottom of the hole with the men!

It was muddy around their feet and the girls' white ankle socks were spattered with dirt. Both of them were crying. They were being bent over in front of the three men with their bottoms up. One of them had her panties pulled down to just above her knees and Maria could plainly see the rosy darkness pressing out from between her young buttocks. One of the men was pulling down the panties of the other girl but they were tight across her bottom and were hard to get off. He had to pull at them roughly and the white, sewn edges cut into the girl's slender bottom.

The girl who was having her panties removed looked up in tearful appeal. Maria recognised her, she was in the fifth form. As the girl turned, the man swung back to her and ripped her panties down violently. She gasped as he pressed one of his hands on her back to force her to bend over even more, then spanked her hard across her rounded bottom. She let out a bleating cry. Maria saw the expression of pain on the girl's face before she was finally forced to turn away by the pressure of the man's hand on her back. There was another smack and an even louder scream and Maria turned and ran.

Her heart felt as though it was going to explode. She felt violated and frightened by what she saw, but even more frightened by what she thought. More than anything, more than fear, or wanting to run away, more than disgust or sympathy for the girls, she wanted to go back and clamber down into the muddy hole herself and have her panties ripped off by the men and be spanked and...

She flushed terribly, wild thoughts spinning uncontrollably through her head as she ran in panic for the sanctuary of the convent school, and when she arrived she dared say nothing.

At the end of the week it was all of this that she confessed. She poured out her wicked thoughts and wrongdoing as normal, but this time she admitted something she did not fully understand. This was no simple misdemeanour. This time she had enjoyed shaking with fear every time the workmen made rude gestures and offered to 'take her little white panties down and give her a good thrashing.' This time, she told him how she had kept her fingers high between her thighs as she lay awake in her bed thinking of the mounds in the men's trousers. This time, she trembled tearfully as she told him how she wanted to be one of the girls in the hole.

As she made her confession to Father Thomas she heard him sigh loudly. She knew he was angry with her and the realisation set off a tingling in her stomach and sent shivering thrills throughout her young body. She pleaded for forgiveness and punishment; she wanted to throw herself on the floor and beg for punishment. She wanted to stretch out before him and kiss his feet until he said she was saved. She felt so guilty and yet so satisfied; she felt so fulfilled with her sinfulness.

"Father," she had begged, "I'm so wicked, I walked past those horrid, smelly men and listened to the horrid things they said. I can't get to sleep at night because I think of them; their muscly stomachs and what it is beneath their trousers that makes them bulge out at the front. I can't stop thinking about what it would be like to be bent over in that muddy hole and have my panties torn down and my bottom spanked by those rough hands. What can you make me do to put things right? What has made me so bad?"

"What did they say again my child?"

"About taking my panties down?"

"Yes, what did they say exactly?"

"They said they would take my white panties down and give me a good spanking."

"Why? Why would they do that?"

"They - they said that I looked as if I would enjoy it."

"And would you?"

"I don't know Father. I don't know what is right any more. Father, perhaps they were right, perhaps I deserved a spanking. Perhaps I still do."

Father Thomas hesitated, then, stroking his beard to its thin point, spoke softly.

"You have been very wicked indeed. Your punishment should be severe this time, very severe, my child."

She shuddered with fear and clasped her school notebook tightly against the tops of her thighs. Suddenly, this

13

was not a game and a sense of real fear spread through her.

"There is only one thing for it,' he continued.

Her hands started to shake and she pressed them down even harder against her thighs. What would it be? Would it be enough to save her?

"No prayer will make this better," he said, "you will have to be punished directly, here and now - by me."

She felt herself beginning to sweat with dread. The pages of her little notebook were sticking to the sweat that was covering the smooth skin of her young thighs. She waited, barely breathing.

"I will have to spank you my child. I must take your panties down and spank you now." He spoke slowly as he adjusted himself on his seat. "Come into my confession box and I will bend you over my knee."

Her head spun dizzily as a sweat broke out on her face and she felt herself flushing all over. This was what she wanted, she knew that, and yet she felt so fearful. She just did not know what to think. She was terrified! She took one frightened glance through the grill, caught a brief glimpse of Father Thomas's flashing teeth, then jumped up and ran out of the church crying and horrified.

When she got home she threw herself down on her bed and sobbed relentlessly. She stayed in her room for three days, weeping and saying prayers. And that had been the last time she had entered this place. That was six years ago...

Now, new feelings of guilt were spilling out and she needed someone to lap them up and guide her to repentance and salvation. It had been six years of an ever-growing need for forgiveness, six years of remorse for refusing her punishment from Father Thomas. There had not been a day that she had not felt guilty for running out of the confession booth all those years ago.

She glanced through the grill and saw the priest's thin fingers stroking his pointed beard and his eyes flashing as he raised his head. She turned away fearfully, shrunk back into the darkness and pushed herself hard against the cold stone wall of the church.

"Father, I need to confess," she said nervously, "I need to confess so much."

There was a pause. Maria anxiously looked through the grill again and saw Father Thomas' white teeth shining between his thin lips. He still reminded her of a wolf. For a second she imagined him slavering at her neck before sinking his teeth deeply into her throat. For a moment she was enthralled by the thought of him sucking her blood and drying her to a husk.

"Begin then, my child."

She turned away and stared down between her legs; her knees had fallen slightly open and she quickly drew them back together again. She pressed the palms of her hands against the tops of her smooth thighs as they stretched out from beneath the hem of her black skirt. She took a deep breath.

"Oh Father, I have been so wicked, I just don't know where to start."

"Start at the beginning," he said.

CHAPTER 2

"It began this morning –"

"Every detail," urged Father Thomas. "Every little detail, don't miss anything out, I need every little detail.

15

Where do you live?"

"I live in a small ground floor flat, actually it's just across the road from here, facing the church. I woke up late this morning, I don't have to go to work -"

"What were you wearing, my child?" he interrupted.

"I was wearing a pyjama top."

"Was it buttoned up?"

"Yes, no, well it had been, but in the night it had come undone. The two sides had pulled wide apart and exposed -"

"What? Had exposed what?"

"My, my breasts, Father, it had come undone and exposed my breasts."

"What are they like, your breasts?"

Maria did not reply straight away, then she realised that this was her only way to be saved, confessing was her only hope, she had to be totally honest and tell Father Thomas everything.

"They are quite small actually, but firm. Sometimes, when I lie on my bed I enjoy rubbing my hands around them. My nipples are small as well, and pink, they stand out from the darker, pink circles around them."

"Did the sides of your pyjama top pull at your breasts? Did they poke out through the gap? Did you feel the tightness of the material against them? Tell me, it's important."

"Yes, Father it did pull at them, and yes, they did poke out as I went to take my shower."

"Did you wash all over?"

"Yes. I washed myself slowly. I splashed shower gel across my breasts and rubbed the foam all around them. The bubbles dribbled down my body, down my legs and off the ends of my toes. I like the way they tickle. Then I splashed more gel onto my hair and ran my hands through it, rubbing it and drawing it out in long strands. A shower always makes me feel sort of glowing and warm. I really do enjoy massaging myself in the shower. Then I dressed in my black suit, the one I've got on now."

"I need the details," said Father Thomas. He was smiling like a wolf again. "What did you put on to start with? Tell me, and then tell me exactly how you put them on."

"I put out a white embroidered bra and a white silky suspender belt with shiny metal clasps, oh, and some flesh-pink stockings. I sat on the edge of the bed, pulled the suspender belt around my waist and did up the two small metal clasps at the back. Then I pulled down the suspenders and pressed the ones at the front flat against my thighs. Then I picked up the white bra and put that on."

"How did your breasts, your beautiful small breasts, fit into it?"

"They fitted well, I like pulling the straps tightly over my shoulders and feeling my breasts press into the soft material of the bra cups. My nipples were quite soft and they didn't stick out, but you can just see their darkness through this bra, it's so thin and silky... then I went to make a cup of tea."

"Was that all you were wearing? Just your bra and suspender belt and stockings?"

"Yes, that's all I was wearing when I went to the kitchen. I looked over to the church. It was so grey and foreboding. Oh Father, every day I see it, it tortures me, just thinking of this confession booth... well, when I looked out of the kitchen window I saw a hole in the road! I could hardly believe my eyes. It was only a few yards away from the hole that I had to run past during that terrible summer when I was thirteen, and the head of a young workman peered out over the rim...

"I went back and looked at myself in the mirror. I stretched my arms up and looked at myself and it made

17

me excited. I pressed my hands across the front of the suspender belt and pressed my stomach out against them. The mound at the base of my stomach, with my hairs, stuck out from beneath the silky material that was pulled tightly around my waist. I felt a bit wicked and sinful when I stretched my thumbs against the inside edges of my hips. It made me sigh, you know, to think of my thumbs working their way slowly inwards across the base of my stomach. But I stopped myself, I really did Father, I stopped myself. Then I heard the kettle crackling like mad because it hadn't got any water in it! I rushed to it and when I lifted the lid, steam gushed from it and burned my hand. It made me yelp. I dropped the lid behind the refrigerator. Look, my hand was burned rather badly."

She offered her hand up to the lattice-work grill then realised he could not see it.

"I had to screw up my face to bear the pain and it made me bite my bottom lip. I leant onto the top of the refrigerator to look at the scald. The metal top felt cool against my skin, it was nice, so I bent further forward and let my breasts flatten out against the cool metal. I stretched right over to see if I could reach the kettle top but couldn't. The refrigerator is in a small alcove and the wall comes out around it and I couldn't get round the sides either. I leant further over the top of the refrigerator, stretching my arm as much as I could. In the end, I stood on tiptoe but it was hopeless."

"Yes, yes, and you had not got any panties on!"

"No, that was the thing, I felt really bad, my bottom sticking up like that, and the more I leant over the more tightly the two front clasps on my suspender belt jammed against the top of the refrigerator. They pulled really tight and dug into my waist at the back, it really hurt."

"Did you like that? Did you like the pain?"

18

"Well, yes, in a way I suppose I did."

"Go on then. How did you feel lying across the refrigerator?"

"Oh Father, I felt really exposed and it made me feel odd, you know, guilty in a way, and yes, it hurt but the pain seemed to make me feel excited. Oh Father I'm so terrible! My bottom was sticking right up, naked, it excited me so much, I could feel the cool air touching the insides of my open thighs and, and it caused me to open them even more. I spread them wider and wider, just to reveal, oh Father, have I got to say? Have I got to say?"

"Yes, my child, you must say. You spread them wider to reveal what? What did you reveal as you stretched your thighs wider like that? Tell me, say the word, I will know if you are lying."

"To reveal my..."

"Yes? Say the word."

"My, my cunt. Oh Father, how can you bear to hear my disgusting talk? How can you stand my filthy sinfulness?"

"I can my child, I can, go on, don't stop, go on."

"Yes, my cunt, my cunt, my cunt, to reveal my cunt."

"Good my child, go on now, don't hold back."

"To reveal the soft edges of my fleshy cunt, my fleshy, fleshy cunt. Oh Father, I felt such pleasure in the pain. It was like a dark power controlling me, but I was not completely lost, no, I was not totally lost to my desires, don't think that, please don't think that Father. I still tried to get the kettle lid, honestly I did. In fact, I nearly got hold of it, but trying to get it made me stretch even more."

"What did you look like, stretched out like that? Tell me what you looked like."

"Well, I was splayed out on the refrigerator. My left leg was pushing against the sharp, metal edge. It hurt so much. My buttocks, they were wide open and my pubic

19

hair -"

"What colour?"

"Black Father, my black pubic hair hung down onto the white, metal top. I was so wide that I could feel cool air wafting against the soft skin of my cunt. I braced my left hand hard against the metal top and... and then I felt the softness of flesh between my legs, my cunt, pressing against the back of my hand."

"You were touching your cunt?"

"Yes, I stopped moving, I was frozen. I was so distracted by the feeling of that warm soft flesh, that warm soft flesh of my cunt. It pressed against the back of my hand and demanded so much attention, I couldn't ignore it. You understand don't you Father? But still I tried to get the lid, really Father, I did. I took a deep breath and forced myself down between the wall and the refrigerator. Then the front of my bra caught in a fastening on the back of the refrigerator top. I tried to draw back but my breasts came out and the bra stayed caught. I was stuck!"

"Stuck? Unable to move?"

"I felt so naked and exposed. My legs were spread so wide and I couldn't move at all. Then -"

"Yes, my child? Go on, go on. What next?"

"I heard a sound behind me!"

"Yes, yes?"

"I could just twist round enough to see..."

"Yes, yes?"

"A man was looking through the window..."

"Yes, yes?"

"It was a tall young man, wearing blue jeans and stripped to the waist! It was the man I had seen peering out of the hole in front of the church. He had a bronzed face, long, golden hair and he was sweaty, it shone on the hairs under his arms and dripped down the sides of his bare chest. He was very muscular..."

"Go on, tell me what happened."

"He could see everything! He could see how trapped I was, how helpless, how desperate, and he could see right up between my legs. Worst of all, I think he could sense my excitement at being violated by his gaze."

"Oh my child, you are wicked!"

"Yes, yes, I tried to wriggle my hand free and I lifted my bottom higher but my cunt just opened more against the back of my hand. Oh Father, I could feel that more than anything."

"Tell me exactly."

"I could feel my cunt more than the pain and panic, I could feel its soft warmth, I could feel it throbbing. That dark force of pleasure was spreading through me, like some sort of evil shadow."

"How wicked!"

"He shouted something through the window. He was standing back and holding a shovel. He pointed it towards the glass, then drove the blade of the shovel right through the glass. It smashed and bits of glass flew everywhere across the kitchen floor. I turned back, I was scared to death, and screwed my eyes up as tight as I could. I was completely terrified, I was shaking all over. Then he smashed the glass that was still in the frame and it flew all over the place. He kept smacking at it and every time he hit it, more bits smashed on the floor. Then he jumped down from the window frame, knocking more pieces of glass all over the floor. He was carrying the shovel as he walked slowly across the kitchen floor. I can still hear the horrible, noisy grinding of broken glass as he crunched over it in his heavy boots.

"At first, he just stood behind me and looked down at me. He stared right up the wide gap between my legs and

I felt so humiliated. Then he bent his head for a better view. He could see - he could see my cunt -"

"Wet?"

"Hot and wet and spread out against the back of my hand. I was so scared. I could see his face and that shock of golden hair, and he grinned as he looked closer between my legs. I struggled and pulled and shouted and yelled. He just kept looking at my cunt, he seemed transfixed by it. Then I felt him come up close behind me, I could hear myself panting, then he banged his shovel down on the floor and pressed his body against my bottom. I tried to squirm but he only pressed harder and I started to cry again."

"Go on, go on."

"He started to say things, I'm not sure what."

"I want to know what he said. Think! I want to know exactly what he said."

"Well, to start with he said something like 'Well, what have we got here then?' Then he said, 'Yes, it's the bitch I've seen running to the bus stop in a black suit, all prim and proper. This is a turn up for the books, you don't look so prim and proper now, do you bitch?' He said something like that."

"What did you say, don't forget that? I want to know what you said as well."

"I said, 'Please, please, help me.' But he shouted, 'Shut up you fucking whore!' Oh Father, I'm sorry. I'm so sorry to have to tell you this, it must be terrible for you."

"It is alright my child, I need to know the words, do not be afraid to say them."

"'Fucking whore' he called me, 'a fucking, fucking whore.' 'Only a slut would show herself like this,' he said. 'Shut your fucking mouth! You're disgusting.' I kept saying 'Please, please, please,' but he wouldn't listen. 'I said shut your fucking mouth! You're a whore so shut your fucking mouth! Sluts like you aren't allowed to speak, so shut your fucking mouth!' When I tried again he did not even let me finish, the next thing I knew I was shrieking in pain. He smacked me Father. He smacked me so hard across my bottom I shrieked out loud. 'Take that as a lesson,' he shouted as he smacked me again, 'any more cackle from you and you'll get it even harder, slut!' Then he smacked me again, really brutally this time, so hard, I shrieked again but he did not stop. Then another one, oh it was so hard and his rough hand caught the inside of my thighs and I screamed like mad. I kept trying to make him stop, 'please, please, please', I really pleaded with him Father, but I just got another smack, right across my bottom and it stung so much.

"I began to shriek continuously, I couldn't help it, I was like an animal, a wild suffering animal. 'Noisy little whore aren't you?' he said, 'let's see if you can do any better,' then he smacked me again as hard as he could. I screamed and screamed and screamed. He carried on saying things, 'what a lovely cunt', 'so good of you to spread it out like this for me' and 'let's have a good look at it shall we?' And while he was saying these awful things, he bent down and looked right up at it, right up at my cunt. Oh Father, it was terrible."

"Good, good, but did he touch you?"

"Yes, he pushed his fingers up the insides of my thighs and grabbed the edges of my cunt. He was very rough and I tried to pull back, I really did, but I just couldn't move. He held the folds of my cunt between his thumbs and fingers and spread them apart. I felt the inner edges opening up. He was looking right up me! Then, he started pinching me! He was so rough, he pinched at it and when he let it go it stung so much. 'Turn your hand over!' he commanded. 'Turn your hand over! I want to see how you play with it.' What could I do Father? What could I do? My face was crushed against the wall, I was blubbering with pain and fear, I just had to do what he instructed. 'Turn your hand over!' he shouted. 'Turn your hand over you fucking bitch!' Father, I just had to. I managed to ease my bottom a bit higher and felt the edges of my cunt peel away from the back of my hand; oh Father, they still stung from his pinching. The soft skin of my cunt was wet and warm and as I lifted it away I felt even more exposed as it was chilled by the cool air from the refrigerator.

"'Too slow!' he shouted, 'perhaps this will help you get going!' Then another terrible smack landed across my bottom. I screeched and lifted myself up as much as I could, but it did not seem enough to satisfy him. He seemed to be getting angrier and angrier, 'turn your hand!' he ordered, 'turn your hand!' I twisted my left arm to try and do what he said but my arm hurt so much and as I twisted it around I had to lift my shoulders as well and the bra straps cut even deeper into me. I felt awful pains, but in the end I managed to turn my hand and laid it back down, this time palm upwards. It was good to feel the warmth coming from my cunt again. Oh Father I'm so terrible."

"Carry on my child, what next?"

"I didn't know what to do next. I didn't know what to do to please him. I was so frightened, I just waited for my next instruction. It was only a second before he started shouting again. 'Get down on it then bitch! What are you waiting for you fucking whore! Get that beautiful wet cunt down on it bitch or you'll get more than my hand across your backside!' Then another terrible smack landed across my bottom and I yelled again. I did not dare to hesitate, I had to do what I was told. My cunt pressed down onto my upturned hand. As it got closer the warmth around its soft

24

folds increased and when it touched the tips of my fingers I felt a thrill run right through me. It was like nothing I had ever experienced before. I pressed my cunt into my hand and let my whole weight press it down firmly. In a way, I felt safe again as I fingered its edges, they had stopped stinging from his pinching now, and I squeezed my eyes tight together and waited. 'Don't just lie there you lazy bitch. I want to see it move. Lift your arse up. I want to see it clearly you fucking bitch.'

"Another smack came down, this time harder than all the others. I didn't think it was possible but I screamed even louder than before, but I had to obey. As I lifted my bottom I kept hold of it, my cunt, I could feel its moist edges, it was so wet and so warm. Feeling it like that, and yelling so loudly, and the spanking I was getting, made me feel really dizzy and confused. I thought I was going to faint. I just couldn't resist him Father, honestly, I just couldn't resist him. Then there was another terrible smack, it hurt so much. I couldn't believe how each smack was harder than the one before.

"I screeched as loud as I could, it seemed to help me bear the pain, but he did not stop. Smack! Smack! Smack! Each one harder than the other. Then another and another and my bottom felt on fire. I was sobbing loudly. He seemed to enjoy that, the more I cried, the harder he smacked me. 'Right bitch, now you can play with your rosy cunt while I see what I can do with your arse. Let's get it good and wide. Yes, open up those red buttocks and let's see your beautiful dark ring, bitch!' Oh Father, he forced his hands right up the insides of my thighs and pressed his fingers around my anus. I shrunk back a bit but he pressed harder. Now I felt raw and wretched but, I thought, at least the smacking had stopped. 'That looks a good place for a wank. Pity you can't look but I'll tell you about it if you want? Would you like that bitch? Would you like a running commentary?' Then another hard smack! 'I said would you like... ah, forget it you fucking bitch!' Then he sent down a rain of punishing smacks. They burned me so much that my whole body strained up all rigid, the pain was terrible and I was so frightened. This time I couldn't scream, I just moaned. 'Just stay like that you fucking cow!' I felt his hands moving between the insides of my thighs again. Then I felt the heat of something in his hands and then I felt the sudden shock of his hard cock against my anus. I stopped moaning and just screamed and screamed as the tip pushed at my anus. It was so tight Father, it was too tight for it to go in. 'Need a bit of lubrication eh?' I felt some wet drips running between my buttocks; he was dribbling spit down me. 'Let's try that, shall we?' Then there was another hard smack! 'I said let's try that shall we?' Another smack! 'Well? Shall we?'

"I could only blubber and then the smacking stopped and I felt a moment's relief. Oh Father, how wrong I was to think it was all over. I felt his cock push again and this time it slid inside me. I felt that hard engorged tip squeeze into the tight muscle of my anus, and my mouth opened wide as I gasped in pain and fear. 'Enjoying it bitch? Enjoying my cock up your arse?'

"He pressed it in further and I felt its hardness penetrating right into my innards. It was terrible Father, so terrible to feel it up my arse like that. 'I said are you enjoying it? I don't see you enjoying it.'

"Then another hard smack landed on my right buttock. I winced and pulled away a bit but he thrust his cock in even deeper, right in as far as it would go. 'What a fucking whore you are. What a fucking arse-fucking whore you are. Ride it bitch. Ride it and get those fingers up your cunt. I want to see you enjoying it!'

"Oh Father, I couldn't resist him, honestly, you must believe me, I couldn't resist him. My buttocks widened under his force and he fucked my arse until suddenly he finished deep inside me. He howled with joy and I cried out in pain. I felt so disgusting, Father, he had fucked my arse so hard and now I could feel his hot spunk running inside me."

"Go on my child, go on. What happened next?"

"For a few seconds I lay there gasping and moaning in pain, then I felt him pull back. His cock slid out of me and my arse tightened up painfully as the head of his cock, it still seemed very big, slipped out. Then I heard his boots crunching over the broken glass. I just couldn't move, my whole body felt racked and my anus was dilating and contracting all by itself, it really burned. Then I began to realise what he had done and what he had seen. I knew he had watched me frantically trying to break free, he had watched me squirming to be released, he had witnessed my captivity and desperation and then, worst of all, he had forced me to submit to this revolting and horrible fucking. I felt his spunk running from my arse down my legs; I felt a terrible wave of self-disgust and I began to heave with nausea, I felt really sick. Then I heard him climb into the window frame, jump down outside and go.

"I relaxed slightly when I knew he had gone. My anus was still pulsating though - his cock had been so big - and every time it swelled and contracted its edges burned with a scorching pain. Finally, I opened my eyes, his spunk was still running down my legs and my hand was still clutching tightly to the swollen folds of my cunt. Oh Father, it was so terrible, lying across the refrigerator like that, my arse was still burning me, but, but I felt so excited, I can hardly say it, but yes, I felt so terribly excited. It flooded right through me and sort of sucked up the pain. I felt such a weird mixture of things, I felt guilty, yes, so guilty, but I felt so excited, so terribly, terribly excited."

"What did you do? Is there more? Have you sinned further?"

"Yes Father. I tried to hold back, I tried, really I tried, but I couldn't stop myself. I felt my hips slowly moving, then I felt my fingers following their movement. They stretched up and started playing against the soft wetness that was making them tingle and shake. They kept themselves close enough to just glance against the delicate folds of my swollen cunt. Slowly, as I twisted my thighs, the soft wetness of my cunt laid drips of sweetness onto their welcoming tips. Then they began to play with those beautiful edges more firmly. The soft folds quivered against my nails and I felt a shiver of delight at the touch of their sharpness. I just couldn't stop them, honestly Father, I couldn't, I couldn't stop them, they were so keen to play with my cunt. I thought of the young man's stare penetrating deeply between my buttocks. I realised that there had been no alternative but to submit to his will whether I wanted to or not. But Father, I was not sure whether I had wanted to resist or not. All the time there had been something inside me that had needed to submit to his words, his stare and that terrible deep penetration of his throbbing cock. I didn't know what to think. There seemed to be a longing inside me that had been driven by the cutting pains, the smacking and the stinging force of that hard cock up my arse. I just had to feel my cunt. As I sank back further onto the top of the refrigerator, my outer labia, those beautiful soft edges of my cunt, fell softly around my finger tips. I probed along their inside edges and those delightful petals, those soft, wet petals, opened as I searched deeper inside. I pulled the inner folds sideways gently and a flow of wetness dribbled onto my fingers as I rubbed them around the insides of those silky wet folds.

"My fingers felt along their edges and worked their way along the opening to my vagina. I felt the hot wetness of my pulsating hole; it was so tight and hot. Then they worked their way to the front. They pulled at the front of my crack and opened it. I felt the hardness of my clitoris and my mouth dropped open with a gasp. For a moment I felt surprised at its hardness and size and drew back, but then the longing flowed through me more violently and I made for it again. I felt it fully, it was swollen and throbbing and as I caressed it my body thrilled and filled with nervousness. My skin flushed hot and my clitoris engorged even more against the touch of my fingers. I pushed it from side to side then grasped it and tugged at it. As I pulled it I did not let my hips follow, instead, I pulled them away to increase the pressure on the pulsating hardness that hung from the front of my full, wet labia."

"Go on, go on, tell me everything."

"My whole body prickled with a thrilling shiver of excitement. I pulled at my clitoris again and again and I felt my hips fighting wildly to plunge my cunt against my hand. I felt my vagina craving to be filled, but at the same time I felt a strange sense of control. Even though my body wanted it I denied the urge to satisfy my cunt by plunging my upturned hand into it. The control I had gratified me, it satisfied my desire for the pain of denial. The conflict was coming from deep inside me and it was driving me towards a level of satisfaction that, though dark and terrifying, felt unsurpassable. I didn't know exactly what to do, all I knew was that I wanted that tantalising pain to continue. I squeezed my clitoris between my fingers and I drew it down their length until it was wedged firmly by my knuckles. Now, I could grasp my clitoris and allow my fingers to be free. I drove my fingers into my vagina and gasped. I lifted my body high on the refrigerator top. My breasts clung sweatily to the shiny metal surface and prickles of pain coursed across their surface. My fingers went deeper into my dripping hole and my knuckles squeezed harder and harder on my throbbing clitoris.

"I strained in ecstasy and banged my head roughly against the wall. My eyes went blurred with the pain and tears and I wanted to scream. Again, I felt the young man's stare deep inside my cunt and his throbbing cock pounding up my arse. I opened my mouth and began yelling. I screamed and forced my fingers even deeper between my sprawling thighs. My body filled with the sensation of penetration, I could feel that cock inside me all over again, but this time it was bigger, and thicker, and harder and more punishing. This time it went so deep, so deep, this time it finished so high inside me with a huge swell of spunk. Oh Father, I felt as if I was drowning from inside and I gasped and choked and writhed and felt as if I was going to die.

"Then my clitoris started stinging with the full flood of my orgasm. I yelled louder and louder and louder, then stopped, suddenly and frighteningly, I stopped. My body went rigid, I held my breath, I could not move. My mouth gaped wide and I squashed my face harder against the wall. My eyes stared wildly. I felt a huge pulse of yearning beginning to flood through me. My limbs were frozen as it took control of me; welling up and draining through my entire body. It centred on my cunt which pulsated and gripped my extended fingers. Then in a huge wave, it poured down through me and my body reddened with the throb of blood and desire. It surged into my head and everything began to spin around me. Still I gaped like an idiot, frozen in the throws of pain and joy, with my face squashed against the wall.

"Still I couldn't breathe and I felt as if I would explode. Then, at last, it released me and I shuddered as if I was in a fit. A flow of satisfaction ran through every part of my shaking body and I quivered and gasped as finally I breathed again. I fell back onto the cold white top of the refrigerator and shouted out loudly, not words, just wild ranting of pleasure and fulfilment. I let out sounds I had never heard before: grunts, screeches, blubbering sounds, and the more they came the more I did them. Then, slowly they died away and I hung my face limply against the wall, making low, guttural gulping noises as spit ran freely from my mouth and down the side of the refrigerator."

"And how did you get free?"

"Oh Father, I just stood up. I - I suppose I never was really trapped, not really and truly."

He had that wolf look again. "You are so sinful my child," he said, slowly, caressing the words as if each one was precious.

"Yes Father," she said meekly. She looked down and found her fingers deeply inside her beautiful wet cunt. "I am so sinful."

CHAPTER 3

"You ran away from your punishment many years ago, my child."

Maria felt a sudden wave of fear. Father Thomas did remember her! "Yes," she said, trembling.

There was a long pause. She could hear him stroking the tip of his pointed beard. Then he sighed heavily and

31

leant forward. His face came close to the grill and she looked up. She could see his staring eyes through the carved wooden lattice between them. She stopped picking at her fingernails and waited.

"This is not an easy matter," he started. "You are filled with such wickedness. It is going to be a long task to purify you."

"Oh Father," she pleaded, sensing that Father Thomas thought there was at least some hope of saving her. "I must be purified. You must purify me. I have to be saved from my sinful thoughts. I have to be punished for my sinful deeds. Oh, please Father, if you can, please do it."

"I think I may have the answer," he said slowly, "but it will not be easy."

She moved closer to the wooden grill and waited anxiously.

"We must begin straight away," he said.

She sat forward, rigid, as he got up and opened the door at the front of the confession box. She listened to his shuffling feet as he stepped around to her side. Then he pulled back the heavy red curtain and looked down at her.

He was tall and angular. He wore a long black robe and around his neck hung a purple satin sash. She thought he looked as if he was going to bite into her with his pointed teeth then eat her while she screamed out her sins. She looked up at him and tried to smile but he did not smile back.

"Caleb!" he shouted without taking his eyes from her.

Maria was shocked, he had been talking to her so softly but now his voice was loud and demanding. She shrunk back against the hard wall of the church.

"Caleb! Caleb! Where have you got to you fucking dog!"

Maria could not believe what she was hearing. She

crouched against the wall, terrified by Father Thomas's shouting and language.

"Ah, there you are, at last."

A small figure sidled up beside Father Thomas. It was a stocky dwarf with an ill-shaved face and jet black hair. He held a long staff with a sharp point on the end and he banged it down noisily on the floor as he came to attention beside Father Thomas; Maria cringed.

Father Thomas turned to Caleb and patted his head as though he was some sort of pet.

"Get some cords, my ugly little servant, get some cords and some tape. We have someone to punish."

Caleb looked at Maria then back to Father Thomas, and licked his lips.

"Yes, pretty isn't she? Lock the door as well, we don't want to be disturbed do we?"

Caleb nodded then turned suddenly and scuttled off into the church. Father Thomas bent towards Maria and she shrunk back.

"Afraid? Of course you are, and with some reason. You have been an evil little girl! Evil! Evil! Evil! An evil little bitch! Your sins are going to be difficult to do away with, but, with effort, I think we can manage to cure you."

Caleb came back, trailing several red cords behind him.

"The tape?"

Caleb put his stumpy arm into his robe and drew out a large reel of heavy silver tape. He held it up and laughed throatily.

"Out bitch!" shouted Father Thomas.

Maria pressed herself hard against the cold stone wall unable to move with terror and shock.

"Out, you fucking, sinful bitch!"

Father Thomas leant towards her and reached out to grab her shoulder. She drew back, gasping and terrified.

He took hold of her shirt and pulled at it but she braced her feet against the wooden kneeling platform and squeezed herself hard against the wall. He pulled again and the shirt tore slightly. Maria winced. She could not believe what was happening.

"Get her out Caleb."

Caleb sprang forward.

Maria saw that he was very ugly: his eyes were large and hooded by dark, drooping lids, the skin of his face was rough with patches of unshaved stubble that erupted amongst sores on his cheeks and chin, and his teeth were yellow and crooked behind fat, pulpy lips. She squeezed herself hard against the wall and drove her feet against the kneeling stool until they hurt. She could feel the skin on her shoulder blades scraping against the cold surface of the wall. All she could think of doing was staying where she was; pinioning herself firmly and resisting the grasping hands that reached forward to drag her into the open.

Caleb smirked at Maria, then took his staff and pointed it at her. She could not draw back any further, so just cowered as he poked the shiny silver point of the staff towards her neck as if he was baiting an animal. It made him laugh, and he poked in time with his guttural giggling and she responded, as if caught in a strange dance, by flinching every time the point came near to her; her eyes widened like a terrified animal.

She could not speak, and like the animal she felt she was, she grunted and whined. Then the point came very close to her neck and she had to dodge aside to avoid it. She gasped and made a shrieking noise. Caleb laughed loudly; her pathetic fear amused him and he prodded at her with increased insistence.

"Get her out Caleb. Plenty of time for fun later. Get the fucking bitch out!"

Caleb grinned and slowly lowered the point of his staff. It followed the line of her throat, down the upper part of her chest then between the top of her cleavage. He held it there for a moment, poised threateningly above the small, embroidered flower, then he scraped it across the front of her jacket and down to her knees. He put it under the top edge of the hem of her skirt. He giggled again, then slowly lifted the skirt and held it aloft on the point of the staff. He did not have to bend much to see up between her thighs.

"White ones!" he shouted excitedly and jumped up and down as he glared at her silky white panties. Then he pushed the silver point of the staff up between her thighs. Maria felt the smooth coldness against the flushed heat of her skin; she was horrified. The point moved further until it touched her white panties and she felt its metal end snagging on their flimsy material. She squeezed her buttocks to try and draw the soft flesh of her cunt away from the probing point.

"Out!" ordered Father Thomas.

She was cowering and cornered and afraid for her life, but she could not bear the fear of being trapped any longer; she felt baited and broken. Even though she was panicking too much to reason, she knew she had to come out into the open. Father Thomas could see that she was ready, and reached over to press Caleb's staff away from its target.

"You will have your fun soon," Father Thomas said, and Caleb screwed up his face in disappointment but stood back obediently. Then he started to shout and dance around, holding his staff above his head like a spear. "White ones! White ones! White ones!" he chanted.

Maria slowly drew away from the wall; she was resigned to leaving her sanctuary. As she relaxed her legs and edgily came forward, she felt the pain in her shoulders where they had scraped against the wall. She stood up with difficulty; she was shaking all over and felt faint and she held onto the red curtain as her knees sagged beneath her.

"In here!" Father Thomas indicated the wooden confession box where he usually sat. "What better place to start your treatment than in here."

Maria's lips were trembling, and she could see her hands shaking as involuntarily they fell to her sides. She wanted to be sick as she stepped out shakily.

Caleb lifted his staff again and prodded at her, its point touched against the sides of her calves and she moved at its insistence. He guided her to the front of the confession box; its wooden door gaped open. The prodding point stuck into her pale skin and left her legs stinging. She went into the confession box like a penned animal.

"Stand and face the wall," ordered Father Thomas. "We do not want to see the face of such a sinner. Face the wall you evil little bitch!" He paused for a moment. "Clothes off," he said. Then he turned to Caleb and smiled. "But leave your panties on for later."

Caleb jumped for joy and danced around and chanted as he poked his staff eagerly at Maria, taunting and baiting her like a cornered bear.

"White ones! White ones! Keep them on for later! White ones! White ones! White ones!"

Now in a state of complete terror, Maria reached up and tried to undo the buttons of her black jacket, but her hands were shaking so much she could not even get a grasp on them. She felt Father Thomas's anger and tried even harder, but she could not hold the buttons firmly enough even to begin pulling them through the buttonholes. Hopelessly, and in a pathetic effort to please, she reached around to the button on the waistband of her skirt, but she could not undo that either.

She wanted to turn around, she wanted to plead with Father Thomas to let her go, she wanted to apologise for being unable to undo her buttons, but she did not get chance to do anything.

"Strip the bitch, Caleb!"

Caleb stopped dancing and threw down his staff. It crashed heavily on the stone floor. He rushed up behind Maria, grabbed hold of her jacket and tugged at it frenziedly until it pulled down over her shoulders then down over her hips. The cuffs did not come over her hands and the sleeves turned inside out. Caleb pulled roughly at them and Maria stretched out her fingers so that the sleeves would pull down. Caleb fell back as they came free and the jacket finally fell to the floor. Then he grabbed the back of her shirt and tore at it until it ripped across the back. She flinched as the material cut into the front of her shoulders and squeezed tightly around her small firm breasts. Caleb kept pulling until the shirt tore down and fell away in tatters, then he grabbed the waistband of her skirt tightly and jerked it backwards. Maria fell against the side of the confession box and gasped loudly as the pressure of his frenzied pulling knocked the breath from her.

"Face the wall!" shouted Father Thomas.

She did not dare disobey; she lifted her arms and braced herself against the sides of the confession box. She put one hand through the lattice-work grill and with the other she hung onto a brass coat-hook. She wedged her wrist painfully in between the grill and its frame and clenched her fist tightly around the coat-hook.

Caleb continued pulling frantically at her skirt and it dug into her waist and made her hips hurt. Then he found the button at the side and ripped it out of the buttonhole.

He grabbed the top edges of the zip and tore at it. The zip came undone and the pressure of the skirt around her shapely hips was released. Then he bent down and squatted on his knees. He bent his head upwards and stared up her skirt, leering at the crotch of her white panties. Then, still in the same position, he grabbed the hem of the skirt with both hands and pulled it down, it fell across his face and he bit at the material leaving trails of spit across it.

Maria hung against the sides of the confession box. Her white bra straps had fallen off her shoulders and were tight against the tops of her outstretched arms. Her white panties had pulled up tight between her buttocks and were cutting into the soft edges of her cunt. Caleb let the skirt fall from his face then turned over and, lying on his back, stared up between her legs. Maria felt giddy and tears blurred her eyes.

Father Thomas bent down and picked up Caleb's staff. He reached the point forward and pressed it against the small of Maria's back. She felt the pressure of its tip. Then Father Thomas slowly slid the point up her back. He held it against the taught strap of her bra, then, with a sudden movement, he pulled it upwards and sliced through the thin material. Her breasts were completely exposed and she felt disgusted and defiled.

Still on his back, Caleb slid forward on the floor and worked his way between her legs. He looked up over the mound at her crotch and ogled at her small, firm breasts. Her nipples were hardened and the tops of the bra cups hung from them loosely.

"Tie her! Ankles and wrists."

Caleb drew back and jumped up and grabbed hold of the cords he had brought. He leapt up onto the wooden seat and started to wind slip-knots around Maria's wrists. One he secured to the brass coat-hook and the other he wound around the sliding lattice-work grill. He pulled them tight and Maria gasped with pain as she was hoisted up on them; she stretched up on her toes to relieve some of the pressure.

Then Caleb jumped down onto the floor and tied her ankles to the legs of the wooden seat. Again he pulled them as tight as he could and this time Maria cried out in pain.

"Oh, please Father, please!"

"Do not worry my child, I will save you. You are in safe hands."

"Please Father, I can't stand it. Please let me go, please, please."

"Shut her up Caleb. The bitch has got too much to say."

"Please Father, please, I can't stand it, please let me go."

Then her words were stifled as Caleb smacked the tape across her face. He pulled it tight and unreeled it so that it went behind her head and back again to her face. He wound it around several times then tore it from the reel. Maria's long hair was caught in it and she could not move for the pain.

"That will do you for the moment, I think," said Father Thomas. "I will give you some time to think over your sins my child, and to think about how you may be saved by appropriate punishment. Come Caleb, we have other work to do."

Father Thomas picked up Caleb's staff and handed it to him. Caleb took it eagerly then closed the door to the confession box and fell in behind Father Thomas. They both disappeared into the depths of the church, Caleb skipping behind Father Thomas's flowing robes as much in excitement as with a need to keep up.

Maria hung on her bonds, tears streaming down her

face. As she stared at the wall she could see the reflection of the flickering light of the candles that burned on the altar. She felt like a sacrifice and sobbed.

She watched as candles burned lower and lower as the night went on. She dreaded them going out altogether; the flickering of the candles gradually got lower and she drifted into a light doze. Her head lolled onto her shoulder as a light mist of unconsciousness crept closer. Then the last candle flickered out and Maria was left, hanging on her bonds in the profound darkness of the empty church.

CHAPTER 4

Maria awoke with a start as a glimmer of sunlight flashed through a high stained-glass window and reflected on the wall outside the confession box. She was slumped heavily on her bonds and instantly felt a terrible pain in her wrists. Her hands were swollen and red and she eased herself up a little to try and relieve some of the pain.

"I see you are awake my child."

Father Thomas was standing behind her with Caleb by his side.

She could only turn her head slightly, her neck was stiff and her shoulders were sore with the strain of hanging all night on the tight cords around her wrists.

"Cut her down Caleb."

Caleb jumped forward and jabbed his staff towards Maria. Her eyes widened with fear as he stabbed the staff forward and, one by one, sliced through the cords at her wrists. As the first one gave way she slumped to one side then, as the other one was sliced through by the point of the staff, she dropped to the floor of the confession box in a heap.

"Bring her!"

Caleb pulled at her shoulders, grabbing and pinching her aching flesh. She winced in pain but slowly allowed herself to be lifted. She clung to the back of the confession box, hardly able to stand. Her eyes were wide with terror as she cowered in the shadows. Her bra hung loosely below her breasts and her white panties were pulled up tightly around her cunt. Caleb pinched the soft skin of her arms and coaxed her out.

Father Thomas walked ahead as Caleb dragged Maria down the aisle of the church. When she stumbled and grasped the sides of a pew to keep from falling, Caleb pinched her arms and drove her on with his sharp staff. When they got nearer to the altar, Caleb ran forward and unhitched the heavy rope that hung loosely in front of it. He prodded Maria with his staff and drove her through into the altar chapel then clipped the rope back onto its brass hooks and ran up behind Father Thomas.

Maria stood limply in front of the altar, her white panties pulled up into the crack of her cunt.

"Here!" ordered Father Thomas pointing to his feet. "Here!"

Maria moved forward slightly but was uncertain what he meant. Caleb ran forward and started prodding the backs of her legs with his staff. He urged her forward then poked her stingingly in the shoulders and drove her down onto her knees.

She knelt obediently in front of Father Thomas and Caleb crouched by her side, looking quizzically into her eyes.

"I have thought long and hard about your sin, my child. Your punishment will be long and arduous, there is no easy remedy for your terrible sins, you will have to suffer

41

much humiliation before you can be cleansed of your wretchedness. You will have to learn complete obedience before you can even think of being saved."

Maria thought she was going to faint, she felt so thirsty and she had not eaten for ages. She began to heave with nausea and felt panicky at the thought of being sick with her mouth gagged by the tape. She looked away from Caleb as he pushed his face close to hers.

"Look at him!" shouted Father Thomas. He stared intensely into her tearful eyes. Then he reached towards her, grabbed the loose end of the tape and pulled it roughly until it started to unwind. As he ripped it away from the back of her head it pulled her hair and made her moan.

"I will now introduce you to the first instrument of obedience, my child. Come."

Father Thomas smiled, reached down and took her hand gently, then led her towards the altar.

"Bend over the altar and we will begin."

He let go of her hand and she bent obediently across the front of the altar. There seemed so much suffering to relieve her awful sins. She pressed her bare breasts down against the white cloth on the altar and looked at the large candlesticks that stood around her with their candles already renewed, flickering and bright.

"This is what will remind you of your obedience my child."

Something smacked down in front of her face and her eyes snapped shut with shock and fear.

"Do not turn away my child, look at the instrument of obedience."

She opened her eyes slowly and looked at the bamboo cane that was tapping on the altar.

"See how it flexes, my child. Is it not a beautiful instrument? Not too thick that it bruises too easily, and not

42

too thin that it cuts too quickly."

Father Thomas lifted it slowly then brought it down with another terrible smack on the white cloth. The candles wavered as the air swirled in turmoil around them.

"Spread out your arms!"

She reached her arms forward and stretched them as far as she could. She turned her head so that her cheek was pressed against the altar cloth. She could see Father Thomas smiling down at her, twitching and flexing the cane in his long bony hand.

"White panties! White panties! White panties!"

"Yes, my little servant, it is time now."

Caleb bounded up behind her and pressed his face against her bottom, sniffing at her white panties and pressing his stubby nose into the soft crease they formed across the crack of her buttocks.

"Naughty, naughty, panties stained and yellow. Not white for Caleb. Stained and dirty. Naughty! Naughty! Naughty!"

"Oh dear," said Father Thomas, "already you are in need of punishment. You have not even started to get rid of your existing sins before you commit more."

"Naughty, naughty, naughty! Dirty little panties. Should be white. Should be clean. Caleb likes white panties, not dirty ones, stained by naughty, naughty girls."

"Get them off!"

Caleb drew his face away from her bottom and grabbed each side of her panties. He wrenched them down in one go. They ripped and pulled down to halfway down her thighs and she tightened her buttocks so that he could not see in between them.

Smack!

She tightened her buttocks even more as Caleb's hand smacked across them.

43

"I want to see!" he chanted. "I want to see!"

Smack!

"Stand back Caleb, she needs a taste of the cane. She needs to learn how to be its servant. She needs much training but the cane will soon become her master." He drew the cane up behind her. "This will be your introduction to the delights of your new master, the cane. Are you ready my child?"

Maria felt so exhausted, but she knew he was offering her salvation, a chance of forgiveness, and she wanted to be freed of her evil so could only assent.

"Yes," she murmured.

"Yes? I cannot hear you, speak up! Speak up you fucking bitch!"

"Yes," she said, trying to clear her throat at the same time.

"Good!"

She heard the cane starting to move upwards through the air. Then a pause, then she saw the candles starting to flicker as the draught caused their flames to bend and break, she felt the silence of a moment's anticipation.

Thwack!

She screamed louder than she thought was possible. It filled her with terror as she listened to her own shrieking filling the church and echoing around its ponderous columns. Tears flooded her eyes instantly and she stretched her hands forward in agony, her bottom felt aflame, she felt as if she had been sliced with a dagger.

Then she heard the sound of it moving through the air again, she saw the flames flicker and bend, then there was the moment of stillness, then she braced herself against the altar and started to scream even before it hit her.

Thwack!

Her scream rent the church and she howled like an

animal. She could not bear it again, she could not stand the cutting pain across her bottom, he could not do it again, she would die, she knew she would. Then the noise again, the sound of the air being rent by the flailing of the cane, then the candles flickering in fear as it came down towards them, then the silence, this time longer, this time more deathly, this time filled with an eternity of fear and degradation.

Thwack!

This time she could not even scream, she did not have the strength, she just gasped in a noisy, throaty roar. The air was torn from her lungs and spit shot out with her exploding breath. She collapsed in agony and the church fell silent as her eyes misted over with a red haze.

She could not see anything even though her eyes were wide open. Then she felt Caleb tugging at her arms, she could not stir, she could not resist, then he was slapping her face but still she could not react, then he slapped her face very hard and she returned from her faint.

"No..."

"No? No? What do you fucking mean 'No'? 'Yes', that is the answer, 'yes'. You will say 'yes' until your master is exhausted, and even then you will beg him for more. 'Yes', that is all there is to say."

"No... Please... No..."

"You will beg him for more. 'Yes, please punish me more, do not stop," you will plead."

"Please... No..."

A cool waft of air breathed against her hot cheeks. She felt the skin on her face tingle as the draft from the rising cane heralded the pain that it held. She winced against it and tightened her muscles as she reached forward and grabbed the candlesticks. She watched their flames flickering and stretched out as tight as she could. Then the silence again; that dreadful moment of anticipation and terror. She waited in fear and gripped the cold metal of the candlesticks. Then she felt it coming again, the cane was splitting the air as it whipped down towards her inflamed buttocks. The flames bent sideways, trembling and shrinking away in fear, as it flew down towards her.

Thwack!

Again she could not cry out. Instead, a gasp burst from her mouth as her lungs emptied their breath in one heavy, bursting eruption. Her stomach flattened against the top of the altar and the candlesticks rocked in her hands, their flickering flames spilling hot wax down their shiny stems.

"Yes?"

"Please... No... Please... No..."

"Again then. The cane will be your master but he must know that you want him. He must know that you demand him and then he will stop. Only then will he draw back from the punishment."

She felt her body shaking. The candlesticks flickered in her trembling grip as hot wax spilled down and ran eagerly towards her hands. She wanted saving, but the pain was too great. She could not imagine how she could plead for more, it was impossible, she could only resist, she could only deny and she would never be saved. She wept loudly.

"Please... No more. Please... No more. I can't stand it. Please... No..."

She felt Caleb pulling at her legs, opening them wide and exposing her cunt. Cool air passed across her outer labia and she felt a dribble of sweat trickling down the inside of her legs. Then the candles flickered again and she buried her face against the altar cloth, gripping it between her teeth.

Her legs were wide apart and she knew she could not stand any more. Her buttocks were stinging from the lashing of the cane and she could feel hot candle wax running down onto her hands. It burned her and she wanted to let go of the candlesticks, but she could not, she needed to grip them, she needed their safety and she tightened her grip as the hot wax poured down onto the tops of her hands then down their back and onto her wrists. She sensed the cane lifting, she felt the moment of silence as it paused at the top of its stroke.

She felt a scream brewing up inside her. It was so intense and deliberate. It was not born of the moment of pain but of the intensity of pain inside her. It came from her bottom and crept across the stinging red skin of her buttocks, it travelled up inside her, through her nerve racked stomach then into her gagging throat. It tightened her neck and for a moment she could not breathe at all. Her face reddened with the tension as it forced its way into her mouth and built up behind the material of the altar cloth that was filling her mouth. Her cheeks were puffed out with it, her mouth was plugged by it, but still the scream built up. Then the explosion broke through.

She spit the cloth from her mouth and the scream burst from her. She screamed enough to rock the columns of the empty church, so loud her body vibrated with its energy, so violently that she felt herself transported on its renting echoes. She screamed like a beast into the silence of the cavernous church and still the cane had not started its downward journey.

She squeezed the candlesticks and shook them. She shook the hot wax from them and ran it across her flesh. She stretched her buttocks higher and opened her legs, exposing her cunt to the gaping eyes of Caleb. She thrust it at him and a wetness of joy ran across the fleshy rim of her glistening cunt. She lifted her bottom higher as if the meet the cane, squirmed herself, lifted her buttocks more.

47

"Alright!" she cried out. "Alright! Yes! Yes! Yes!"

Her buttocks went higher and the soft edges of her engorged cunt shone in the flickering light of the candles.

There was a momentary pause, then...

Thwack! Thwack! Thwack! Thwack!

Each one landed heavily across her upturned buttocks. They rained down on her but the more she had the more she screamed. Finally, the flickering of the candles dimmed as her eyes saw less and less, the sound of the cane became more distant and even her screams seemed far away. In the end, all went dark and silent. Occasionally she sensed the pain of the writhing cane but it did not seem part of her experience any more, it seemed part of another world, a world of unbelievable pain.

When Maria awoke she was lying on her back on a cold wooden trestle. She rolled onto her side and her bottom hurt terribly. She looked across the small room, it was some sort of antechapel. Around the walls, heavy, green curtains hung from brass curtain rails and her clothes were piled up on the floor. She looked down at herself, her bra was still hanging loose and her panties were twisted up around her knees, her wrists were red and her hands were still swollen. She started to sit up and winced as she felt her weight on her bottom. She went over to her clothes and started to pick amongst them absently. Then she turned as she heard someone draw back one of the green curtains.

It was Father Thomas!

"Come back this evening child, after you finish work, we will continue then. You have made a good start, you have been introduced to the cane and I am pleased with you. You may yet be saved but you will have to suffer much more. And remember, I will be watching you from now on, and don't forget your new master, the cane; it will be him and his friends who will be testing you and leading you to forgiveness. If you go astray again it will be them to whom you answer. This evening then, as soon as you finish work."

"Yes Father."

"Good."

Ten minutes later she ran from the church, sweating and breathing heavily. She had managed to dress herself fairly well but still looked dishevelled and distressed. She could not repair her bra and had thrown it in a dustbin together with her dirty panties. As she had tossed her underclothes into the overfilled bin she noticed a man looking at her. He looked like a tramp, he had a dirty red beard, his hair was tangled and matted and he wore a long brown overcoat. He watched her inquisitively and it made her feel disgusted and ashamed to think he had seen her dirty panties and torn bra, so she ran behind a wall near some derelict buildings and, gasping for breath, threw herself down amongst some rubble. When she realised that the man was not following her she relaxed. She sank down against the wall and squatted with her hands clasped together between her knees. The cool air blew up her tight skirt and she felt it fanning her naked cunt.

She stared down at a green, cider bottle that was lying on the ground in front of her. She had kicked it as she had hurried behind the wall and it was still rocking back and forth on the litter strewn ground. It tinkled rhythmically against a squashed can which lay alongside it; it reminded her of the swishing of the cane and the savage punishment she had just endured. She reached her hands down between her legs and ran them up the underneath of her thighs. She jerked back as she touched the swollen weals that laced her buttocks.

She rubbed the raised stripes gently and the stinging gradually faded. She kept rubbing them and sank into thinking about her punishment and the more she thought about it the more she realised that it was her only hope of salvation.

As she rubbed her bottom she found her fingers straying to her anus. She felt its edges and squatted down more as she felt its tingling pleasure at the touch of her fingertips. Almost without thinking she pressed the tip of her forefinger inside. The firm circular muscle gave way and her finger sank in easily. She squatted down more as it entered and she drew it inside.

The palm of her hand pressed against her fleshy cunt as her finger worked around the inside edges of her anus. She looked down between her legs and watched the flat of her hand massaging the soft flesh between her legs. Her finger went deeper and she gasped as it drove in up to the knuckle. She drew it back then pushed it in again even more deeply. As it drew back her muscles contracted and held it tight, making it throb under the pressure. As she pushed it back in her muscles relaxed to let it enter and sucked it up eagerly. She dropped her head and raised and lowered her squatting buttocks rhythmically. Her hair fell down across her face and she stared through its tangled strands at the green bottle.

She moved her finger up and down faster. She started panting as her anus pulsated around her finger, gripping it tightly then relaxing and sucking it in again. She stretched her finger as much as she could and plunged it in as deep as it would go, but it was not enough. Her body craved more penetration than her finger could provide and she reached forward with her other hand and grabbed the bottle. She turned it upright and planted it firmly on the ground then, lifting herself higher, she moved the bottle back between her legs, feeling its smooth edges as they glanced the insides of her thighs.

She drew her finger out and felt the dissipated ring of her anus throbbing for more. She placed the neck of the bottle directly beneath her demanding anus, lifted herself some more, then slowly dropped down until the ring of her hot anus touched the round top of the neck of the green bottle. She pushed herself down onto it, it went in smoothly and she gasped as she felt its coldness inside her.

She pressed down more and it slid in eagerly - first as far as her finger then, more satisfyingly, deeper. She opened her legs wide and sat down on it, and as it sank in, her anus opened to accommodate the widening neck. She took as much as it could offer and, as it plunged deeply inside, her eyes widened with the cold delight of its smooth penetration.

She plunged her hands between her legs and pulled her outer labia wide apart. Her clitoris hung down, throbbing and hot, and she tugged at it and massaged it. She thought of her punishment, of the cane and the pain that it had inflicted on her, of the red weals across her bottom, of her bestial screams and the feelings of humiliation.

Then she felt the pleasure of the bottle as she dropped even further onto it, she felt so degraded and delighted, and she sensed a feeling she had never had before, she was spinning relentlessly from dirtiness to purity and back again. As she bore down on the bottle she realised that her self-defilement would lead her back to punishment and, when she was punished, that would help cleanse her, but after her punishment she could defile herself again and once more enjoy its painful fruits.

It was an endless cycle from which she now knew she did not want to escape! The realisation rushed through her and she felt a deep delight as her anus gripped the neck of the bottle and her cunt dilated and ran with the moisture of her joy.

She plunged herself wildly onto the bottle and as she looked up she saw the tramp watching her, he had his hands deep inside his long coat and was moving them slowly at his groin. For a moment she was afraid, then, staring at him, she opened her legs wider and pulled at her clitoris until, still with the green bottle deeply inside her anus, she collapsed in a gasping orgasm of delight and humiliation.

An hour later she arrived at the agency. Lesley, her boss, was in her small office talking to a man, so Maria had to wait. The man had his back to Maria so she could not see his face but he had a shock of golden hair like the man who had beaten her as she had lain across the refrigerator earlier. The sight of the hair and the thought of her beating made her shiver.

Lesley seemed to be having a heated argument with the man she was calling Kirk, and Maria watched as she banged the table between them with her hand then shook her fist at him, shouting his name and swearing at him. Maria had seen Lesley's anger before - she was very dominant and, indeed, had been a prefect when they had both been at the same school and had beaten her. She was frightened when Lesley banged the table so hard some papers fell off the edge, which put her into even more of a rage. She pointed angrily to the door.

As Kirk left, his golden hair swirled across the side of his face and, as he turned, Maria saw that it was indeed the man who had beaten her. He sneered at her, then stamped out and went down the street.

Lesley came out of the office and drew back in surprise when she saw Maria leaning against her desk. Maria noticed a puzzling mixture of compassion and anger in Lesley's eyes as she asked her to come into the toilets to 'sort things out'.

Maria followed her like a lamb.

"You look terrible!" said Lesley as she helped Maria sit on a small stool which stood by a wash-hand basin in the back room. "What on earth has happened to you? Here, let me dry your face, you poor thing."

"I'm alright really, really I'm alright," Maria stuttered, still shocked by the sight of her attacker but not daring to ask what he had been doing there.

As she tried to sit down she winced and had to hold herself away from the chair.

"You don't seem alright at all. What's happened? Are you in pain?"

"Well, yes."

"Here, let me look... My God!"

Lesley hurried for a flannel and ran some cold water over it. She got Maria to bend over the small stool and gently dabbed the wet flannel across Maria's bruised bottom. Maria felt safe in Lesley's hands and let her put the flannel wherever she wanted. After a while, Lesley stepped back, rested against the basin and looked again at Maria's naked bottom.

"Now, what is all this?"

Maria was too ashamed. She just shook her head.

"Oh well." Lesley shook her head, "At least I'll go and find you some fresh panties - hand on, I answer the phone first."

The telephone call was a very angry one, with Lesley shouting and banging on the desk, but when it ended she came back and gave Maria a pair of skimpy red panties. They felt smooth as Maria pulled them up over her stinging buttocks.

As the day went on the stinging subsided, but the fear of what lay in store when she next visited Father Thomas caused Maria's stomach to ache with a pain that mixed terror with anxious excitement.

That evening, Maria stood with Lesley as she locked the door of the agency. Lesley put her arm around Maria's shoulder and gave her a squeeze.

"Where are you going now?"

"To the church near my flat."

"Why?"

"To confess."

Lesley smiled. "Make sure you go straight there then. We don't want you to get into more trouble do we?"

"I will. Oh, I will."

CHAPTER 5

It was not long before Maria arrived at the church. She stood at the huge door and held onto the large iron latch without turning it. For a moment she thought of turning and running away, but she knew that was pointless, she had started on the road to her salvation and she had got to see it through. She pushed open the heavy door and went inside.

Father Thomas was standing inside and Caleb was crouched by his side holding his pointed staff.

"We have been waiting. Do not be late in future or I will not be able to let you out again."

Father Thomas turned and Caleb prodded Maria with his pointed staff. She twisted to avoid it, but he still managed to stick it into her calf. It was sharp and she winced but did not cry out. Father Thomas led the way to a small chapel behind the altar. Against one wall was a small table upon which stood some candlesticks and in the centre was a low wooden bench. Just above the bench hung the ends of a slender rope which was pulled through a large iron hook bolted to the ceiling. On one of the walls there hung some shiny metal rings. Candlelight flickered on their burnished surface and gold coloured cords dangled loosely down from them.

Father Thomas reached beneath the small table and took out a black leather whip. It was quite long, plaid from shiny leather strands, with a smooth, thick handle and a plain, sharp tip. He flexed it between his hands then suddenly smacked it down on the table. Caleb giggled and Maria felt her body filling with fear.

"Now, your first lesson with the whip, my child. You have tasted the cane but the cane is only the whip's gentle brother. The whip is violent and uncontrollable, see how it flexes in anticipation of the pain it can administer."

He flexed it again. She saw how strong it was and how eagerly it wanted to return to its natural straightness. Then he smacked it against the top of the bench and Maria's body shook at the hard unforgiving sound it made.

"You have not been truly beaten yet. You did not need to be tied down for the cane, you could bear its thrashing without bonds, but not so with the whip. The whip is too hurtful to bear without firm bondage to keep you in place. For the whip, you must be tied down tightly. The whip is too savage to bear without restraint."

Maria stared at him, waiting for her instructions. She heard his words but could not really believe that this could be more painful than the cane. This time, she thought, she would not struggle, she would accept her punishment gladly.

"Caleb!"

Caleb jumped to attention with his staff by his side. "Bring her!"

Caleb pointed his staff at Maria's legs and shepherded her towards the wooden bench.

"Down!" ordered Father Thomas. "Down on your knees. Get down you fucking bitch!"

Maria was suddenly frightened by Father Thomas's angry words, her composure was disappearing and her fear was mounting. Perhaps the whip was more painful, perhaps it would be too much for her to bear? As the thoughts came so did a wave of fear that quickly turned into a desperate desire to escape. She fought hard against it, but her terror heaved through her in floods of nausea.

"Down, you fucking bitch. Down on the bench! Crawl onto it. Now you will be tested. Now we shall see how much you can really suffer. I am going to test you with the whip. I am going to give you pain you never thought existed. Get down! Crawl!"

Caleb prodded her and she moved to the bench, bent down and rested her hands on it then looked up at Father Thomas for her next instruction. She looked weak and defenceless, like a fawn.

"Get on your knees! I am losing patience. Get on your knees!"

He flexed the whip impatiently between his hands. Maria lifted her legs and knelt on the bench. The wood felt hard against her knees and she squirmed them about. The ends of the rope which hung from the hook in the ceiling draped loosely across her back and against her waist.

"Tie her Caleb."

Caleb ran across to the rings on the wall and drew out the gold coloured cords, then, twirling them around like lassoes, rushed back to the bench where Maria was crouching in fear. He grabbed her shoulders roughly and thrust them downwards towards the bench. The abruptness of the movement hurt her neck and she dropped onto her elbows and gasped. Quickly Caleb wound the cords around her wrists and secured them beneath the bench, then he put his foot on its edge, leaned back and pulled on the cords so tightly that she cried out.

"Please... Stop... Oh please..."

But he took no notice and kept pulling until they cut deeply into her wrists. She felt tears forming around her eyes.

"How does that feel bitch? Do you want it tighter?"

"No... Please... No..."

"Silence you fucking bitch! Silence!"

Caleb ran around to her legs and wound the cords around her calves but this time he let the other ends dangle free at the sides of the bench.

"Hoist her up, my servant!"

Caleb began to dance around the bench, darting in front of Maria's face, performing a curtsy, then running on frantically in giddy circles.

"Hoist her up I said!"

Caleb stopped prancing and threw down his staff; it crashed on the floor and bounced against the wall. He took hold of one end of the rope which hung from the hook in the ceiling and pulled it around Maria's waist. She gasped for breath as he tightened it. It bit into her skin and she contorted with pain but did not dare cry out. Caleb pulled the rope tighter then fixed a knot in it. Maria could hardly breathe. Then Caleb grabbed hold of the other end of the rope and looped it through the knot at her waist. He jumped up on the bench and reached as high up the rope as he could, held it tightly, then swung out and jumped back down onto the floor.

Maria felt a terrible pain around her waist as the rope snatched her upwards under the weight of Caleb's body. He dragged it back through the hook in the ceiling and her waist was drawn up until she was bent over and suspended by the pinching rope. Tears fell from her eyes, she felt captured and humiliated and hung her head low so that Father Thomas could not see her shame. Caleb tied off the end of the rope and ran to Father Thomas's side.

"Panties Caleb?"

"Panties! Panties! White panties! White panties!" Caleb cried out wildly.

He ran to Maria's side and lifted her dress slowly. As it lifted he saw her red panties and shrieked.

"Red panties! Red panties! Horrid! Horrid! Hateful red panties!"

"Disgusting!" said Father Thomas. "Shameful! Get them off! Pull them off the harlot! Shameless child! Pull them off my servant, as quickly as you can. Pull the vile, red panties off the shameless bitch! Bitch! Bitch! Shameless bitch!"

Caleb grabbed the red panties and angrily tore them down, ripping them and dragging them down to just above her knees. As the material tightened against her thighs Maria flinched and wriggled anxiously, but Caleb gave her a heavy smack across the bottom to make her stop. Then he grabbed the loose ends of cord at her calves, tied them tightly underneath the bench and pulled them with all his strength until they dug deeply into the flesh of her calves. She could not move them at all; she could only feel the tingling of the blood trying to run through her constricted veins.

"We'll soon stop her wriggling, eh Caleb?"

Caleb jumped around the bench, circling and prancing.

"Stop her wriggling. Stop her wriggling."

Maria hung like an animal on the rope, her forearms and calves secured painfully to the bench and her waist bowed under the upward strain of the rope from the ceiling. Her buttocks were bare and exposed and the red panties which Lesley had found for her were pulled in shreds around her knees. She began to cry.

"Oh, my child," said Father Thomas softly, "do not cry yet, you are a long way from being saved, it is too soon to cry, wait until you really suffer before you cry. It is a good thing that you came to me when you did. It is a good thing that I have the whip to bring you to obedience. Are you ready to begin the punishment?"

"Please Father. I don't think I can stand any more!"

"Still! Be still! The whip will be your master. When he has had his way with you, when he has striped your buttocks with his marks, then you will plead for more, not less! ... is she bound tight enough Caleb?"

Caleb nodded excitedly.

"Good! It is time and we will begin. This time you will taste the unfathomable pleasures of the greatest inflictor of pain there is, the whip. Oh yes, the whip is a vicious master, but it brings obedience like no other, even the cane shrinks back in fear of its power. But, I have to warn you, the whip is its own master and it punishes its victims in the ways that it chooses. Though I can wield it, or try to direct it, I cannot control it, the whip itself will inflict whatever pain it decides you must suffer. I cannot prevent it or hold it back for I am its victim as much as the body which stretches out before it. We begin!"

Maria hung on her bonds terrified. Her buttocks were stretched tight and the flesh of her cunt was exposed between her tied legs. Her hard nipples rubbed sorely against the inside her dress. She felt petrified but she could only submit. Then it started.

Whack!

The whip came down with such ferocity that Maria lurched forward on her bonds and screamed out.

Whack!

Another painful slash across her buttocks and she screamed again.

Whack!

This time it burned deep into her skin and she cried out fiendishly.

Whack!

She felt slashed by the scorching whip as she roared like a savage monster and the cavernous church echoed with her pain.

Whack!

She felt herself going giddy, she screamed again and again and tried to pull away, but her bonds held her completely fast.

Whack!

Another scream, another deep cut and her eyes went blurred, she felt herself losing consciousness, she could not bear any more.

Whack!

This time she could not scream and just hung limply on the rope that suspended her by the waist. The pain was so great, and she could not bear it, but she could not escape it; somehow her body would not let her fall unconscious. She felt totally hopeless as she realised she would have to suffer whatever the whip decided.

Whack!

Another scream but this time fainter, it was so weak it was hardly a scream at all, more a pathetic, begging whimper.

Whack!

No scream this time, she only blubbered, she wanted to beg but words were no longer hers.

Whack!

She could not speak, nor scream nor blubber, she wanted to beg for forgiveness but she could not find the strength or will to beg. She could not move, she could not even wince under the flailing of the whip, and now she could not even hope. She hung loosely and the rope around her waist dug in deeply as it pulled against her weight.

Whack!

There was nothing left to do but suffer, she could not lose consciousness, she could not plead for it to stop, she could only absorb the terror that the whip was dealing out. The pain was so great it ran through her in huge, uncontrollable waves and her tortured body rose and fell against its bonds as if caught helplessly in a mighty tide.

Whack! Whack! Whack! Whack! Whack!

They were coming so fast now. Somehow she realised that Father Thomas had lost control, she knew that the whip was in command and she was suffering the pain that only the whip knew she deserved. One after the other the whacks from the whip struck her buttocks, the terrible pains from each stroke merging into the next as she writhed in a paroxysm of continual agony. Spit dribbled freely from her mouth and ran disgustingly down her chin as she hung like a tormented animal under the frenzied punishment of the uncontrollable whip.

But through this feeling of disgust, beyond this sensation of relentless torture, she sensed something different. Through the blurring intensity of her suffering she realised something other than just the feelings of disgust and hurt, it was something deeper even than the cuts that were being inflicted by the uncontrolled flailing of the whip. She sensed a glimmer of her salvation. It was as though, beyond all the pain, there was a radiance of purification. She pressed her buttocks to the whip, wanting the flogging to continue forever so that she could approach closer to the light that promised to cleanse her of her sinfulness. Then suddenly it stopped.

Maria sensed it was all over and she sagged desperately on the rope. She felt as if she was being burned all over and her bottom felt as if it was on fire; pain filled her whole body. She gasped and spit bubbled messily from her mouth then she gasped again and started to come back to the realisation of what was happening to her. Then she felt the rope around her waist and let out a terrifying scream. It was not a scream in response to direct pain but a scream born of all the pain that had gone before. She thought she would not be able to stop. She knew she had to take a breath before she could scream again, but when it came, it was only enough breath to continue the frightening scream that burst from her like steam from an engine. She could not stop, she thought she would die before it would end, she felt her whole life would be eaten up by her terrible all-consuming scream.

After what seemed an age, the beating finally stopped and, although in the empty silence of the church her screams still rang in her ears like trumpets, she faded away into an uncomfortable unconsciousness. Then she felt the strain at her waist loosening and she dropped heavily onto the bench. For a while at least, she had been released.

As the drumming in her ears subsided she could hear Father Thomas talking to someone. She could not hear the other person and could only pick up fragments of what Father Thomas said but Maria could sense fear in his voice.

"I'm sorry, I'm very sorry, yes, I know it was wrong, I thought it would be alright to let her go during the day, I felt sorry for her... Yes! Yes! I'm sorry, I know it was wrong, yes, I know, please forgive me."

Then the drumming in her ears returned. The next thing she knew Father Thomas was standing beside her, speaking to her, but now his voice had changed, it was no longer fearful, it was taunting and cruel.

"So, you want more do you?"

Maria shrunk back in terror.

"I think you do. Ah yes, I can see it in your eyes. You want more! You little bitch, you fucking little bitch. You want more! Whether you do or not, you are going to get it. You have got me into trouble, appealing to my better self. Yes, you are going to get more and this time there will be no release!"

He sat down on the edge of the bench beside her and flexed the whip across his knees.

"I have never seen the whip so angry. I have never felt its power so great. It nearly tore itself from my hands in order to punish you enough, and yet, I can see it has not brought you to heal. Even suffering as much as it can give, the whip has not been enough to save you from your sinfulness. You are a wicked little bitch, that is for sure. This is going to be such a long road. Of course, you will have to stay. Ah yes, you will have to stay. I cannot let you go now. I thought I could, but ah, no, not now, not now I have seen how much it will take. You will have to stay now, oh yes, you will have to stay alright."

"Please Father," she murmured, "please, I have to go to work."

Father Thomas laughed and stood up beside her, he looked down at her red striped buttocks and laughed again.

"Impossible! Now you are mine for as long as it takes."

He flexed the whip again then tapped it against his knees.

"But the whip has a kinder side, my child. Yes, it can

63

bring the most excruciating pain, but it can also bring un-fathomable pleasure. It is the bearer of both terror and desire. See how it flexes with anticipation. See how it tenses along its full length at the thought of the pleasures it can bring. It is letting me know that now it is time for you to take its pleasure. Of course you will demand more pain from it, but before you beg for more pain it needs to show you its kindness. Lie there my child, Caleb has slackened the rope around your waist so that you can respond to the gentle delights of the whip. Raise your bottom, yes, I know it is still sore, I can see the red slashes that the whip has inflicted on you, but raise it up, pull it high so that your flesh pokes out between your burning buttocks. Let the whip see your rosy cunt and the dark ring of your beautiful anus, raise it high and welcome its attentions."

Her calves and wrists were still tightly bound, but her waist was free and, although her body ached all over, she eased herself up. Her back ached and she could feel the pain around her waist where the rope had suspended her full weight, but still she eased her bottom higher. She felt the skin stretch against the red marks that the whip had inflicted so punishingly, but she did what she was told.

"Ah, yes, what a beauty. I can see that soft flesh coming into view. What a beauty. Its rosy edges shine with moisture. Open your buttocks my child, I want to see it all, I want to see it gaping at me, show me your beautiful arse."

She eased herself higher and bent her back up in the same way that she had been hung on the rope. She felt Father Thomas's penetrating eyes staring in between her buttocks and wanted to show him more. She wanted him to see her cunt, she wanted to open her buttocks and show him the muscular ring of her anus and show him how it was dilating with the joy of her exposure.

"What a beauty my child. Show it to me and I will introduce it to the kindness of the whip."

She did not know what he meant, but she felt within her an urgent demand that was forcing her to move towards whatever pleasure was there. So, she lifted herself higher and opened her buttocks even wider, squeezing the insides of her thighs apart as far as they would go. Then she began to moan with the anticipation of whatever awaited her. Deep inside she knew she wanted pain but the temptation of pleasure drew her in like the sucking wet lips of a ravenous wolf.

Father Thomas drew the tip of the whip into the firm valley of flesh that puckered between the base of her buttocks and the smooth curves of her thighs. He probed its hard end lazily into the crack and pushed it slightly open, exposing the darkness of her anus and revealing it from the protective pleats of her soft skin. He pressed the sharp tip around its edges and it dilated under the pressure.

As she felt the sharp tip she sensed the pain again, but it was not really a pain, she knew it was only an introduction to something entirely different. She felt the heat of pleasure and her body sought it out as she squirmed her buttocks, trying to find the end of the whip and get it to the centre of her aching muscular ring. The whip bent as he pressed harder and she pulled back a little as the hard edges of the whip's tip bit into the edge of her anus. Then she squirmed some more and as it found the centre of her readily pulsating ring, she pushed hard against it and the end slid in.

"See how he slides in so freely. Feel him tickle your innards. Feel him prickle against the inside edges of your beautiful arse. Is he not indeed a bringer of pleasure?"

"Oh yes Father. I can feel the point. It is so fine and yet it is tracing every sense that I have. It is finding every vein and prickling it as though I was an instrument. Please, Father, more."

Father Thomas pressed the point of the whip in further, he twisted it around, and Maria twisted with it. She moaned with every movement and her mouth fell open, gaping with both anxiety and fulfilment. She wanted to feel her cunt, she wanted to slip her fingers between its wet folds and seek out her burning clitoris, but she could not, she could only ache and suffer the frustration of her bonds. She dropped her tongue onto her bottom lip and let it dribble the spit which ran down and dripped from its end. She raised her bottom as high as she could and submitted eagerly to the penetrating point of the delving tip.

"Father, please smack me. Smack me as my punishment for enjoying the whip. Smack me for enjoying its pain and its pleasure. Please Father, I want to feel your hand across my bottom. I want to feel you punishing me."

"No, my child, you cannot be smacked while the whip is enjoying you like this."

"Please Father, smack me. Please, I need smacking. I want to feel the sting across my bottom. I want to dribble as it shocks me I want to squeeze my buttocks under the shock and squeeze the whip inside my arse. Please, Father smack me. Smack me!"

Father Thomas sighed in despair.

"No, my child. I have told you, no."

"Father, please, please smack my bottom. You can smack it as hard as you want, I don't care how hard it comes. I want it hard, I want to be punished, I want to be in pain. The whip is so exquisite, I need some pain to dilute it or I think I will die. Please Father, smack me hard, smack me for the rest of the night, smack me and don't stop, smack me forever. Please Father, I can't survive without it."

Father Thomas sighed again as he twisted the tip of the whip deeply into her anus. Maria groaned loudly, then submissively bent her head and licked at the pool of spit that was running from her mouth. She drooled and salivated, sucked at it noisily and spit back into it, she felt like the wolf.

"Smack me! Father, smack me! I beg you, smack me! Keep the whip inside me and smack me as hard as you can!"

"What a wretched bitch you are. Here bitch, take that!"

Smack!

The tingling in her arse built into a sharp, searing sting of delight as Father Thomas's hand smacked down on her bottom. She lurched forward, shocked and satisfied.

"Again! I'm a wretched bitch, I know I am! Smack me again!"

Smack!

She pitched forward again as the smack knocked the breath from her.

"Again! I'm a wretched bitch! Beat me more!"

Smack!

She gulped as she was knocked forward. The whip twisted inside her and the pale, tight cheeks of her bottom were set on fire with the weight of the stinging smack.

"Again! Harder!"

Smack!

"Again! Harder! Harder! Harder!"

Smack! Smack! Smack!

"Father, please keep the tip inside. Force it in as far as you want. I can feel myself coming, my cunt is filling with it. Harder! Harder! The bitch wants more! Please Father, harder! Harder!"

Smack! Smack! Smack!

Maria lifted her bottom even higher, forcing her scorching buttocks back onto the unremitting smacks and her anus further down the pointed end of the whip. She gasped a deep, throaty gasp and she felt her cunt running with moisture. She gasped again and fell forward, her face splashed into the pool of spit that was spread out on the wooden surface of the bench and she licked her tongue out and drank it up, drooling and salivating with her wretchedness and giddily drunk with the pleasures of pain and delight. When she had sucked up all her spit, she squashed her lips against the bench and let her bottom fall back.

"Thank you Father," she muttered quietly. Thank you for beating me."

Father Thomas withdrew the whip and stood in front of her.

"Now my child, we are finished for the day and you must be taken down to the place of captivity. We will continue with your training tomorrow. Caleb!"

Caleb danced up and undid her bonds, they fell away loosely but she did not move, even when he began prodding her with his staff. In the end, she got up shakily and stood with her red panties still hanging torn around her knees.

"Take her down to the vault, my servant."

Caleb stabbed the point of his staff at the backs of her calves and forced her forward into the darkness at the end of the chapel.

CHAPTER 6

"Bitch! Bitch!" screeched Caleb as he prodded her angrily with his staff. "Dungeon! Dungeon! Bitch in the dun-

68

geon!"

Maria stumbled as he forced her forward through a dingy corridor. She stubbed her toes on protruding stones in the floor and realised that she had left her shoes in the chapel. Every so often there were candles stuck into recesses in the stone walls, flickering like greasy pools of false safety. Each time she reached one she rested on the wall to steady herself and feel some comfort from the nearness of the flame, but Caleb moved her on, stabbing her legs and making her yelp. The floor was wet and cold and as she trudged on she felt slimy water running between her toes.

"Move! Move! Bitch! Bitch!"

She tried to pull her red panties up but Caleb jabbed her hard and she had to leave them hanging loosely and torn just above her knees. It was difficult to walk and the more she stumbled the more angry it made Caleb. Once, when she tripped and had to hold onto the wall to stop herself from falling, he lifted up the back of her dress and smacked her bottom hard. After a while she saw the tunnel opening out into a huge vaulted cellar. Caleb pushed her forward and as she looked in she gasped.

"In bitch! Dungeon for a bitch!"

It was a huge stone-built dungeon. Candles were stuck in recesses and flickered with a sickening and uneven yellow light. The walls were studded with iron rings that hung from heavy metal chains and in the middle of the room were benches and various wooden and iron contraptions. Maria could hardly believe what she saw. On each of the walls there were young women hanging from the rings. Their heads hung down limply in fear and exhaustion, and all of them had a wide piece of tape pulled tightly across their mouths. They were all naked except for one whose clothes seemed to have been partially ripped from her and

69

dangled down in pitiful tatters. As Maria looked at her she saw that this one had high cheekbones and dark eyes.

"Over there!" shouted Caleb as he prodded Maria forward.

Maria tried to hold back but Caleb forced her on. She shrunk from the strange benches and instruments in the middle of the dungeon floor and tried not to look at the desperate women as they slumped heavily in their chains.

"Wake up! Wake up! New friend! New friend!"

Caleb started dancing around the dungeon, going from one woman to the next, the first he slapped on the leg and she looked up in shock and fear, another one he prodded with his staff and she groaned and lifted her face slowly. Then he went to the one with the tattered clothes and reached up and pulled at her dress. It ripped and her firm breasts were exposed but she just stared forward vacantly, her face pulled tightly beneath the shiny silver tape.

"Over here!"

He motioned to Maria with his staff. She walked towards him and he grabbed her viciously, pulling her towards the wall and turning her so that she stood against it facing the centre of the dungeon. Then he ran and fetched a wooden stool and dragged it over. He jumped up on it and pulled one of Maria's arms as high as he could. She cried out as he stretched it higher but he took no notice and thrust her wrist through one of the manacles that hung from the wall and clamped it firmly together. It pinched her skin and she cried out again, but he only laughed, then shackled her other wrist and jumped down.

She hung on the manacles limply, her hair wet and tangled around her face and her red panties twisted up above her knees.

"Please -"

"Silence! No talking! Dirty little bitch! Dirty, dirty little bitch!"

Angrily he picked up the stool and smashed it towards her, she managed to twist sideways and it hit the wall and broke in his hands.

"Silence!"

Then he picked up his staff, ran out of the dungeon and disappeared back down the tunnel. Everything went quiet and Maria started to sob. She drifted into an uncomfortable sleep, then suddenly woke with a start. Her eyes opened wide as she heard the sound of footsteps coming down the tunnel. She pulled on her manacles and felt terrible pain in her arms and wrists. Father Thomas entered the dungeon and approached Maria. She looked at him briefly then hung her head, afraid of what he might say or do.

"Lift your head my child," said Father Thomas. "There is nothing to be afraid of here. I am here to help you. I am here to help you cleanse your sins. Now, let's have a good look at you."

He reached forward and lifted her chin.

"You really are quite a beauty my child. But there is still much work to do if you are ever to be saved."

"Oh, yes Father Thomas, I must be saved."

"And are you prepared to suffer for it my child?"

"Yes, Father, oh yes, you know I am."

"Well, that is a start but I must find out what you have got to be saved from first. We cannot start training you properly until we know exactly the nature of your sins... Caleb! Bring her to the table."

Caleb jumped up, braced his feet against the wall, then clung like a bat to Maria's manacles. Maria could feel the heat from his body as he strained to undo the metal rings around her wrists. She turned away from him as he pulled and tugged at her bonds until finally they came undone

71

and she dropped to her knees. He jumped down by her side and pushed her to the centre of the dungeon.

"Sit here my girl," said Father Thomas pointing to a wooden trestle. "So, what are your sins my child?"

"Father, you know that when I was younger I refused a spanking from you. You wanted to save me then, but I ran away from you. Oh Father!"

"That was very bad my child."

"Father, I have been so bad since. I have enjoyed spanking and the feel of -"

"Yes, the feel of?"

"I can't say Father, I don't like to say."

"You must not be even more sinful my child, you must say everything."

"Well, Father, I have enjoyed the feeling of a man's -"

"Go on."

"I have enjoyed the feeling of a man's... thing. His, his cock, Father."

"And where did you enjoy it my dear?"

"In my bottom Father."

"Up your arse you mean."

"Yes, I enjoyed a man's cock up my arse. Yes, I enjoyed a man's cock up my arse."

"And did you know the man?"

"No, Father, I didn't know him, he was a stranger."

"And what else?"

"I pushed a bottle up there as well, and enjoyed a man, a dirty filthy man, watching me while I did it."

"Did you know him?"

"No, Father, he was a stranger as well."

"What else?"

"I have tasted the cane and the whip as well, and I have enjoyed the pain they gave me. I have been spanked and smacked and no matter how much it has hurt I have wanted more. Oh, Father, can I truly be saved or am I too evil?"

"But that is not all is it my child?"

"Father, that is all I can remember."

"Yes, but that is not really all is it? You have more desires, I think. I can see in your eyes that you have more desires and it is those that I must know about. Tell me your secret desires, tell me your secret fantasies, I can see you have them, I must know them so that I can lead you to salvation."

"Father, oh Father, you're right. I am so bad! I am so evil! I have terrible thoughts, I have terrible desires, I don't dare admit them though, they are too shameful, they are too terrible."

"Tell them, tell them all. I must know them and then I can help you. Tell me all your fantasies my child."

"Oh Father I can't. I just can't."

He leant towards Maria and offered his hand, she reached forward and took it.

"Here my child, come here I can see that you need help."

She stood up and he led her gently to a large contraption that was near the trestle. It was about ten feet long and made of heavy timber. At one end there were black leather thongs attached to iron pegs and at the other was a wide, wooden drum with handles attached to each side. More black, leather thongs were wound around the drum and trailed from it onto the heavy, wooden base.

"I think this will help you tell us your sinful thoughts, my child. When you feel the strains from our friend here, I think your tongue will loosen and you will be keener to tell us how dirty you really are."

Maria shrunk back as she realised that she about to be tied onto a rack!

73

"Lie down on it my child, prepare to feel the caress of its thongs around your wrists and ankles, prepare to sense the strain from the wheel as it squeezes your evil fantasies from you."

Maria sat on the edge of the rack, then obediently lay on her back. She felt the wood of its base, cold and smooth against her skin, and it made her shiver. She looked around the dungeon and saw that all the women hanging in their manacles were watching her. She stretched her arms above her head submissively and widened her legs as far as her red panties would allow. As she felt the tension of her panties cutting into her legs, a wave of terror ran through her and then a flush of unbelievable excitement. The rack would be her means of salvation, at last she would be made to confess her sins.

Caleb started prancing around the walls of the dungeon, prodding the women with his staff as he passed them. One of them screamed loudly as the point of his staff pricked deeply into her thigh.

"Caleb! Come here and secure her."

He came over and began tying Maria's wrists to the thongs that trailed from the wheel of the rack. He pulled them tightly and she squirmed as the pain intensified, then he clambered across her and crouched down by her ankles, tied them as well and leaned back against the knots in order to pull them as firmly as he could. She lay splayed open on the rack, her arms were pulled up close to the sides of her face and her hair lay in sweat covered tangles across her cheeks. Her black skirt was pulled up around her thighs and her red panties dug into the sides of her knees that were pulled as wide as they would go by the taut thongs. She breathed deeply and waited.

Caleb played with the hem of Maria's skirt, lifting it, peering beneath it and giggling. She felt his glare and squirmed, she felt so exposed but could do nothing to cover or protect herself. She hoped they would leave her skirt on, she dreaded being completely naked.

Father Thomas called Caleb over and gave him some instructions, he sniggered and ran out of the dungeon with a sense of excitement and purpose. Father Thomas then walked over to the woman who still had some clothes on, he ripped the tape from her face and began feeling her breasts. Maria craned her neck to see. The girl looked at Father Thomas and smiled as he cupped her breasts in his hands and massaged them firmly. Then her grabbed her by the neck and she gasped. He slipped his hand higher and squeezed her cheeks together so that her lips pursed out, then he lurched towards her and began kissing her mouth. He salivated all around her face and licked her eyes and she started moaning and writhing her hips and legs.

Then Father Thomas thrust his hand down between the tops of the woman's thighs, grabbed the flesh of her cunt through the rags of her dress, and tugged at it roughly. She writhed more and began moaning loudly as he pulled at the top of her dress and ripped some of the material that hung raggedly below her breasts. He tore some more away and, as though it was a signal, she bent her face and started frantically kissing the top of his head. Her arms strained in the manacles and her fingers spread wide then clenched in repeated, rhythmic pulses. Then Father Thomas stood back from her and watched. She did not stop writhing and even though there was nothing to kiss she did not stop kissing. Her body pulsated wildly and her hands opened and closed madly. She started to dribble and moan even more loudly. Then she started to scream out loud. At first her words did not make any sense but then Maria could hear clearly what she was saying as she screeched and screamed in complete abandon.

"Fuck it Father. Stick your cock in it Father. Push your throbbing cock up my cunt, up my arse, stick it wherever you want to. Wank it in my mouth, let me suck it down, right down, let me suck it down my throat. I want to feel your swollen cock in my throat Father. Stick it in until I can't breathe. Finish down my throat Father and let me swallow everything you've got. Let me draw it out of you, let me suck it out, suck, suck, suck it up. Then fuck me again Father, fuck my wet cunt, fuck my aching arse. Fuck me, fuck me, Father. Fuck, fuck, fuck, fuck... Yes, yes, then you can spank me, you must spank me, harder, harder, harder. Then you can cane me for fucking you, cane me so hard I bleed, harder, harder. Then you can whip me for sucking you, oh whip me Father, sting me with the whip, all over my body, whip me, sting me, harder, harder. Then you can punish me in any way you want for wanting your dick up my arse. Oh, Father, fuck, fuck, fuck!"

She she rose up on her shackles and, tensing her whole body in a violent convulsion, she let out a terrible scream. She hung there, her body pinioned to the wall of the dungeon in a spasm of tension and relief. Then suddenly she dropped down heavily to the clanking sound of her straining chains and hung there gasping for breath and drenched with sweat.

Maria's eyes were wide. She had become so excited watching the woman, she had not wanted it to stop, her screams, her words and her response to Father Thomas. Yes, the way she had succumbed to him, that was what had excited the woman most of all, and her passion and dirtiness, it had been so instant, so overpowering.

Maria wanted to see more, she wanted Father Thomas to go to another woman and set her into a frenzy of excitement, she wanted to see him grabbing her cunt and licking her face, but most of all she wanted to see how she boiled into a frenzied seizure, an overpowering and uncontrolled frenzy of desire and abandon. It was that uninhibited outpouring of desire that had made her own cunt so wet with desire, it was the wild words and the dirtiness of it all that had made her cunt ache to be grabbed and violated.

Then Caleb pranced back through the tunnel swinging a small canvas bag in circles above his head.

"Got it! Got it!"

"Ah good," said Father Thomas. "Lift up her skirt, Caleb, and I will get to work."

Caleb jumped up onto the rack beside Maria, leered at her, then turned quickly and lifted her black skirt. The smooth skin of her flat stomach lay stretched in its shadow and he looked underneath it and put out his stumpy tongue.

"Lift it high. I need light to work. Here, pass me the bag Caleb."

Caleb stretched out his hand and passed the canvas bag to Father Thomas. He undid it and, after rummaging around inside it, took out a razor, some shaving soap and a bristle brush, all of which he placed between Maria's outstretched legs.

"Higher Caleb!"

Maria's skirt was pulled up higher until the waistband pulled painfully at her back. Father Thomas began working the brush into the soap, it was already wet, and soon it foamed up into a mass of white bubbles. He reached forward and started painting the soap around the black hairs that curled above her cunt. He rubbed the brush hard, working it between her legs so that all her hairs were covered in froth, then he took the razor and held it above her soap covered cunt.

Maria flinched at the first touch of the blade then relaxed slightly as she felt the silky pull of the blade across her flesh. Father Thomas dragged the razor smoothly across the base of her stomach until all her pubic hair at the front was cut away and she was smooth and clean-shaved. He felt her skin with his fingertips to check that he had not missed anything. Then her worked the shiny razor carefully between her legs, sheering off every hair until her outer labia were completely exposed and surrounded only by naked skin. He pushed his hand between her legs to inspect his work, her outer labia glistened and shone, their pinkness glittered in the yellow flickering of the candles; he sat back pleased. Then he felt in the bag and drew out a large pair of shiny silver scissors. Maria saw them glint as he held them up and she drew back anxiously.

"Do not be afraid my child. This is for your benefit. Here, see how they snap. Caleb! Loosen the skirt, let it fall so that she can feel the cold metal of the blade as it strips the whorish clothing from her body."

Caleb let the dress fall. Maria felt a momentary comfort as the black material fell down and covered her. Her skin felt sensitive and cool where it had been shaved and when the material of her skirt touched it she quivered with a mixture of excitement, fear and safety. Then she heard the scissors snapping again, and the feeling of fear overtook anything else she was experiencing. She heard the clicking of the blades getting nearer to her legs, then she felt Father Thomas's hand touch the inside of her knees and the cold metal blades glance the tender skin of the insides of her thighs. She felt them contact the material of her skirt, she felt them sheer through it and sensed it falling apart under their sharpness. Then the blades came higher, she could feel them approaching her naked cunt and the skirt was slowly parted as the scissors cut it higher and higher. She felt their coldness as they sheered around her cunt and their edges touched the naked base of her stomach as they worked their way towards the waistband.

Their back edges pressed deeply into her skin as Father Thomas opened them wide enough to accommodate the extra material at the waist, then he brought them together sharply and her skirt fell aside.

Now she felt completely exposed.

But the scissors did not stop, they carried on up the front of her blouse. He clipped them on one side of the buttons and the flimsy material began to peel away. He brought them up between her neat breasts and she felt their sharp coldness in her cleavage as he snipped them to the top of the last button. They stopped snipping when the blouse fell aside and he rested them for a moment against her throat.

She began trembling with fear as she suddenly realised her predicament: lying outstretched on the rack, shaved naked with her clothing cut apart and lying at her side, totally exposed and at the mercy of Father Thomas. She shuddered as she shrunk back from Caleb's mocking taunts and stared fearfully at the manacled women hanging limply in their chains. She could hardly believe it, but she knew it was happening, and she shook all over and felt the pain in her wrists and ankles and when she pulled at them the pain intensified. She struggled and tore at her bonds, her wrists hurt terribly as she writhed her pelvis and tried to turn her body to hide her nakedness. She twisted frantically and as she threw herself to one side she knocked Caleb off the side of the rack. He fell on the floor with a thud.

There was a moment of silence; she stopped moving, there was no noise; then there was uproar. The dungeon exploded into a turmoil of anger and noise. Caleb sprung to his feet and started screeching at the top of his voice, his face was purple with anger and he sprung at Maria like a wild animal. The woman on the walls all pulled frantically at their manacles and their chains clanged under the writhing of their limbs. Maria twisted herself wildly in distress and fear.

Caleb leapt between her legs and jumped up and down on the wooden base of the rack. He pulled the zip of his trousers open and his cock fell out into his hands. It was long and half erect. Maria could just see it as she strained her chin down towards her naked chest. He grabbed it and started pulling at it and it grew instantly into a huge, engorged member completely out of proportion with the size of his body. Maria twisted and turned, throwing her head from side to side in blind panic.

"Fucking bitch! Fucking bitch!"

Caleb held his throbbing cock up high then bent onto his knees and pressed its head against Maria's shaven cunt. She felt its heat and then its width as it began to penetrate her, the swollen glans forcing her outer labia apart with ease as it drove in without pausing.

"Caleb!" shouted Father Thomas. "Down Caleb!"

He took no notice and started thrusting his cock even deeper. Maria gasped as she felt the monstrous cock pushing painfully inside her, her thighs were stretched so tight that she could do nothing except let it enter. Caleb thrust again and his cock went even deeper. She gasped again as she felt its hot tip going higher than she had ever known.

"Caleb! Caleb!"

Father Thomas rushed forward and grabbed Caleb's shoulders, he tried to drag him off but Caleb was too strong and too angry. He thrust again, this time even deeper, and Maria screamed as his cock went in up to its base.

"Caleb! Caleb!"

Father Thomas struggled to get Caleb off but Caleb

was now thrusting at Maria like a dog. His pelvis moved frantically as he dropped his body on top of Maria and she gasped as his weight knocked her breath from her. He clasped his arms around her waist, buried his face into her breasts and held on tightly as he fucked her harder and harder refusing to let go. She screamed again as she felt his cock swelling even more, its tip was expanding against the insides of her vagina and she could hardly stand the strain, she felt as of she was going to explode. Father Thomas pulled frantically at Caleb's shoulders to get him away, but his grip was too tight and he was impossible to prize off.

As she contorted under the weight of the frantic dwarf, Maria felt her own body beginning to respond, not in fear but with desire. She felt her breasts pushing at his face and she felt her cunt driving onto his cock. She was beginning to match his frenzy. She could not hold him but she could follow the wild rhythm of his body and she could suck at his cock with her cunt. Her screams turned to yells, they matched his movements as well and she squeezed her cunt around his mighty cock even more. Father Thomas pulled as hard as he could and suddenly Caleb was wrenched from his prize, lifted bodily and thrown down onto the floor, his huge cock sticking up throbbing and wet.

Maria let out another yell, a yell of anger and dismay, her cunt stayed open and she wanted it filled, she looked at Father Thomas and stared deeply into his eyes.

"Fuck it Father, please fuck it."

Father Thomas stared back, then recoiled when he heard her words.

"You bitch! You evil little bitch!"

"Please Father, fuck it please. Please Father, fuck it, please, or Caleb, please, either of you, both of you, fuck it please, fuck it, fuck it, fuck it. I want a cock in my cunt. I want my cunt fucking. Please fill it, please fuck it. Fuck it, fuck it, fuck it, fuck it -"

She would not stop, she kept repeating it over and over again. Father Thomas rushed to one of the walls and pulled something down from a hook. He came back to Maria and held a leather gag with a ball at its centre above her mouth and shook it threateningly.

"Fuck it, fuck it, fuck my cunt, I want a cock in it, fucking, fucking, fucking -"

He slapped the gag across her face, the ball filled her mouth and she was silenced as he tied it tightly behind her head. Even so, she was still trying to make sounds, somewhere deep in her throat she was growling out her needs and her eyes blazed and her cunt ran with her delectable perfumed moisture.

"Caleb, you evil little bastard! Come to the wheel and put some turns on it."

Caleb folded his cock back into his trousers and zipped them up, then went obediently to the wheel of the rack, grabbed the spiky handles and waited for instructions. Father Thomas looked down at Maria, her mouth forced wide by the leather ball that filled her mouth, and the sides of the gag cutting deeply into her cheeks.

"I can tell there is much evil in you my child, so much evil. We are going to have to prize it out. We must get started straight away. A few turns on the wheel will let you know what is in store for you. I have already heard some of your filthy thoughts, now I want to know them all, all your dirty ideas, all your fantasies, all your evil desires. I want you to tell me all of them in every detail, then and only then can we begin to save you and cleanse you of your sins. Caleb! Give her the first turn!"

Maria's body strained under the turn of the wheel. She

felt the ropes at her wrists and ankles pull into her flesh as the huge wooden drum pulled them tighter. She could not move, her whole body was stretched on the rack. Her cunt still ached from Caleb's frantic thrusting and as the ropes tightened she felt a thrill of fear and desire creep all over her, it centred on her cunt and she wanted it filled again.

"Another turn, my little friend, another slow turn will stretch her enough for the moment."

Maria felt the ropes tightening even more, her arms pulled terribly and she felt her hip joints straining as if they were going to come apart. Still, the throbbing in her cunt did not ease, the fear of the rack only mingled with the overpowering desire to have a cock thrusting deeply inside her. Her eyes were wide and ablaze with passion as Father Thomas bent down to her.

"That will do for the moment my child, reflect on your sins, reflect on your fantasies, and when I return you can tell them all."

The dungeon fell silent and Maria was left stretched out on the rack. Her head was filled with thoughts of the delights of sex and the raptures of pain and, as she stared around the walls at the manacled women, she could only think of ways of fulfilling her desires and suffering more.

CHAPTER 7

Maria awoke to the rattle of chains. She turned to look in the direction of the noise, then realised that she was still racked and only able to move her head. She tried to clear her throat, but the gagging leather ball in her mouth made her choke. For one terrible moment she thought she was going to be sick, then it passed. Someone was untying the women from the walls.

It was the golden haired man who had attacked her! It was Kirk!

She watched silently.

He reached up to the first woman and with a large key undid her manacles; she fell to the floor in a heap, he kicked at her and she groaned.

"Up bitch, you're needed. I hope you've been thinking of ways to please. It's an important client and I wouldn't like to be in your shoes if you fail to please him. Christ no!"

The young woman got up slowly, rubbed her wrists and looked over to Maria but turned quickly as the young man punched her in the back.

"Attention! Wait for your orders!"

One by one he untied the other women and soon they all stood in a row rubbing their wrists, their faces reddened by the tape as it clung to their cheeks. The last woman to be released was the girl whose clothes were all in tatters. The young man put his hand between her legs before he undid her.

"Nice," he said. "I hear you're always keen for a bit. How's this?"

He pushed his fingers into her cunt, she looked straight at him and began to writhe.

"Nice cunt. Sorry though, you'll have to wait for the moment."

He removed his fingers and smeared them across her cheeks, then he undid her and she stood obediently with the rest. As she stood with the others Maria could see her buttocks through the tears in her dress, on her right cheek there was a strange red mark that looked as if it had been branded into her skin, Maria thought it spelt a name, 'Barbara'.

"Line up now slaves. That's it, line up and follow me."

They all fell into a line and, as he walked out into the tunnel, they all followed dutifully with their heads bowed. Maria was left alone. There was no point in trying to get free, she was completely captive. She thought about her sins and how at last she was beginning to be cleansed. Then she thought about Barbara and how she had screamed to be fucked by Father Thomas. Then she thought about Caleb rutting at her like an angry animal and she wanted to reach down and feel herself. Then she heard someone coming down the tunnel.

Father Thomas!

"Maria, my child. I hope you have been doing what I instructed. I have come to relieve you of your terrible fantasies and desires. I hope you are ready to explain them to me. If not..."

He reached up to one of the chains that hung from the wall and drew it from its ring, he shook it by his side and it rattled heavily.

"If not..."

He sidled over to Maria and sat on the edge of the rack.

"Have you enjoyed the tension of the rack my child? Have you enjoyed having your limbs stretched and pulled? Have you enjoyed not being able to cry out and be a filthy little bitch?"

He reached down and started to untie the gag. He let the thongs dangle at the side of her face and she made no effort to remove the ball, she just lay there staring up at him and kept it firmly inside her mouth. She licked the back edge of it as if to show him that she did not want to let it go. Father Thomas lifted the sides of the gag but Maria bit down hard on the leather ball and when he pulled it she bit even harder. He tugged at it hard but she would not let it go and gripped it between her teeth like a dog with a bone.

"Bitch!" he shouted. "Bitch!"

Again he tried to get the gag from her mouth but Maria clung onto it tightly and he could not get it free.

"Bitch! Let it go! Let it go or you will never be saved. You cannot save yourself like this. Let it go bitch!"

He pulled hard at the gag until finally the leather ball exploded from her mouth. She gasped loudly and, with her mouth still open and gaping, growled and snarled like a savage brute.

"You are a little bitch; a real little animal. Here, bite on this."

He dangled his finger in front of her still gaping mouth and she made a snap at it, he pulled it away and laughed. Then he dangled it again and she snapped again but he was too quick and she could not move her head enough to pursue her prey.

"Bitch, bitch, bitch," he said tauntingly as he kept dangling his finger in front of her mouth and she kept snapping at it without success.

"Now, stop your silly animal games. It is time to begin your treatment. Your confession has begun in earnest."

Father Thomas held up the chain and rested it across her breasts, drew it slowly across her skin then dangled it in front of her face. She snapped at it and he pulled it away quickly.

"So, what have you been thinking about overnight, my little animal?"

Maria did not speak at first. She knew she would have to in the end, but she still wanted to snap at something, to bite into something or miss it and have it dangled at her again. She wanted to be taunted and played with, but she also wanted something in her mouth, she wanted it filled and plugged, she wanted to run her tongue around it and suck it and taste it.

"Can I suck your cock Father?"

"What! Is this the start? Is this your first fantasy? You are an evil little bitch indeed. Perhaps you will be impossible to save. Again, what did you say?"

"Can I suck your cock Father? I want it in my mouth, I want to feel how big it is, I want to draw it fully in, I want to feel it throbbing as I suck it across my tongue. Oh Father, give it to me I want to suck it until it finishes and fills my mouth, then I want to drink it down and feed on it. Father, I need to suck it. Get it out, give it to me. Please Father, stick it in my mouth."

"Quiet, bitch!" he screamed. "Quiet! This is not your confession. How can it be? This is not your deepest fantasy, this is just lust, this is just craving."

Without warning he lifted the chain and brought it down across her breasts and she howled in pain.

"Now, you know what I want, I want you to confess your fantasies."

"Oh Father, I'm so sorry. Please Father, forgive me, I'm so sorry, I will tell you what I must, I promise, I will hold nothing back."

"Good. So, let us start."

Maria took a deep breath and began.

"Father, I want sex with men, lots of them, not just one after another but all at the same time. I have always wanted it like this, even when I was very young I used to think about what it would be like, but then I could never imagine how it would be best. Now I know, now I know how I want it."

"Continue my child. Tell me everything you desire and tell me in detail. Only if you tell me can I help you. Everything now."

"I want to go into a pub, into a bar, I want to go up to

the bar and order a drink. I will be by myself and I will sit on a stool at the bar. I will be wearing a very short skirt and my white panties will be easy to see as I stretch my legs up on the stool. The barman will eye me up and down and I will lean forward so that he can see how my breasts curve nakedly inside my blouse. There will be a group of men at a table in the corner, they will start looking at me and they will nudge each other and laugh about what they would like to do to me. I will drink my drink quietly and, every so often, I will turn on the bar stool and re-cross my legs in such a way that the men at the table can see my white panties. I will have made sure to wear very thin ones that slip against the soft edges of my cunt as I cross my legs.

"After a while, as they drink more, the men will get more boisterous so I will walk over to the pool table and pick up a cue. I will bend over the table and start to hit some pool balls around the table and as I bend I will make sure that my thin panties can be seen by the men at the table. I will hear them saying things about my bottom and how they would like to fuck me. Then I will reach over the table to get one of the balls and my skirt will rise right up over my bottom, it will be in full view of the men, but that is what I want and I will keep reaching for the ball. I will feel the hard edge of the pool table against the front of my hips and I will press against it. Then, so that I can reach further, I will put the cue down at the side of the table."

"What then, what will you do then?"

"I will wait, I don't want to reach the ball you see, I just want to show my bottom to the men and I will stay there showing my bottom until they do something. Then one of them will sidle over and pick up the cue. He will hold it up above my bottom but I will not move, he will place it against my bottom and rub it against my silky panties and still I will not move. Then the others will come up and gather around me, but still I will stay there, leaning as far as I can cross the table. I know what they want to do and I am going to let it happen. I know they want to rape me and I will not stop them though I know that when they start I will pretend to resist. I will give them the pleasure of thinking that I don't want to be violated, but all the time I will be enjoying their violence."

"Go on my child, go on."

"I will feel the cue against my bottom and it will make my cunt wet, it will need to be wet because of all the fucking it is going to get. I will lift my bottom against it and feel how it rubs against my smooth panties. Then I will feel an extra pressure from it, I will not be able to lift it any more because the man will be forcing me to stay lying across the table. I will wait for what happens next, I know they are going to rape me but I don't know how and the thought of not knowing will excite me and I will start sweating and feeling flushed. Then I will feel someone else holding one of my wrists then someone holding the other and I will be pinned down to the table. The cue will lift away then come smacking down on my bottom and I will yell loudly because it will hurt but still I will want it more. Then it will come down again and I will yell even louder. I will smell the sweat of the men holding my wrists and I will hear them shouting encouragement to one of the gang as he undoes his trousers behind me. They will call me names, whore, bitch, cow, and I will get more excited each time I hear the words.

"Then I will feel my panties being grabbed by the waist and they will be torn down. My bottom will be exposed and my cunt will show out between the crack of my thighs. I will start screaming as though I don't want them to fuck me but all the time I will be screaming with delight at the thought of their cocks and how they are going to use them."

"Go on, what will you do then?"

"I will scream a lot but I will be waiting for the first cock. My face will be flattened against the green cloth of the pool table and I will dribble onto it. I will not be able to see what is going on behind me but then I will feel the heat from the first cock, it will be massive and it will force its way straight in. I will squirm as though I am trying to resist but all the time I will be sucking it inside my cunt and it will go right up all in one go. The men will be laughing and taunting me as the first man fucks me hard and deep and soon I will feel the throbbing of his spunk surging up his cock. I will feel it spurting deeply inside my cunt, then I will feel his cock being pulled out and his semen running out after it. Then, straight away, another one will come inside me, this one is even longer and it will bury itself right up me. I will scream again and this time I will be screaming because it really hurts."

"Go on, what will happen next?"

"This cock will be fucking me and then I will see one in front of my face. The men holding my wrists will grab my hair roughly and lift my head while one of the men kneels on the table and holds his stiff cock in front of me. While I'm being fucked from behind he will stick his cock in my mouth and I will be forced to suck it. It will go very deep and I will choke but I will not stop. Then another will start fucking me and the one in my mouth will finish right down my throat.

"Then they will turn me over and hold me down on my back, they will rip my skirt off and tear my blouse and my panties will be pulled down around my ankles. One of the men will sit astride me and wank all over me. He will rub his cock around my breasts and then squirt his spunk into my face. Then they will lift my legs high and one of them will stick his cock up my cunt then pull it out, all wet and silky, and stick it up my arse. This will make me scream because it is a big one. While he is fucking my arse one of them will crouch over me and lick my cunt. He will force his arse down over my face and I will have to stick my tongue up it."

"How will they make you do that?"

"They will not have to, I will want, I will want to lick my tongue deeply up his arse and feel his balls hanging down across my chin. Then I will feel the man up my arse finishing and I will scream for them to stop. I will plead with them to let me go, but they will get even rougher and wilder. One of them will lie down on the table and I will be held above him. He will stick his cock into my arse, it is already wet from the spunk of the man that has just finished in it. This cock is very thick and I will squeal as he plunges it into me. Then one of them will get on top of me and fuck my cunt, then two of them will stick their cocks into my mouth at the same time. I can hardly get them in my mouth and I will choke as they force their nobs to the back of my throat, then another will wank over me and finish so much I will hear it as it splashes all over me. Then the one in my arse will finish and the one in my cunt, then the two in my mouth will come at the same time and then they will bend me over and beat me with the cue for being such a whore. Then, as they take turns to beat me with the cue and as they call me names and abuse me and spit on me, I will finish. I will shout to them to fuck me more, beat me more, fuck my arse more, wank over me more, all the time I finish I will shout to them that they have not been able to give me enough and I will demand that they give me more. Because I want more they will beat me even harder but it will only make me scream louder. Then when they have had enough of beating me they will leave me lying on the pool table, covered in spunk and gasping for breath."

Father Thomas was silent for a few moments. Then he spoke quietly.

"Oh my child, my dear child, you are so terrible, your thoughts are so evil."

Then his face hardened and he shouted at her.

"You are such a fucking bitch!"

He stood up abruptly, pulled the heavy chain across her breasts then threw it down across her hips. She screeched.

"What else? I know there is more, what else? Tell me or be damned forever. Tell me your sinful fantasies, all of them, you fucking little bitch!"

"Oh Father I'm so terrible I've finished while I was telling you my fantasy. Oh Father, can you help me? Can you save me?"

"Tell me the rest."

"Oh Father, I want to be tied up, I want to be held captive, I want to be violated, I want to be fucked, I want to be tortured. Oh Father, save me please."

"Tell me, tell me how you want to be tied. Tell me bitch!"

"This is terrible, I never thought I could admit it, even to myself."

"Tell me, you must, tell me how."

"Oh Father, I want to be abducted, I want to be stolen in the night, I want to be ripped from my bed and taken away blindfolded and tied, I want to be bundled into the boot of a car and driven for days until I am starved and thirsty, then I want to be released into the bright daylight and tortured."

"Tell me how my child, do not spare me the details, tell me how you want to be tortured."

"When I am released from the car boot I want to be dazzled by the sun, it will take me ages until my eyes adjust, but as soon as they get used to the light I will be knocked unconscious and thrown back into the car boot. The next thing I know I will be having water thrown over my face and I will be in a hot foreign land, I will not know how long it has been since I was kidnapped and I will be terrified. I will be starved for a few more days and then released into a compound, a dusty pen where animals are corralled and branded. Everyone there will be black, they will lean over the side of the corral and prod me with long spears. I will run around in the dust terrified of what they are going to do to me, then I will fall in the dust exhausted but they will keep prodding me until I get up and run again."

"What are they going to do to you?"

"That's it, I don't know, I'm so afraid of what might happen to me, I'm not sure I will even live through it, but at the same time I'm excited because I've no idea of what they are going to do. I feel so humiliated running around the compound, so dirty, my clothes are in tatters and my feet are cut and bleeding and they taunt me as I run around the ring, I just feel so terrified. Then one of the men leaps down from the side of the corral, he has a large dog on a heavy chain and the dog bares its teeth at me. The man uses the dog to drive me towards the edge of the ring and as I back up in fear I am grabbed from behind by two of the men. All the rest cheer as I am caught, then the two men jump over the fence, drag me to the ground and roll me over face down."

"Do you still feel afraid of what will happen?"

"Yes, oh yes, terrified. One of the men sits on my back and the breath is knocked out of me. I choke in the dust and the dog barks and growls in front of me. Then I hear more cheering and shouting and I feel something hot going past me. I turn to see what it is but someone hits the back of my head and forces my face deeper into the dust. I choke some more and cough to try and get breath but I feel as though I am suffocating. Then I hear men gathering around me and, as I pull my face out of the dust, I can see their feet dancing up and down as they shout and chant at what is happening."

"What is happening? Do you know yet what they are going to do to you?"

"No, I still don't know. Then I feel hands around my bottom and then I feel my skirt being torn off. It rips and is flung down into the dust, then, I hear the men cheer loudly as my panties are grabbed, torn down and pulled off over my feet. Then I feel the heat again and I sweat with fear and struggle for all I'm worth but still they will not let me go. My eyes fill with dust and I feel as though I am being buried, I choke terribly, then..."

"Yes, then, then what?"

"Then I feel it. Oh, it's so terrible Father, I can't explain it."

"You must, you must."

"It seers me, on my bottom, the heat is awful, they're branding me Father! Oh Father, they're branding me with a red-hot iron. The men cheer and, as the iron sizzles against my bottom, I feel the terrible scorching pain and I hear my skin burning, and Father, I can smell it! I shriek and scream and howl and screech so loudly. I just can't bear the pain and I think I'm going to die. Then it's over, the pain subsides and I'm lifted to my feet. One of the men ties a rope around my neck, all the others gather around and I'm led away from the corral towards a railway engine. It's a steam engine and it's roaring with smoke and noise. I'm dragged up to it and the heat that comes from it is unbearable. I feel faint but the man with the rope around my neck keeps tugging at it and when my legs crumple he pulls harder and makes me stand up straight. He says that now I'm a slave, that I have been branded, I will have to do everything that I'm told."

"Yes, yes, what does he do with you?"

"He takes me right up to the locomotive, steam gushes out and burns my legs and I try to pull back but he is too strong, he drags me to one of the wheels. Some of the other men gather around me and tie me to a wheel, a huge steel wheel that's all hot and greasy, they tie my wrists and legs so that I am spread-eagled against it. I can feel the spokes cutting into my breasts, then the engine sounds it's whistle and steam belches from beneath it, it surges between my legs, wetting my skin with its scorching heat and I scream in horror."

"What next? What next?"

"Then, while the man holds tight to the rope around my neck the others come up behind me. My bottom is still burning from the branding and one of them smacks it hard, the pain is almost unbearable, the pain of the smack on top of the burning of my branded skin is just terrible. Then they all take it in turn to smack me. It seems to go on for ages and all the while the man with the rope keeps it taut and my neck is strained so tightly that when he tugs it I choke. Then the first one takes his cock out and thrusts it up my arse, I hang onto the iron spokes of the wheel and feel him thrusting me deeply, I feel totally filled up. My neck it nearly throttled as he comes and the man with the rope squeals with delight. Then another, this time up my cunt, then another, in my cunt again, then another, first up my cunt and then up my arse. The steam from the engine bursts out against my legs and scolds me and they keep fucking me, sometimes in my cunt, sometimes up my arse,

95

sometimes they go from one to the other, I feel completely humiliated and overcome with pain."

"Do you feel pleasure?"

"Oh, that's what's so terrible Father. I finish every time I'm fucked. Every time! Each cock gives me a fresh orgasm, each one is better than the one before. The pain, the heat, the captivity, all blend into amazing orgasms, one after the other, I just can't stop finishing. I revel in the delight of the terrible pain and the repeated fucking, every time one of them finishes I come as well and straight away, yes straight away, I want fucking again."

"How many times are you fucked my child?"

"I can't tell, but at least fifty, maybe a hundred, whatever it is, it's not enough, I end up screaming for more and they keep coming. Only when none of them can get their cock hard do they stop but even then I still want more. I beg and plead for more, anything, fucking, smacking, I beg to be branded again, I plead to be dragged along in the dust by the rope around my neck, I beg to be splayed wide and fucked by anything, I beg for the growling dog."

"You are so evil, so evil! Is there nothing you will stop at? Tell me, is there anything else? Do you have any other secrets to confess?"

"Oh Father, I do."

"Then tell me, let me hear them all, it is the only way you can be saved. I can hardly bear it but it is my duty to listen to your filthy fantasies."

"Oh Father, Father, fucking is not enough for me. I need more than just cocks, I need more than just spunk up my cunt or up my arse, I need to suffer, more than anything Father, I need to be humiliated, I need to be treated like an animal. I think about it all the time. My mind is filled with the pleasures of defilement and degradation. I'm so evil, I know I am, but I can't stop the feelings. Like an animal, that's how I want to be, I want to growl and snap and I want to be fucked like a beast. That's what I am, I know it, I'm a beast, I want to be stripped naked, so that I am like an animal, then I can snarl and bite, then I can be kicked when I am disobedient, then I can be punished if I fail to please my master."

"What would your master ask of you?"

"Anything, there is nothing I would not do for him. I would beg him for instructions, I would plead with him for tests of my obedience, I would be a grovelling slave-beast for him, he could command me to do anything, anything."

"But don't you have any desires of your own?"

"My only desires are to please my master, to flinch when he scolds me and to twist away in pain when he kicks me for my disobedience."

"What has this master done to you then? What has he forced you to do to show your obedience?"

"He takes me to the pit, the pit is where he takes me. It is a fighting pit, other animals like me snarl and fight and draw each others blood in the pit. But when he takes me there the fighting is all over, there is blood in the sand on the floor but the other animals have gone. Some have left as victors and others have been dragged out ripped and torn to pieces by their stronger foes. When my master brings me in, men line up around the ring, they are inflamed with all the fighting that has gone on. They are chanting and jeering, they have seen much blood and many horrors and they are satiated but they know, when my master brings me in, they know that they will be even more satisfied, they know that the pleasures they have had so far will be nothing compared to what my master will force me to do for them."

"Tell me how he makes you please them."

"My master drags me in, I am naked and around my neck is a thin leather thong. He trails the other end loosely in his hand, it is very thin and the slightest pulls cuts into my skin. I have to crawl on all fours, my master will not let me stand, my hands and knees are cut and raw from all the grovelling I do for my master but still I have to crawl. The men around the ring cheer loudly and when my master snatches the leather thong and drags me to heel, the men roar again wildly. My master makes me sit like a dog, and I crouch down on my knees and hold my hands like paws just below my breasts. I look up at the frenzied faces of the men around the pit and they throw scraps of food down in front of me but, even though I am starved because I rarely get fed, I am not allowed to pick them up. The men laugh at me and spit down onto me, then my master lets go of the thong and commands me to sit obediently while he goes to the side of the ring. The men taunt me as much as they can but still I sit obediently, waiting for my master's return. When he comes back he is carrying a leather saddle and the men cheer loudly because they know what is going to happen to me."

"Are you excited?"

"My cunt is dribbling Father. I want it licked but I dare not move. Then my master grabs the thong again and pulls it hard, I know this is the order to get up onto all fours again. I whine like a sick dog as the thong cuts into my neck and the men go quiet as they watch intently. Then my master throws the saddle across my back, I slump under the weight of it and I gasp for breath and the men all cheer as they see me flinching. My master ties the girth around my waist, he pulls it so tight I can hardly breathe, then he picks up the bridle and drops it over my head, I open my mouth and wait, then my master pulls the metal bit between my teeth. It clanks against them and he tugs the leash around my neck which is my order to bite down onto the bit, I bite it hard.

"Then my master jumps up onto my back, I can hardly bear his weight but I arch my back to take the strain. Then he pulls on the bit and drives me around the outside edges of the pit, he rides me in front of the jeering men and they throw things at me and spit down onto me. When my master wants me to move he whips me across my buttocks with a leather whip and he makes me go faster by whipping me harder. He rides me wildly and whips me harshly and I bite the bit harder to stave off the pain. Then my master pulls back hard on the bit and backs me up to some of the men. He pulls me back so that my buttocks are presented to them, then he pulls harder so that the bit digs into the sides of my mouth and this is the order to stop. Then, as he sits astride me, the first man comes up behind me and sticks his cock into my arse. I can't scream because of the bit between my teeth, and the man fucks me madly as my master jumps up and down on the saddle that weighs so heavily on my back. When the first man is finished my master drives me to the next, and the next, and the next, until I have been fucked up the arse by all of them. Then all the men come down into the pit and take turns at whipping my bottom and licking my arse and my cunt, then, when they have all enjoyed me as much as they want, my master rides me out of the pit and ties me tightly in a stable where I stay until the next time.

"I wait all night, growling in the stable, then the next morning my master comes again, this time he brings with him a -"

"Enough!"

"But that's not all Father."

"Enough of your filth!"

"But Father, I need to tell you all the other things. I

99

need to tell you about how I want to be pierced: through my nipples, my nose, my clitoris. Oh yes, I want to be pierced painfully through my clitoris, then I want a chain tied through the ring and I want to be dragged around by it, dragged and pulled and punished and violated. Oh, and there's so much more Father, I want to be chased through the night by men and dogs, I want to feel the fear of being captured as the dogs bay and snarl at my heels, then I want to be caught and violated and tied to a stake and have flames lapping round my feet, and then, oh Father, I can hardly say it, and then I want -"

"Enough I said! You need cleansing of your fantasies, I cannot bear to hear any more of your evil, you must go for training straight away, you filthy little bitch! You evil little whore! Caleb!"

Caleb sprang out of the shadows of the dungeon.

"Take her from the rack and throw her in her cell, make sure you tie her tight though, she is very evil and will need much training before she is saved."

Caleb jumped up to the wheel of the rack and released the tension, Maria slumped limply, then he untied her and dragged her away down the tunnel. He pulled her along roughly until they came to an iron grating door, he reached up to the heavy handle and swung the door open.

"In slave-bitch! Quickly! Quickly! Quickly!"

He prodded at her with his staff and she tumbled into the dark cell. She could hardly see anything and she was so exhausted that she let Caleb do what he wanted. He put her wrists in some steel manacles that hung from the wall and then manacled her legs to a solid steel bar, her legs were forced wide and the bar was almost too heavy for her to lift. When he had finished, he jumped back and eyed her with satisfaction.

"Naughty girl! Naughty girl! Naughty girl!" he jeered,

then he sprang round and ran off up the tunnel, leaving her alone, naked and tightly manacled in the dark cell.

CHAPTER 8

Gradually, Maria's eyes got used to the dark. She peered around the cell. The opposite wall was draped with a heavy white curtain and there seemed to be something underneath it, it looked like the outline of a person! She shivered, then looked to her side and saw that she was not alone, there was another woman hanging in chains beside her, it was the girl with the tattered clothes that had her name branded across her buttocks, it was Barbara!

Maria turned painfully in her shackles and looked at the limp figure. She was very beautiful, her arms were stretched up high and her hands lay crookedly in the metal rings that secured her, her face was dropped and her long, dark hair fell in swirls around it but Maria could still see her full red lips and high cheekbones standing out in the murky darkness of the cell.

"Are you awake?"

Barbara did not respond.

"Is your name Barbara? Are you awake?"

Barbara stirred slightly then slowly lifted her head, the opened her large, dark eyes.

"Yes, I'm awake. You're the new girl aren't you? I saw you earlier when they strapped you to the rack, and I think it was you I saw in the confession box."

"Yes, yes it was, I remember your face, my name's Maria. How long have you been here?"

"A long time. I'm fully trained now, I am one of their fully trained slaves."

"I have come here to be saved from my sins, I hope to be made better, I hope to be cleansed, I've been so bad, so terribly bad."

Barbara lifted her head higher and looked at Maria inquisitively.

"Don't you know what's going to happen to you?"

"Not really, except I'm going to be saved."

"I don't know about being saved, but you are certainly going to be sold! That's what happens to us all in the end, we are all sold."

"What?"

"We all get sold as slaves. It'll be you and me next. It's that bitch Lesley who arranges it all, the 'Mistress Lesley' they call her. She arranges it all, she's down at the docks now, that's where we'll be shipped out from. That's where all the others went and I expect we'll follow soon."

Maria did not know what to say. She could hardly believe it. Then Barbara looked closely into her eyes.

"You're beautiful," she said. Then her dark eyes darted towards the cell door. "Quiet, someone's coming, don't let them catch us talking, quiet, we can try and talk later."

The heavy door creaked open and Father Thomas came in. Barbara dropped her head as he strode straight past her and went up to Maria.

"Oh my child, things are looking very bad for you. These terrible fantasies, these awful thoughts, and I know there are even more terrible things that you have not yet admitted. You are so evil, so bad and dirty, we have to act quickly. I must introduce you to the punishment regime now, before it is too late, we must not lose any time, your salvation is at stake. We must train you to control your terrible fantasies. Caleb! Undo her manacles we shall begin her training now."

Caleb sprung in through the door and, in one bound,

jumped up and clung to the shackles at Maria's wrists. He undid them with a large key and, as her arms fell to her sides, he leapt down and grabbed her hair tightly. She yelled in pain as he dragged her down onto the floor and pulled her on her back to the middle of the cell. He let go of her hair and she dropped heavily on her back, her legs splayed wide with the iron bar that braced them apart.

"Your road to redemption is absolute obedience," said Father Thomas. "You must never question your orders, you must be a submissive and humiliated slave, only then can you hope to be saved. What are you?"

Maria did not answer.

"I said, what are you, bitch?"

"Please Father, a slave."

"Again, you fucking bitch, what are you?"

"A slave Father. I am a slave."

"What do slaves do?"

"They, they, they do what they are ordered Father."

"Good, yes, they do exactly what they are ordered. Now kneel before me and we will begin."

Maria struggled to get to her knees but the heavy iron bar made it almost impossible and she fell clumsily to one side.

"Quickly slave, to your knees! That is an order!"

She twisted and turned and in the end managed to crouch in front of him.

"Good, a little reward I think, so that you know when you have done well. Caleb! Show her our warrior. Just the sight of him will make you wet with desire, my child, and when you see what he has to offer I am sure we will see just how much you are prepared to suffer to turn that desire into pleasure. Caleb!"

Caleb bounded to the other side of the cell, reached up as far as he could and pulled at the heavy white sheet, tugging it hard until it peeled away from the wall. It revealed a huge and heavily muscled black man chained tightly to the wall. His vast arms were splayed out wide and his wrists were secured by heavy chains to large iron hooks. His neck was pulled tightly by the links of a shiny metal chain and another chain pulled his forehead back against the wall. He had a wide leather gag pulled painfully across his mouth and his legs were strained apart by a wooden beam that was strapped to his ankles with leather thongs and bolted to the wall.

There was a black leather belt buckled around his waist but otherwise his body was completely naked. Hanging from his groin was the biggest cock Maria had ever seen, it was so thick and long and as it stretched down flaccidly its uncovered glans swung heavily against the middle of his hugely muscled thighs. Maria gasped as she saw him, she was shocked by his mightiness and the way that he was restrained and she was overawed by the size of his massive, pendulous cock.

"What do you think of our black warrior my child?"
Maria kept silent.

"Big cock eh? Bigger than you have ever had I warrant. Bigger than she has ever had I bet, eh Caleb? Enough to satisfy that wanton cunt I think, even a cunt like hers, dripping and hot and ready to be filled. Yes, I think she should get some pleasure from our black friend eh? Check that he is secure Caleb, the last time we used him he wriggled like a panther and broke his chains and I do not want him to break free again."

The whites of the warrior's eyes flashed from side to side as Caleb jumped around him, pulling at his chains and bonds and wrenching and tugging at his shackles. When he had tested them all several times, he jumped back satisfied.

"All secure! All secure! Ready for cunt! Ready for cunt!"

"Do you like him, bitch? Yes? I think you do. Yes? Stuck for words eh? Well, let's see how much you really like him, shall we?"

Maria moved slightly as if to get up and Father Thomas was enraged.

"Down bitch! Stay down! Do not dare move until I instruct you! What did I tell you. Complete obedience! Fucking bitch! I will not warn you again. Hang your head! Down bitch! That will be your last warning!"

Maria quickly crouched down again, shivering with fear and panting quickly as she fought unsuccessfully to keep herself calm.

"Ah, but of course, as you know, with every pleasure there is pain. You think you have had pain? Yes, it is true you have had some, you have been caned, you have been whipped, you have been fucked and racked, you have been shaved and chained and you have tasted the pleasures of humiliation. You have learned that if you get things wrong, if you are disobedient, then you have to be punished. But to think you have experienced real pain, to imagine that you have been truly punished already, that is a mistake. No, my child, you have not even tasted true punishment. See how the warrior waits for you? He is eager I assure you, even though that massive cock dangles down his legs he is still eager, he is always eager for a young cunt. And you? Ah yes, I can see you are eager too. But how eager I wonder? How much are you prepared to suffer in order to please the soft flesh of that warm cunt of yours? Ah, my child, we shall soon see whether it is pleasure or pain that satisfies you most. We shall soon see whether the pleasures of your cunt are stronger than the pleasures of the flail across your back. Caleb! Rouse our warrior."

Caleb stabbed the point of his staff into the warrior's muscular chest. His eyes widened in pain as he stiffened against his bonds and gurgled deeply in his throat as he tried to throw his head from side to side like a terrified savage.

"Rouse him I say!"

Caleb reached forward and stroked the huge cock that hung down between the warrior's powerful thighs and straight away, it began to stiffen and rise. Maria lifted her head slightly, being careful not to let Father Thomas see her move, and watched the growing cock as it hardened readily beneath Caleb's stubby fingers, gradually filling and swelling and growing even longer. To begin with it reached down and began to throb then, as Caleb pulled more firmly at the shaft, it began to stand upwards.

It was massive!

Caleb could not get his fingers around it and as it grew he used both hands to pull the loose black skin along the hardening shaft. The glans became swollen and reached upwards, drawing its weighty length after it. Finally, Caleb let go and stood back. The black cock was at full length, its veins standing out roughly along its shaft as it throbbed and pulsated.

"What a fine sight. Does that make your cunt wet my child? Does that stir your young juices. Just think of it, just think of that massive shaft running inside you, just imagine its hardened veins pulling at the soft flesh of your vagina, just think. Caleb! Get her ready! We shall soon see whether it is her eagerness for pain or her desire for pleasure that takes control. Get her ready!"

Caleb pranced around Maria.

"Bow your head! Bow your head! Bow your pretty, pretty head!"

Maria did not dare move and waited, trembling with

106

fear, until she felt Caleb slipping a thin leather leash over her head. He pulled it down around her throat then, after tightening it in a noose, he stood back trailing the loose end in his hand. She felt like a dog on a lead as he tugged at it roughly and she looked from side to side as she crouched on her knees. Then he threw the end up over a steel bar that stretched across the ceiling of the cell above the warrior and caught it again as it dropped down on the other side. He tugged it hard and Maria gulped as it tightened and nearly choked her. He pulled it harder through the ring and, as her head tilted sideways under the pressure, she started to cough and gasp for breath.

"Ah, good. You can feel it then, good and tight and ready to draw around your lovely throat if you should resist. Good, good, you can move now my child. I said you can move! Move! That is right! Get up! Stand! Stand in your shackles bitch and go over to our beautiful warrior. See, his cock is throbbing with desire for you, it wants to be inside you, it wants to thrust inside your soft cunt, see how it wants you. Ah, but it is not that easy. You must get up, get up onto the warrior, climb up our muscular friend my child, but be careful, do not touch that throbbing cock, do not dare touch that wonderful, throbbing cock. I warn you, climb up his muscular body but do not dare touch that thing which you desire so much. Ah yes, I can tell how much you want it, I can see the lust in your eyes, but beware, you touch it at your peril."

Maria stood in front of the black warrior. Her neck was bent by the strain of the leash and she stumbled as she tried to balance herself with the iron bar shackled between her ankles.

"At your peril," repeated Father Thomas.

Maria turned to look at him and shrunk back as she saw what was dangling from his hand. I was a wide, black leather whip, solid and stiff for half its length, the rest of it shredded and pulled out into a tangle of split and broken ends.

"At your peril," he said again as he smacked the terrible whip against his side and caused the flailing ends to bend keenly in tangles around his robe covered thigh.

Smack!

Maria shrunk back and, unable to balance because of the bar between her ankles, fell forward, stretching her hands out to save herself and pressing them against the hard stomach muscles of the black warrior. She had barely glanced the warm oily skin before she shrieked with pain.

Smack!

The whip smacked loudly against her back. She recoiled in fear and pain and almost fell over backwards but managed to regain her balance and stood quivering in her shackles.

"Oh please Father. Please."

"At your peril! Now climb up onto him and keep away from that throbbing cock, no matter how much you want to grab it, keep away!"

Maria hardly knew what to do, she was shaking all over. She tried to lift one of her feet but it was impossible, the shackles around her ankles dug into her skin terribly, she was petrified and confused, she felt so humiliated.

Smack!

Another searing blow on her back. The whip slashed down right between her shoulder blades and she screamed loudly. She tried again to lift her foot but could not, then she reached forward and put her hands on the warrior's shoulders. His wide eyes stared at her and he looked savage and fearful. His mouth was pulled horribly by the leather gag and as he tried to move his head his eyes widened more with pain. His shoulders felt warm and oily and she started to pull herself up his rigid body but as she moved higher she felt Caleb pulling up the slack of the leash. It tightened around her neck and she drew herself up more to ease its tension. She pulled hard with her hands to get a little higher, but the weight of the bar between her legs was too much.

Smack!

A terrible blow came down across her back and she fell to the floor. She started to scream but no sound came out. She tried again but still nothing, she was being throttled, Caleb had not slackened the leash and she could not breathe. She was panicking, she wanted to beg to be released but she could not even gasp.

"Oh my child, you cannot go back again. Did you not realise that? There is only one way to go, higher, higher, up the body of the black warrior, there is no going back. Caleb will not slacken the leash now, you have made some ground and you must make more, there is no way back. Get up! Get up!"

Maria realised her plight. She felt a terrible desperation and scrambled frantically back up again, this time grasping the warrior's shoulders tightly with her fingers and digging her nails in deeply. For a moment she felt the tightness at her neck ease slightly, but she also felt the touch of the huge black cock against her stomach and realised she had not been careful enough to keep away from it.

Smack!

Another terrible blow, this time lower down her back. The force of it knocked her forward and the cock pressed harder against her, she felt its heat and its pulsating massiveness. A thrill went through her, she could not stop it, just one touch of that massive cock sent a shiver of ecstasy through her, but at the same time she knew she would have to suffer, even for that single moment of pleasure.

Smack!

"I said, do not touch it!"

She scrambled furiously now, like a terrified animal. The weight of the shackled bar between her legs kept trying to drag her down as, in frantic movements, she clawed her way higher up the body of the black warrior. But it was impossible to keep away from the cock, it pressed firmly against her again and she shuddered at the pain to come.

Smack!

She gulped as the wicked whip sent scorching pains across her back. As she climbed higher Caleb took up the slack in the leash, but once or twice she managed to get some breath back and let out a terrible scream which echoed around the cell. Frantically, she pulled her stomach past the throbbing cock and at last found herself above it. Her knees were pressed either side of the warrior's chest, her shackled feet were twisted back and pressed hard against his stomach, her hands were forced down onto his shoulders and the leash was pulled tightly around her neck. She panted with exhaustion and relief as spit dribbled from her mouth and she felt the heat from the warrior's cock rising up between her legs.

"Now, the choice is yours my child. The choice between pleasure and pain is in your hands. Do you feel the heat from that pulsating cock? Yes, I think you do. Do you feel your cunt warmed by it? Does its flesh shiver with excitement and anticipation? I am sure it does. But you feel something else I think. You feel the tension around your neck, you must fight against it or you cannot breathe, but then you shiver with the fear of touching that object which you desire, touch it and you feel the flailing lashes of the whip. What do you do? If you drop down to encircle that mighty cock you will throttle yourself and as you touch it you will be beaten until you finally draw away. What pain, what pleasure, oh my child, what sinfulness."

Maria gasped as she tried to keep her grip on the warrior's shoulders. He was breathing hard through his flaring nostrils and the heat of his breath blew across her breasts. It made her skin tingle and her nipples stuck out long and hard. Again, she sagged a little and felt the intense heat from the cock that reared up between her legs. The leash at her throat tightened but this time she did not respond, the strain against her throat was just about bearable. She dropped a little more and struggled to breathe, but the heat from the cock, the warrior's hot breath across her breasts and the tightness at her throat all seemed to conspire to make her want to get closer to that massive cock. The leash was only offering her pain but the cock was offering her pleasure and pain. She dropped a little more and the heat got greater, she could feel it radiating against the insides of her thighs and when she looked down to see it, it was mighty!

It stood up like a massive staff, the glans swelled and pulsated and it still seemed to be growing! She was not dropping down any more but it was still getting closer. Now, she could not breathe at all and she forced her hands down onto his shoulders for relief. The leash was pulled to take up the slack but she was still able to grab a quick breath. She looked down again at the cock and saw that it was still getting harder, still swelling and lengthening and all the time it was coming closer to her cunt. She did not know what to do, she did not know whether to commit herself to its pleasures or not, she knew she would, in the end she knew she would, but that would mean it was all over. To commit herself now would bring the delectable tension to a close, but her cunt was so wide, so forced

111

apart and gaping and her inner labia were exposed to the heat of the cock. She dropped to meet it, they touched, she could not hold back.

Smack!

"That is the pain my child."

Smack! Smack!

She could not stand it, she braced her arms against the warrior's shoulders and pulled herself off. Caleb took up the slack on the leash straight away. The warrior grunted and his eyes widened as he tried to wriggle in his bonds, frantically trying to force his cock up to her. She felt his effort, it was as though he wanted to save her, it was as though he knew that she wanted it but could not get to it. She tried to go down to meet it but the leash was so tight now, her face felt red and full, she was not breathing at all, she felt as if she would explode.

Smack!

She must have touched the cock again, she was not sure.

Smack!

Yes, she must have reached it, the pains across her back said she must have reached it, but the beating was no longer a threat, she strained her neck as high as she could, then bore down to the massive cock that was still swelling between her legs.

Smack! Smack!

Her back was burning from the flogging but it was only inciting her, the pain was only driving her down towards her goal.

Smack! Smack! Smack!

Down she went. Then suddenly the leash relaxed, it broke away from her neck and she fell with all her weight onto the massive, throbbing cock. She felt the whip flogging her back but more than that she felt the huge cock surging up inside her. She screamed and yelled in a frenzy of agony as the cock drove in. She felt as if it was going to rent her apart, but she bore down more then thrust her hands down to it. It was inside her as far as it would go, but there was still masses of it left outside the distended edges of her sucking cunt. She grabbed it with both hands and tried to push more of it in, dropping her body heavily and opening her legs as much as she could. The fierce lashes of the whip rained down on her back but she drove down harder and harder. Wildly she forced herself onto it but it would not all go inside. She screamed for it, she screamed in pain and anger, she shouted at the warrior to give it to her, she wanted it all.

"Fuck me! I want to your cock inside! Get it in! I want it all in! Fuck me! Fuck me! Fuck me!"

All the time the whip came down then, as suddenly as it had been released, the leash tightened again, this time with a terrific and awkward jerk. It pulled her neck right up at an angle and instantly she lost her breath. As she felt it dig into her throat she felt a spasm inside her cunt and she drove back down to it, one more second, that was all she needed. She drove down harder and harder and then, in one final paroxysm of breathless delight and pain, she froze into a massive orgasm. She screamed and yelled and again the animal noises came out of her breathless mouth, growling and snarling amongst the dribbling spit that spilled from her bitten lips. She slumped, not knowing whether she was conscious or not, unsure of whether she would ever breathe again, then she fell, like a shackled wreck onto the still hard cock that held her up like a huge, black skewer.

CHAPTER 9

Maria had only been vaguely aware of being lifted off the warrior's mighty cock. She had felt someone holding her up under her arms and she had felt the massive cock sliding out of her cunt. She had felt the coolness against the distended edges of her cunt as she had been prized away, ravaged and exhausted. She had felt the manacles being clamped around her limp wrists and the pull on her arms as she fell back, but she had remembered nothing else. The next thing she knew she was opening her eyes as the cell door creaked open. For a moment she was confused, but, as she looked towards the door, she saw someone coming in, it was the golden haired man.

Kirk!

He entered the cell carrying a plate in each hand and pushed the door shut behind him with his foot. Maria saw that Barbara was still hanging by the side of her and that the black warrior was still chained to the wall opposite them. Kirk laid the plates down in front of them and as he reached up to undo Maria's manacles she shrunk back in fear.

"Fucking bitch, fucking, fucking bitch, you got me in trouble you fucking bitch!"

He spat in her face and she winced as his spit dribbled down across her mouth. Roughly, he undid the heavy metal rings around her wrists, her legs buckled and she dropped down to the floor. She barely had time to wonder what was happening to her before she felt a hard kick in her side and she screamed in pain.

"That's just a start you fucking bitch!"

Then he reached up and freed Barbara, rubbing his knee between her legs as he unlocked her shackles. She collapsed as they came undone and banged her head on the floor as she dropped down heavily.

"Like some food would you? Well you're not fucking getting any! Not until you beg, and beg enough to please me. Fucking bitches! You're not going to get me into any more trouble with the Mistress Lesley."

Maria was shocked again at the mention of Lesley but she could think of nothing except the food.

"Please, I'm so hungry," begged Maria. "Please, please, I'll do anything, please."

Kirk sneered then kicked the plates towards Maria. She grabbed some food in her hands and started stuffing it into her mouth like a hungry animal. Barbara pulled herself up painfully, then took some of the food in her fingers and poked it eagerly into her wide mouth.

"That's enough!" he shouted as he kicked the plates aside. "If you want more you'll have to work for it. You'll have to beg and grovel and do what I ask, you fucking bitches."

Maria felt so hungry, she could not take her eyes off the food that now lay spread across the dirty floor.

"I will, I will, please, ask me anything. I beg you, please, please give me your orders, I will do anything you say."

Kirk picked up a piece of food and dangled it in front of Maria.

"Anything?"

"Yes, anything."

He snatched the food back and laughed.

"Then kneel down in front me you fucking bitches."

Maria and Barbara got to their knees and waited. Barbara tried to wipe her mouth with the back of her hand but Kirk kicked it away and she whimpered in pain.

"You are my slaves. Is that correct?"

"Oh, yes. we are your slaves. We will do whatever you say."

"Then you must call me 'Master' whenever you address me."

"Yes, Master."

"Yes, Master."

"And you must do exactly what I order."

"We will, we will do anything you say, anything."

"Yes, anything."

"Anything what?"

"Anything Master."

"Anything Master."

"Better. And if you do not please me, what then?"

"You will not feed us and you will punish us, Master."

"Yes, so you'd better please me, and please me well."

"Yes, Master. Please give us your instructions, we promise you will not be disappointed."

"Feel yourselves, bitches. I want to see you playing with your cunts."

Maria glanced over to the black warrior. His cock was hanging loosely at his groin and she felt a tingle of excitement in her cunt as she remembered the pleasure of riding him. She reached down and felt around where they had shaved her, her skin was so smooth and sensitive. Her fingers went lower and found the crack at the front of her cunt. She probed into it and felt along the edges of her labia, then she rubbed her fingers against her clitoris and a hot thrill shot through her stomach. She started massaging it and she felt the glow of pleasure surging through her veins.

She looked at the black warrior again and opened her still shackled legs a little wider so that he could see what she was doing. She stared at his cock and saw that it was beginning to respond, so she opened her legs more and showed him the edges of her outer labia. Then, she probed more firmly at her clitoris and forced her pelvis forward so that he could see clearly what she was doing. Moisture started to cover her fingers and she rubbed them fervently along the edges of the soft flesh that encompassed her cunt.

Then Maria felt Barbara leaning against her shoulder. She was feeling around the edges of her cunt as well and, pulling at her clitoris which was sticking out prominently from the front of her crack, she rose and fell against Maria as she began to squirm rhythmically and breathe harder and quicker.

Kirk watched them for a while then lay down in front of them and snapped at Maria.

"Now undo my trousers bitch! Let's see what you can do with a cock!"

Reluctantly, Maria took her fingers from her clitoris and knelt down beside Kirk. Her ankles were still splayed wide apart by the bar that was attached to her shackles and, as she bent down, she felt the strain of her captivity and another thrill of excitement ran through her. Then, obediently, she reached down and undid his zip, he lifted his pelvis and, like a slave, she pulled his trousers down to his knees. Then she grabbed the waistband of his under-pants and slid them down as well. His cock fell loosely to one side, exposing his balls which hung heavily at its hairy base.

"Now suck it bitches!"

"Yes, Master."

"Yes, Master."

Barbara knelt on his other side and they both bent their heads, their faces came close and, before they reached the large, soft cock, their cheeks glanced lightly together. Maria felt the smooth skin of Barbara's face and she turned towards her, Barbara's lips were full and red and, as Maria looked at her, they opened in a wanton pout. Maria leaned towards them and pressed her mouth gently onto them, they opened more as she made contact and Maria opened her own mouth to fit it. Their lips pressed together. Maria tasted Barbara's lips and pressed harder, then she felt Barbara's tongue gently lapping into her mouth. It probed further until it touched Maria's tongue and then began to play with it.

Maria wanted to be gentle but could not hold herself back and she pushed her tongue out and thrust it deeply into Barbara's mouth. She felt Barbara suck it in and it folded deeply into her warm mouth. Spit ran between their mouths and Maria screwed up her eyes in delight, then the pressure slackened and their lips slowly and reluctantly peeled apart. Maria gasped a little then turned to the already hardening cock that lay below them, the skin covering the glans was being forced back by the pressure as it swelled and grew in length, and they both watched as it rose towards their mouths. It did not ease back at all, it continued to swell until it just touched Maria's lips and she parted and let it reach up inside her mouth. Barbara pressed her lips against the side of Maria's, slid them down the shaft, then back up to Maria's wet mouth which opened to take another kiss.

Their mouths opened together as Kirk's cock slid into them and, as they closed their lips around it, they came together in another sweet kiss. This time their tongues shared the throbbing glans as they probed for each other, then Maria ran her mouth down the shaft and Barbara followed.

With their mouths open they could keep their lips in contact and still surround the stiff, pulsating cock. They pulled their longing mouths up and down it and licked its hardened veins, then they felt it filling and moved their kissing mouths to its end. They locked their lips in a tightly

118

sealed kiss and waited as the surge of semen began to flow. Maria opened her eyes and watched Barbara as together they felt the hot spunk shooting up the shaft then they bore down hard together and sucked at the glans and wove their tongues around it. They tasted the first drop and both sucked harder, then a huge wave of spunk shot from it and they sucked at it as hard as they could, slurping and sucking and together drank it all down, sharing it and enjoying it until there was not a drop left. Only when the cock began to unstiffen did they finally release their grip on its hot and throbbing end.

Maria sat back and smiled at Barbara, then she wiped her lips with her hand and looked over to the black warrior. His cock had grown to its full length, its massiveness throbbed weightily and its tip glowed like a hard ball in the light that came in through the cell door. Kirk noticed her interest and smirked.

"So you need more, do you?"

"Master, Master, we only need your orders. What do you want us to do? Give us your instructions, please, give us your orders."

"Tell me what you want you fucking bitches!"

"That, Master," said Maria staring at the warrior's cock.

"Shall I lift you to it bitch?"

"Yes, Master, lift me to it, any way you want. Yes, oh yes, lift me to that marvellous cock."

Kirk scrambled up, kicking his trousers off from around his ankles.

"Cunt first, then arse," he shouted.

He got behind her and lifted her by the waist. She drew her legs up as high as she could and pulled her ankles hard against the metal bar.

"Are you ready bitch?"

"Yes, Master. Take me to it. Present me to that mighty

119

cock."

He carried her over and held her in front of the black warrior, the cock reared up in front of her and she gasped at the sight of it.

"Please, lift me on Master, please lift me on!"

Kirk raised her up until her splayed out cunt was above the throbbing glans of the huge cock.

"Tell me how you want to be placed bitch. Tell me how you want lowering and how you want to feel it. You're a fucking slut and I want to know how a slut takes such a huge cock."

"Please Master, I just want to feel the end of it first. Lower me, lower me please. Can I tell you when to stop?"

"Yes, I want to know it all, you dirty little bitch."

Kirk held tightly around her waist and she could feel his muscular arms straining under her weight as he lowered her slowly towards the warrior's huge cock. When she felt the first touch of it her cunt widened more, this time she knew how big it would be, this time she knew how much she would have to stretch to accommodate it and she strained her legs wider to open her cunt as far as it would go.

"More, a little more!"

Kirk let her down slightly. The massive glans forced itself against her outer labia, they pressed back and folded inwards painfully, she needed to open herself wider and she stretched her thighs even further apart.

"Please Master, I beg you, lift me off, I need to be wider before I can even get it started!"

She forced her hands between her legs and pulled the silky edges of her labia wide apart. She held them splayed open and felt the heat from the massive cock radiating upwards and penetrating the opening to her vagina.

"Please Master, down again, please let me down, I'm

ready now."

Kirk let her down again and this time, as she kept the edges of her cunt pulled back, the tip of the cock began to sink inside and she wriggled on it to ease it in. She gasped as it entered.

"Please master, keep going! Please keep going!"

It went in further, her eyes widened and she threw her head back as she squeezed herself onto it until she could feel its throbbing deep inside her. Kirk kept letting her down until she could take no more.

"Please Master, stop! That's all I can take."

"You're taking more than that you fucking bitch!"

He thrust her down further and she gasped as the huge cock plunged deeply into her already filled vagina. Its tip pressed hard against her innards and she felt as if she was going to be sick.

"Now let's see how you ride it!"

"Please Master, please, I can't take any more, please!"

But he took no notice. He plunged her further, drew her back then plunged her down again. Maria yelled out loudly as she felt the swollen veins of the cock pressing and dragging against the insides of her vagina but Kirk ignored her pleading and just kept holding her firmly around the waist and forcing her mercilessly up and down the pulsating cock. As the warrior's cock swelled even more, and tightened inside Maria's cunt, Kirk found it difficult to move her at all, but he did not stop and she gasped and shouted as the pain drove through her and ignited her desire for more. The thought of shouting for release passed away like a forgotten dream.

"Fuck it! Fuck it!"

He kept her going but the more he moved her the more her cunt tightened onto the huge member and the more difficult it became. He gasped with the effort of pulling

121

her up and down as he fought against the pressure of her cunt as it held onto the warrior's cock like a grasping fist.

"Fuck it! Fuck it! Fuck it!"

She stared into the writhing face of the gagged warrior and was inflamed by the sight of his captive savagery.

"Master, Master, take me off! Take me off! I want to try it up my arse!"

With difficulty, Kirk pulled her off the cock and the edges of her cunt pulled together sharply as the glans finally slipped out. Kirk turned her around and, holding her breasts against his face, he lifted her up into position. She pressed her buttocks out and waited for a moment, then she dropped her face onto Kirk's golden hair, took some of it between her teeth, and bit and pulled at it to urge him on. She felt his hot breath against her breasts and pressed them hard against him and her stomach thrilled anxiously as she felt her anus dilating in expectation and fear of the throbbing glans.

"Please Master, now!"

He lowered her anus towards the tip of the warrior's cock, she felt its heat and her muscular ring opened wider. Kirk lowered her some more and, when it touched, a terrified thrill shot through her and she screeched in panic.

"Please Master. Down! Down!"

Kirk kept lowering her. She opened her anus as much as she could and the glans, still dripping wet from her cunt, stretched it wider and pushed in.

"Please master. Down! Down!"

Then she wanted to ask him to move her slowly, bit by bit, but she could not say words any more. She started howling and braying like an animal, her throat gagged then she choked and coughed and howled even more. Kirk kept lowering her down and her eyes widened until she looked mad. Her face flushed red-hot and her anus was passing excruciating pain throughout her whole body. She kept howling, now she had taken as much as she could, she wanted to scream to Kirk to stop. She wanted to tell him to pull her off, she wanted to command him to release her from the plunging, painful cock, but she could not make any sense, she just screeched in pain and delight. Her cries and howls only excited him more and he forced her even further onto the huge, pulsating cock. Maria yelled but only animal noises came out, she yelled so loudly her ears rang with her screams, but Kirk kept forcing her down onto the massive thing.

Barbara watched as the shaft disappeared, inch by inch, into Maria's arse, Maria still yelled to be lifted off, but Kirk kept pushing her down. Barbara reached forward and grabbed the lower part of the massive shaft in her hands and tried to encircle it, she could just touch her fingers around it. She pulled it up and down and watched as it kept slipping deeper into Maria's anus. She held onto it and pulled at it wildly hoping to keep a grip on it, but slowly it disappeared and, in the end, her hands were forced away as it plunged in up to its base.

Kirk could hardly hold on to Maria as she squirmed and writhed. Her howling was terrible as he lifted her a bit then plunged her down again and she screamed and bayed in pain and fear. Every time the base of the massive stem appeared Barbara grabbed it and felt its might. Maria bit more of Kirk's hair and pulled at it to try and get him to release her, but he just kept going. Then she reached down his back and clawed her nails into his skin, cutting him deeply and watching blood pouring from the wounds, but still he kept plunging her up and down. Then she felt the cock widening and stiffening even more, she could not believe that it could get even bigger, it swelled inside her and she felt the flow of semen roaring up it like a huge

123

tide.

She clawed deeply into Kirk's back and bit into his hair, she choked and screamed and threw herself about in panic, as all the time, the surge grew stronger and she felt the veins on the warrior's cock hardening and pressing against her innards. Then suddenly his spunk exploded into her. It was hot and poured out in incredible volume, scalding her from inside. As it spurted out she felt the huge cock expand for one last time, then she collapsed in horror and felt her muscles contracting as a vast orgasm ran inside her. The pain had gone, she was filled completely and now her body was giving her the pleasure it had earned.

She pulsated and throbbed as her cunt delivered the thrills that ran into her arse and throughout her whole body and all her limbs tingled and burned as she fell forward onto Kirk.

She gurgled and blubbered and still could not speak, then he lifted her off and the expended cock came out of her but her anus stayed open and dilated.

Kirk dropped Maria down heavily on the stone floor of the cell, she lay on her back, panting and gasping for breath. Then, as if in a fit, she started screaming again. She twisted and turned and beat her heels on the floor, she howled like a wolf and dribbled and spat from her mouth, then, with a terrific bang, the cell door opened and Caleb rushed in brandishing his staff.

Caleb stood over Maria and pointed his staff at her stomach. She went quiet, then Father Thomas rushed in behind him, flushed with anger, and Kirk shrunk back against the wall.

"Caleb! We have no time to deal with this. The Mistress Lesley has ordered us to send six slaves to her tomorrow so we had better get going. Send the branded one

124

to make up the numbers, the other one, our sinful child Maria, obviously needs more training, much more training. For the moment, release their legs and take them both to the holding cell."

He turned to Kirk who was now shaking with fear.

"And you, Kirk, you fucking fool, will you never learn to behave yourself? You can stay and keep the warrior company for a few days, perhaps that will give you time to learn some self-control. Fucking fool!"

Kirk shuffled back along the wall and hung his head in shame. His golden hair dropped loosely across his face and his wide mouth tightened. Maria glanced at him meekly, but she looked down as she caught his angry gaze. Then Caleb dropped his staff on the floor, took a key from his trouser pocket, jumped between Maria's legs and started to unlock her shackles. He pulled at them roughly and she twisted her body and tried to resist.

In a way she did not want the shackles removed, she did not want to be freed. The more she wriggled the harder he pulled and, when she let out a shriek, he turned and slapped her hard across the face. She looked at him hard then shrieked again, then she leant up onto her elbows, still staring at him, and shrieked harder. He slapped her again and again she shrieked, then he slapped her several times across the cheeks and, although her head was knocked from side to side, still she kept shrieking.

In the end, he drew a dirty handkerchief from his pocket, pulled it tightly across her open mouth and tied it behind her head. She still tried to scream but the only sound that came out was the wild rush of air through her flared nostrils. Then he went back to the shackles, undid them and in one action, lifted them up and threw them into a corner of the cell.

Then he jumped across to Barbara and released her as

125

well. This time he threw the shackles across the room angrily and they crashed against the wall above Kirk's head.

Maria and Barbara struggled to their feet and shrunk back in fear as Caleb picked up his staff and prodded at them both until they moved out of the cell and into the dark tunnel outside. He forced them forward into the darkness and soon they reached a very small door set low down into the tunnel.

"In there! In there! Dark little hole! Dark little hole!" he shouted.

They bent down, crawled inside and the door slammed shut behind them.

CHAPTER 10

Maria and Barbara lay with their arms wrapped around each other on the stone floor of the tiny low-roofed cell. Maria nuzzled her gagged mouth into Barbara's neck as they both shivered in the cold dampness.

Maria clung tightly to Barbara. She did not want to let her go, she felt as if she had found a friend and was afraid of losing her before she could even get to know her. Some tears fell down her stretched cheeks and she nuzzled even closer into Barbara's neck. She wanted to kiss her and lap her tongue around Barbara's face while Barbara's lips pressed softly against her skin, but because of the handkerchief gagging her mouth, she could only press herself closer and breathe on her through her nostrils.

Suddenly Maria's eyes widened as she started to think about how disgusting she had been with the black warrior. Her sinfulness seemed to have completely overtaken her, she must surely be beyond salvation. Then she re-

126

membered what Father Thomas had said about being trained and she felt a sense of relief to think that at least she was still on the path to redemption, that no matter how evil she was, there would still be more chances to beg him to hear her confessions. But she wanted to be taken straight away, she wanted to be punished and cleansed now. How could she last the night out in the sensual comfort of Barbara's arms when things seemed to be getting worse and worse? How could she wait when her wickedness was increasing with every hour? She thought of her craven desires and the pain she had felt when she had the black warrior's cock up her arse. Just the thought of it made her tingle.

She wanted to whip herself for having such feelings, but that only increased her feelings of pleasure. Everything was all mixed up together. She shuddered as she imagined that no punishment, no matter how severe, could cure her of her wickedness, because every punishment she received increased her desire for the pleasure of more pain. Gradually she sank into a dazed sleep.

She was woken by the sound of scurrying in the tunnel outside, her face was buried deeply into Barbara's hair and she inhaled its sweetness deeply through her nostrils, then drew away and waited anxiously.

"Off we go! Off we go!" chanted Caleb as he unbolted the small door to their cell.

He leaned in, grabbed Barbara's ankles and hauled her out roughly. She trailed her arms longingly towards Maria as she was dragged out of the door and into the darkness. Maria wished so much that she could say something to her, but it was hopeless, the door slammed shut and everything went silent again.

A few hours later Maria sat up suddenly as the cell door

was flung open noisily. Caleb reached in and started to drag her out by the ankles, her face scraped against the stone floor as he pulled her out savagely. She looked up at him and breathed hard through her nostrils as he slipped a slender rope around her ankles, pulled it over his shoulder and hauled her like a heavy sack along the dark tunnel. The stone floor became increasingly wet, then muddy, and when Caleb released the rope and Maria fell in a heap, she was lying in sloppy red mud. She looked around and saw light coming in through a heavy iron grill, she was in the muddy hole that she had seen the workmen in!

A wave of fear passed over her as the memories of her past flooded into her mind. She shivered and tried to wipe the mud from her eyes but Caleb prodded her hard with his staff, then she heard footsteps.

"Ah, my child," said Father Thomas. "Your road to redemption is going to be a long and tortuous one. You are even more sinful than I thought. Perhaps there is hope, but you need to have your fantasies drawn from you, they must be expelled before you can be saved, they must be released by rigorous training. I have decided that a visit to the Brothers may cleanse you of your dirtiness, perhaps they will help expose the full extent of your sinfulness. I will come with you so that I can watch you and hear your confession when you are ready. Perhaps you can begin reflecting on your sins while we wait?"

Maria lay in the mud and stared up through the iron grill. Caleb waited by her side, occasionally poking her for amusement. Maria turned and looked at Father Thomas. She wanted to plead with him to hear her sins now, she still needed to confess so much. She wanted to throw herself at his knees and beg him to lead her out of her evil ways, but he just stared at her impassively and she realised from his look that he had done all he could for the moment. She was too sinful for him to deal with without further help. She looked at him again, but he turned away.

A van drew up outside and two men dressed in robes came over to the grill. Caleb pranced around excitedly as they climbed down into the muddy hole.

"Do not worry, my little servant, you will see her again soon." Father Thomas turned to the men. "Total obedience! That's what we must have, and Mistress Lesley wants her ready in a couple of days. I have told you what she has said, we must work the evil out of her and make her ready, but I warn you, her desires are very powerful."

Caleb released the lock on the grill and the two men grabbed Maria, tied her wrists behind her back and, without a word, dragged her to the rear of the van. Father Thomas went through the grill after them and climbed into the front. Maria took a last look at the church before the two men threw her down in the back, slammed the doors and drove off.

Maria lay in the darkness on the floor of the van. She was bounced about roughly as it sped through the streets, and when it went around corners at speed she was flung against the ribbed metal walls. She was unable to protect herself and gasped through the tight gag as she hit the sides and rolled about the floor. She was covered in mud and her black skirt was dirty and crumpled, her white blouse hung in tatters from her shoulders and she felt bruised and disgusting. After a while the van stopped and she was thrown forward in a heap.

The doors opened and the men dragged her out. She was blinded by the light at first, but soon saw that she was being dragged through the large double doors of a mansion house. They opened into a large hall with a high ceiling and bare brown walls upon which hung dirty oil paintings of monks and nuns. The men dragged her in roughly by the ankles and as the doors were slammed shut behind her, tossed her down on the floor.

"Take her to the dining hall Brother Arnold."

"Yes, Father."

Brother Arnold grabbed Maria's wrists and hauled her through the hall and down a corridor, then he flung open a door and threw her into a room full of men sitting at long trestle tables. They all wore brown robes with loose, brown cords tied around their waists. Father Thomas came into the room and stood at the door.

"This child needs some intensive training, Brothers. She has found too much pleasure in our punishment and she has to be ready for the Mistress soon. I implore you to help her expel her dreadful fantasies, to make her ready to serve as a slave and bring her to salvation."

"Ah, a muddy slave to be sure," said one.

"Filthy little slut!" said another.

They started to jeer and bang knives and forks on the trestle tables.

"Dirty bitch!"

"Filthy whore!"

Maria cowered on the floor and looked nervously around like a frightened animal.

"Here slave," said one of the Brothers, holding out his bowl, "fetch my food and be quick about it!"

Maria was too terrified to move.

"Fetch my food, slave!" he shouted angrily.

She crawled over to him and looked up helplessly, drew herself onto her knees and bowed her gagged face. The Brother leant down to her and sniffed at her muddy hair. She pulled away but he grabbed her hair and pulled her head back sharply.

"I want serving, you fucking bitch. Here!"

Maria did not know what he wanted her to do, she could

not take the bowl because her wrists were tied behind her back and she could not speak because of the gag that pulled tightly across her mouth. The Brother yanked her hair tighter and she breathed hard through her nostrils, her eyes widening as terror swept over her and she felt her skin flushing with fear.

One of the Brothers jumped up from his seat and held a knife high above his head, then he rushed over to Maria and held the blade in front of her face. She tried to draw away but her hair was pulled even tighter. The shiny blade of the knife was pointed at one of her cheeks and she shivered with fear and tried to pull away but it was impossible. Her nostrils flared wide as she panted in panic, staring at the blade of the knife, shivering and shaking and consumed by a hot surge of frantic terror.

"Fucking bitch!" shouted the Brother with the knife. "Fucking disobedient bitch!"

He drew the knife back a little then put it underneath the tightly pulled handkerchief that strained across her mouth. She stopped breathing and waited, frozen with terror, then, with one sudden movement, he slashed through the handkerchief. The tension across her cheeks was broken but, as the handkerchief fell away, she still kept it clasped between her teeth.

"Drop it, you dog!"

Slowly, she unclenched her teeth and the handkerchief fell onto the floor, her mouth was sore but she opened it wide and started screeching straight away.

"Please, please, please -"

"Get my food bitch!" shouted the Brother with the bowl, then, without warning, he pushed it between her teeth. "Get my fucking food and keep silent!"

The metal bowl crashed noisily against her teeth and she fell back under the shock. He pushed it at her again and this time she gripped it tight. The metal felt stinging and cold against her teeth and its edges forced the sides of her mouth out wide as she looked around for instructions. The Brothers were pointing and jeering at her as she sat like a dog carrying a food bowl, then she saw that they were all pointing towards a large table with food on that stood at the far end of the room. With the bowl firmly clenched in her mouth, Maria tried to stand, but a Brother knocked her back down to her knees.

"Get my fucking food slave! But crawl! Slaves do not stand in the presence of their masters! Crawl like a dog and fetch my food you dirty slut!"

Holding the bowl in her mouth, she shuffled on her knees towards the food table. She felt dirty and humiliated as she crawled between the jeering Brothers and the metal bowl hurt her mouth and her knees were sore.

"What have you brought us here Father Thomas? A filthy slut to be sure. Covered in mud and yes, unless I'm mistaken, no panties on. Brothers, Brothers, I do believe our slutty slave has no panties on. A filthy bitch with no panties on. Come on bitch, I'm waiting! Where's my food?"

She struggled on between the Brothers, then one of them lifted the muddy hem of her skirt and revealed her smooth bottom.

"Yes, no panties Brothers! What a slut!"

"Spank that little bottom, Brother. Give her a good spank for not wearing her panties!"

She flinched as his hand smacked down across her bottom and her teeth bit hard into the metal bowl.

Spank!

She screamed as she fell forward under the heavy smack, then he held her skirt up high and brought his hand back again, this time even harder.

Spank!

She shrieked but as she shuffled forward her skirt fell back down and covered her naked bottom. She ducked and cowered as she made her way between them, all the time clenching the bowl between her teeth until finally, she got to the table and stopped. A fat Brother stood in front of her holding a ladle above a huge, wooden bowl.

"Soup?" he asked

She waited.

"Soup?" he demanded.

Maria nodded slowly.

He dipped the ladle into the big bowl and drew it out full and spilling over with hot soup, then, clumsily, he poured it into her bowl and hot soup splashed over the sides. It ran scoldingly down her chin and onto her breasts. She tried to hold the bowl steadily between her teeth, but could hardly bear the stinging of the hot liquid as it poured over the sides. Then he ladled another helping into the bowl. It sloshed all over the sides but although she stung with the pain of the hot soup dribbling down her chin, she did not dare let the bowl go.

"Take it to your master, slutty slave!"

She turned and started to make her way back to the table. As she shuffled along on her knees all the Brothers shouted and jeered and more of the soup slopped over the sides. She gripped the bowl hard in her mouth and pressed her lips against its sharp edges but still soup splashed out, running down her face and trickling across her breasts. When she arrived at the Brother who had sent her for the soup there was hardly anything left in the bowl. He reached down and pulled it from her mouth and she flinched in pain as he wrenched it from between her teeth. He lifted the bowl and turned it slowly upside down, a single drop of soup dripped from it and the Brothers started to shout loudly and bang the tables even harder with their knives and forks.

"Oh dear," said the Brother. "You are a fucking, hopeless bitch."

He stood up, grabbed hold of the long, brown cord that held his robe at the waist, slowly untied it and pulled it free.

"Please, please, plea -"

"Silence!"

"Plea -"

"Hold her Brothers, we need to punish our dirty little slave. She does not seem to know how to follow orders!"

Two of them came up on either side of her and grabbed her tied arms, they wrenched them back and she cried out as the one with the long cord stood in front of her and looked her up and down.

"Complete obedience, that's what you're here for, complete obedience! And what a start! What a start, you fucking bitch!"

He reached forward, grabbed the muddy tatters of her blouse and ripped them down exposing her firm breasts. He grabbed the material of her skirt and pulled it hard. It parted completely at the front but still hung from the torn waistband, and her shaven crotch came into full view. She felt terribly exposed but at the same time a surge of excitement ran through her as she felt the Brother's eyes staring longingly at her naked cunt.

"No panties and look Brothers, she is shaved!"

The Brothers shouted excitedly.

"Hold her tight Brothers!"

Her arms were pulled back hard and her breasts were forced forward, She felt her already hard nipples tingling with anticipation as soup mingled with mud dripped from them in long, streaky dribbles. Then the Brother drew back the cord, she stared up at him and waited, then it came lashing down.

Thwack!

It struck her full across the breasts. She screamed and wanted to bend forward but when she tried her arms were pulled even more tightly behind her back.

Thwack!

Her breasts stung as the cord lashed across them again.

"Hold her tight Brothers!"

Thwack!

The cord slashed across her dripping nipples and they sent two lacerating pains through her breasts.

Thwack!

She tried to squirm but was being held so tight she could not move.

Thwack!

Red lines appeared across her breasts as the cord slashed against them.

Thwack! Thwack! Thwack!

She screamed loudly as the flogging continued.

"Let me serve you. Let me try again. Please, let me try again."

Thwack! Thwack! Thwack!

"I can serve you properly. I can, really I can. Just let me try. Please, no more. Please let me be your servant. Let me be your slave."

Thwack! Thwack! Thwack!

The lashes rained down on her breasts relentlessly. She sagged at the knees and felt the draft from the lashing cord between her thighs. Her naked cunt pushed forward and its fleshy lips swelled fully, their pinkness glistened as a moisture of desire spread across them and the more lashes she received the wetter it got. She felt her clitoris swelling and rising between the crack of her cunt, it was aching and tingling and probing forward, she wanted it held, she wanted it massaged and pulled, then she felt the draft from the cord getting closer. Her clitoris swelled and engorged, she could feel it poking between the wet lips of her cunt, then the draft got closer and then it was not a draft but a terrifying pain as the cord beat down across the front of her cunt.

Thwack! Thwack! Thwack!

It slashed across her raised clitoris. The pain was terrible but still she pushed it forward and still it grew as her desire swelled inside her like a vast wave.

Thwack!

This time right between her crack. She pushed her pelvis forward for more and struggled against the tension on her arms, but not to get away, not to protect herself from the lashes, but to expose herself for more.

Thwack!

She wanted more thrashing, the beating was inflaming her, she wanted more and more. She struggled against the restraining hands, but not to get free, nor to offer herself for more beating, she wanted to feel their strength, she wanted to feel her captivity, she wanted to feel the tension of their grip and the pointlessness of her struggle. She felt a drawing inside her cunt, a pulling, a tension, a release, her clitoris was being beaten into an orgasm.

She wanted more, she wanted it whipped until it released her with a climax, she needed the pain to give her relief with that final convulsion of passionate frenzy. It built inside her as the cord came down, it touched her anus and she heaved up on the arms that held her then fell forward with a gurgling, convulsive shriek. The thrashing stopped and she was dropped to the ground, but she was given no time to recover.

"Now, fetch my soup!" the Brother ordered.

The bowl was thrust into her mouth again while she

still lay on the floor gasping. She struggled to her knees and started back to the serving table, again her dress was lifted and she was spanked, but it was so delightful now, her body was flushed with her orgasm and the spanking felt like a gentle massage. Each smack pulled at her buttocks and tugged the swollen edges of her cunt and she wanted to bend over fully and take it harder, she wanted to bend over and demand spanking from them all until she finished again, but she knew she did not dare and kept going with the bowl firmly between her teeth.

The bowl was filled and she started on her way back. The soup spilled again and then she dropped the bowl and it rolled across the floor with a noisy clatter. For a moment she froze where she was, then she bent over, wanting to be smacked. She bent her shoulders down to the floor, laid her face down and lifted her bottom as high as she could, her cunt opened wide as she pressed her thighs apart desperately wanting to be spanked.

Smack!

A hand smacked down on her upturned buttocks.

Smack! Smack!

Another and another until they blurred into a stream of delectable pain and pleasure She raised her bottom high and lifted it towards the pain as the hands rained down on her. Then she was dragged to her feet, held from behind again and thrashed with the cord even harder across her breasts. Now they were covered in red stripes and, as she looked down at them, her cunt filled and finished repeatedly.

Then the bowl was thrust into her mouth again and, after it was filled, she carried it back to her master. He took it from her, looked at its contents and smiled approvingly but, before she had a chance to do anything, another bowl was forced into her mouth. She went to the serving

137

table and crawled back again and again, each time the bowl was filled to overflowing with splashing soup. Her ripped dress trailed at her sides and her reddened breasts stung as she went from Brother to Brother carrying their bowls in her mouth.

Whenever they were not pleased she was held again and beaten. She was forced to continue until they had all been served and then she was ordered to kneel in a corner and wait for further orders.

Maria curled up in the corner of the dining room while all the Brothers ate their soup. She pushed her hands between her thighs and felt the warmth of her soft cunt. Her fingers played around its edges and pulled longingly at her erect clitoris; it stung from the beating it had taken but the delight that it caused when she played with it was intense. She wanted to be beaten again, she wanted to serve the food and be treated like a slave.

Soon the Brothers wanted more serving and the whole process started again. She crawled around the dining room with the bowl in her mouth, serving their food and taking her punishment whenever she spilled anything from their bowls. She felt desperately ashamed and wretched but also desperately excited and suffused with overwhelming pleasure.

When they had finished eating she was dragged to the serving table. Two of the Brothers undid the ropes at her wrists, then pinned her on her back on the wooden trestle. She did not think she could stand any more, her cunt was throbbing from the pain of the beating and the repeated swelling of her orgasms, and she wriggled her hips to try and protect herself, but two others held her ankles and spread her legs wide apart.

"Total obedience!" shouted Brother Arnold. "Now, my girl, let's test your ability to be totally obedient. Who'd like to fuck the bitch first?"

A tall Brother came forward.

"We will tell you how to be fucked, bitch! You must only do what we say!"

A surge of panic ran through her.

"Yes, Brother," she said meekly.

"This one is going to fuck you hard. He is not going be gentle, he is going to plunge his hard cock inside you and fuck you until he comes. Is that alright bitch? What did you say?"

"Yes, Brother."

"Yes, what?"

"Yes, he will fuck me hard until he comes."

"Good."

The cock plunged straight into her cunt, driving itself deep into her vagina in one sudden thrust. Maria yelled as she felt its thick base forcing the lips of her cunt wide apart. Then it drew back slightly but quickly thrust again and immediately spurted a hot stream of semen deeply inside her. As he drew it out the semen trailed from the end of his cock and dribbled stickily down the insides of her thighs.

"Who's next my Brothers?"

Another came forward and Maria was spread even wider. The Brother lifted his robe and held his hard cock in front of her open cunt, squeezing it tightly until the swollen purple glans spread out wide at the sides.

"Open up for the next one bitch!"

He rammed it in and she gasped. The edges of his flared glans squashed hard against her inner labia as it plunged deeply inside her. She felt her vagina pulled by its edges as he thrust her rapidly, then another spurt of semen and he drew it out, dripping the remnants of his orgasm across her legs.

"More bitch?"

She did not speak.

"I said, more bitch?"

"Yes, Brother, yes, more."

"Give the bitch some more! The dirty slut wants more! Give it to her my Brothers!"

Another approached and rammed his cock into her. He finished quickly and, while he was still wiping the sticky end against her legs, another pushed him aside and stuck a massive erection in. Maria yelled because it was so big. This time, when it began to surge with spunk, the Brother drew it out and let it spurt across her stomach, where it ran in hot floods and completely soaked her.

The next was inside. She felt her clitoris standing out and rubbing against the veins on the cock as it thrust at her. She yelled again but this time she was yelling for more, she wanted more fucking.

"More! More!" she shouted.

Every time she demanded more another cock plunged into her widespread cunt. She strained her arms and legs as they were held fast, and she stretched her fingers wide and as each cock thrust inside her, and as the semen ran hotly into the depths of her vagina, she shouted louder and more frantically.

"Give me more! Another dick! Stick it in!"

She heard her words and they inflamed her. She stretched her fingers wider and felt the blood pounding through her wrists as they were pinned to the top of the table.

"Here, here, in my hands! I want dicks in my hands."

Then she felt the hot stiffness of a cock drop across her outstretched fingers and she grabbed it, then the other hand was filled and, as she screamed with pleasure, she pulled at her wrists and her ankles and raised her pelvis high to receive the next one.

"In my mouth! In my mouth! Deep in my mouth. More!"

Her mouth was filled and she sucked wildly at the throbbing cock that was thrust in.

"More! Another. Fuck me! Fuck me! I want more to suck! Give me another!"

Another cock squeezed into her mouth and her lips were forced wide under the pressure, she sucked them both and wanked the ones in her hands, and all the time she was fucked by cock after cock. Her body lurched and strained and she felt the desperate heat of pleasure as it surged through her limbs and streamed over her flesh. She could not get enough, she choked as she tried to shout for more and another cock finished in her face. She wanted her arse filled and she wanted beating while she held onto the cocks in her hands, she wanted to feel the deep fucking inside her cunt, she wanted so much more and they were not satisfying her. She struggled and sucked and fucked as madly as she could and orgasms spilled through her like ravaging torrents but still she had not had enough.

Then, for a moment, her mouth was open and not filled and she yelled and screamed at them for more, then it was filled again and she choked as one of them ran deeply down her throat, she spit it out and screamed for more but her words were lost to her howls and screams.

Then there was a strange silence, the Brothers had fucked her enough. Maria lay, unrestrained, on the trestle, still spread out and covered with sticky semen. It ran across her thighs, over her stomach and breasts, covered her face, ran from her mouth and dripped in sticky strands from her hair. As she panted and growled, her pelvis kept thrusting out for more and the heat in her cunt was still unsatisfied.

Then she heard Father Thomas calling her over. His

141

voice sounded gentle and forgiving and she went and crouched before him. He rested his hands on her wet hair and sighed heavily.

"Oh my child. I wonder if you can ever be saved? Your fantasies are so terrible and your desires are so strong. Even living your fantasies does not seem to satisfy you. Oh, my child, will I ever be able to absolve you?"

He patted her head and she dropped her head in despair, then she lay down and curled up like a faithful dog at his feet with her semen soaked cheeks pressed softly against his black leather shoes. Occasionally, she pushed her tongue out between her lips and licked it across the shiny leather and when she lifted her face to get more comfortable, the lace-holes left an impression on her smooth, wet skin.

As she dreamed about the fucking she had just had, she was aroused by the feeling that she had wanted so much more and, as she slipped her fingers inside the soft folds of her still dripping cunt, she wondered if Father Thomas was right.

CHAPTER 11

Maria awoke to find herself lying on the floor of the dining room. When she tried to move, she found that she had been tied with a rope that led from a noose around her neck, down across her stomach, and to her ankles.

"I think the slut needs a bath!" she heard someone shouting, then she heard Father Thomas's voice, but it was no longer wistful and soft, it was angry and loud.

"We only have today Brothers. The Mistress Lesley has ordered me to deliver her in a few days and she will

142

not take kindly to a slave who is only half-trained. Do whatever you have to, but make sure she is ready!"

Maria saw the hems of brown robes gathering around her and she was pulled to her feet. The rope tightened at her neck and she could not stand upright. The Brothers lifted her at the elbows. The strain from the rope at her ankles pulled hard at the back of her neck and her feet were lifted off the ground as they carried her away.

Brother Arnold led the way as they marched her down a long corridor. They stopped in front of a black door at the end and Brother Arnold grabbed her chin and lifted her head.

"Well, slave, we do not have long to bring you to heel, but I know we can do it. Father Thomas has told us of your evil ways, yes, all of your evil ways, we know your fantasies and your terrible deeds and we have seen your wanton craving for ourselves. But do not worry, we will lead you to salvation, we will show you how to be saved. Take her in Brothers! We know she likes to be washed, at least when she does it herself, so first let's clean the little bitch before we take her for the training she needs!"

Maria felt frozen with fear by his words but she did not have time to think about them. Before she could begin to understand what he meant, the door burst open and the Brothers carried her into a large, white, tiled room, it was hot and steamy and at its centre was a huge sunken bath.

"In the bath with her, let's get the little bitch clean!"

They dragged her across the room then threw her into the steaming water. The breath was knocked from her as she hit the surface, then, as she quickly sank to the bottom, she was confused and disorientated and, when she tried, she could not stand up because of her bonds. She swallowed some water and fought to get some breath, but she was lying face down and could only gulp hopelessly in panic. Several of the Brothers pulled off their robes and jumped in behind her, they grabbed hold of her and, just as she thought she was going to drown, they lifted her up and held her above the surface. She gasped wildly and managed to get enough breath to start screaming.

"Please, no, no, no!"

But they took no notice of her cries and plunged her back down again. The water ran up her nose and into her mouth and again she fought desperately for breath, then they lifted her out again and she gasped once more in panicky relief.

Her frantic begging for mercy went unheeded. Two of the Brothers grabbed her ankles and held her upside down in the foaming water. Then another plunged his face between her legs and stuck his tongue deeply into her cunt. She felt it go in and wanted to cry out but she did not dare open her mouth because she knew it would fill with water and she would drown. Then they lifted her again and again she gasped and begged again for mercy.

At last she was lifted up, but a Brother grabbed her from behind. He bent her forward, forced his hands between her legs, grabbed the rope that ran from her neck and pulled it down hard. Her head was snatched forward and her face plunged into the water. She choked and bubbles burst around her gulping mouth, but he kept her face firmly under the water as he pushed his hard cock between her buttocks. The stiff shaft prized them apart and the throbbing end pressed hotly against her anus, then he relaxed his grip on the rope and she flung her head upwards for breath.

It was a short relief.

He only allowed her a single breath before he grabbed the rope and pulled her face back underneath the water. This time she was more prepared and she held her breath

144

as he pushed the throbbing end of his cock against the tight muscular ring of her anus. She felt it giving under the pressure and the hot tip began to enter, then he released his grip on the rope and again she burst to the surface. She choked and gasped frantically as he grabbed the back of her hair and forced her ear close to his mouth.

"Slut! Arse-fucking slut! Can you feel it? Can you feel my dick?"

"Yes, yes, but -"

"Good. I know you like it, that's all I want to hear. That's all you are allowed to say. Do you hear me? That's all you are allowed to say."

"Please, what must I say?"

He plunged her head under the water again and held it there for ages until he pulled it back, then, as she came back to the surface, water burst from her mouth and she choked convulsively.

"You must only say that you want more!"

"But please, oh, please -"

He grabbed the rope and pulled her down again. This time the warm water lubricated it and his thick, hot cock slid in easily. Then he released the rope and again she burst to the surface.

"Please -"

"Not learnt yet have you? Scream for more you fucking bitch!"

He grabbed the rope again and forced his cock further inside her arse, she wanted to gasp as she felt its hardness penetrating her but she bit down on her lips to keep her mouth tight shut. Then he let her go and yet again her panic-stricken face broke into the air.

"Yes, more!"

He pushed his cock in further.

"How much more bitch?"

"Oh more! More! More! I want it deep! Please, more, more..."

He grabbed the rope again and down she went into the foaming water. He pushed his cock further in and she bit her lips even harder. The pressure in her arse was enormous and she felt the stiff rod getting higher and higher, then the rope was released.

"More! Give me more! I want more of your dick up my arse!"

He gave her more and she spluttered and choked as he grabbed the rope again and forced her head down low under the water. This time he pushed his cock in up to its base. She wanted to scream but knew she had to wait until she was released, she had to hold her breath and suffer the deep fucking until he decided to let her go. She bit down hard onto her lips but could not stop her mouth from opening, water ran in and she felt it washing around her tongue. She pulled back against the pressure of the noose around her neck, but it was too tight and cut deeply into her straining throat. As she held on, she felt her body filling with unbelievable desire. It was wanton and bestial, it felt like the desires of an animal, a wolf, a terrible, roaring beast. As the noose throttled her the animal feelings grew, they emanated from the tightness in her throat and cascaded through her body like a gigantic waterfall of sexual images.

She saw cocks and spunk, she saw cunts around her mouth, she saw dicks wanking in her face, she saw herself being flogged with a chain until she begged for mercy, and she saw herself drowning and still being fucked as she floated dead in the water. When she came to the surface she could only think of one thing.

"Give me a dick in my mouth, I must have a dick to suck. Give me more in my arse but I must have a dick!"

One of the Brothers crouched down in front of her and held his stiff cock under the water.

"You asked for it bitch!"

The rope was pulled violently, she opened her mouth wide and her face plunged under the water again. The stiff cock went straight into her mouth and plugged it completely. She sucked at it ravenously, she did not think of breathing any more, sucking was breathing, her arse was full and she sucked at the cock until she felt its head at the back of her throat. It made her want to choke but she welcomed it and pulled it in further, then she felt the hot surge of spunk up her arse, it was a huge torrent, and she forced the cock in her mouth right down. Then she choked and tried to pull her face above the water but she was being held down too tightly.

Then, as she thought she could not stand it any further, the cock in her arse swelled with its final burst of semen and the rope was released. She broke to the surface heaving and choking and, as she fought desperately to breathe again, she felt her body heating up with the pressure of an immense orgasm.

It broke and ran through her in searing, convulsive waves, her head spun giddily, for a moment she did not know if she was alive or dead, then she shuddered all over and started to scream for more.

"More sucking! More fucking! I want more! More! More! More!"

She felt the Brother behind her let go and she floated out into the water, rolling over and screeching at the top of her voice. Then her legs were grabbed and parted wide and another cock drove hard into her open cunt, she gasped for a moment and then lurched forward to draw it in. She sat onto it and felt its heat burying deep into her soft vagina. Then the noose pulled on her neck again and this time her head went backwards under the surface, her mouth filled and water ran up her nostrils. Then a cock was pushed into her mouth and then another, she grabbed them both between her lips and sucked them hard. Her ears were bursting and the frenzied bubbles exploded all around her, but this time she did not think of breathing, she just stayed down until the cocks finished together in a massive flood of semen. Then the rope was released and, even as she was sucking the last drops of spunk across her tongue, she burst to the surface.

"Fuck her, Brothers," shouted Brother Arnold. "Fuck the bitch until she can take no more!"

"Give it to me," she shouted. "I want fucking with every cock and I want to suck them all as well. More! More!"

She was rolled over in the foaming water and another stiff cock penetrated her cunt at the same time as a huge one was forced into her arse. She yelped for an instant but was dragged back choking under the surface where her mouth was filled with two more eager cocks.

Maria felt the last cock drain into her arse as the rope eased for the last time. She floated on the surface of the water, giddy and exhausted, with her legs apart and her mouth filled with sticky spunk, she felt completely dissipated, then she heard Father Thomas shouting.

"Is there no limits to your sinfulness my child? I have watched you being ravaged, I have seen you revelling in your evil fantasies. What must I do to train you and make you ready for slavery? You are such a slut! I almost despair with you."

She pulled herself to the edge of the bath and laid her elbows over the tiled sides.

"Can you forgive me Father? Can I ever be saved?"

"Not yet my child. Brother Arnold, you know your task!

This slut needs more work. Take her!"

"Oh please Father, please, what must I do? The more I suffer the more I want to suffer and the more pain I have the more desires I have. Oh Father, can I ever be saved?"

"Perhaps your suffering has not been enough. Brother Arnold! Take her!"

Brother Arnold reached down, grabbed her arms and hoisted her from the bath. Her naked body dripped as she stood on its edge and her hair stuck in wet strands across her face. Some semen dripped from the edge of her mouth and she licked it with her tongue.

"Enough, you evil bitch! Take her!"

Brother Arnold grasped her by the hair and dragged her out into the corridor. He closed the door behind him and pinned her roughly against the wall, he pressed his face close to hers, he was red with anger and she shrunk back in fear as his hot breath blew across her wet face.

"We have never failed with anyone yet bitch and we are not going to fail with you! Have no doubt slut, we will make you into a slave before you leave us. What will you be?"

He grabbed her by the throat and squeezed it tightly, she could barely speak and her eyes widened with terror.

"What will you be, bitch?"

"A slave!"

"Yes, a fucking humiliated slave. We will knock the pleasure out of you! We will make you crawl and beg. We will make you serve your masters and never think of your own pleasures again. What will you be?"

"Please, a slave. Please sir, I will be a slave, a sla -"

He yanked her by the hair and hauled her away down the dark corridor. The other Brothers followed, one of them was holding a straining mastiff on a long leather leash. It pulled at its lead and its teeth dripped with saliva. Maria cried out as the huge dog barked behind her and she felt its hot breath panting on her still wet calves as she was pulled along.

Brother Arnold lugged her roughly down some steep stairs and she stumbled and fell. The mastiff barked loudly and snarled at her as she struggled to regain her balance. She was too slow and Brother Arnold held her up off the ground by her hair and she screamed in pain.

"Good, that's what we want to hear!"

As they went down the stairs she could hear a loud rumbling sound and feel and increasing heat. By the time they reached a huge, steel door, she was sweating with the heat and the noise was almost unbearable. One of the Brothers flung open the door and Brother Arnold dragged her inside. Fluorescent lights flashed on and Maria was dazzled by their brightness.

"Open your eyes bitch! See what awaits you!"

Slowly, she opened her eyes and as she looked around she saw that she was in the boiler room. The ceiling was covered with a tangle of differently coloured hot pipes of varying thickness and in the centre stood a flamed a huge boiler. Steam billowed from joints in the pipes and valves attached to the boiler and the heat was incredible.

Brother Arnold shouted something but she could not hear him for the terrible hissing of steam, the loud roar from the burners of the boiler and the snarling and barking of the mastiff that still snapped at her calves. Then she felt hands holding her arms and dragging her forward towards the roaring boiler.

Sweat dripped from her skin as she got nearer. She felt the heat scorching her face and she tried to pull away. Fear ran through her, she was aware of her nakedness and the men's bodies around her, but any sense of pleasure had evaporated with the hot steam pouring from the huge furnace. Even the pinching of her arms as they forced her forward and the feeling of terrible captivity brought no delight.

She was overcome with terror and felt at last, amongst all the turmoil of noise and heat, that her fantasies had been removed, that her pleasures had been drawn from her and that at last she could be saved. Even as she was dragged forward towards the terrible thing she felt a sense of elation, just the thought that at last she might be saved from her terrible sinfulness gave her a new sense of hope and joy.

But as they flung her against the side of the boiler and her breasts were squashed against the asbestos coating that encased it, she screamed in pain and her excitement turned again to fear. As they pressed her hard against the boiler, she felt she could not bear it and tried to pull back, but she was held too tight. She screamed louder and heard her cries joining the wild barking of the mastiff that strained at its leash behind her.

Her hair pulled out in long wet strands as streams of sweat poured down her face. It ran down her neck and onto her flattened breasts, she felt it on the insides of her thighs and draining down to the soft flesh of her cunt, but even that gave her no joy. She screamed again in pain and fear.

Then one of the Brothers tied cords around her wrists and threw them over some of the pipes that trailed in the ceiling. Others pulled the cords up and she was hauled up onto tiptoe. Sweat ran down her arms and her armpits swilled with its hot moisture, from there it streamed down the sides of her chest, past her taut waist and into the crevice of her buttocks. The cords were pulled even tighter and she felt her toes lifted off the ground, the mastiff barked loudly and the Brother holding him strained to keep him

151

under control.

Maria's full weight hung on the cords as she revolved in a slow, sickening spin. As she turned helplessly on her bonds she saw the group of Brothers standing near the door, Brother Arnold near the boiler with two others and the Brother with the straining mastiff on the opposite side.

The two Brothers nearest the boiler bent down and opened the fire door. She flinched as a terrific burst of heat blew out from the hot furnace, scorching her cheeks and singeing her hair. She screamed as loud as she could, she wanted to let them know that she felt no pleasure, she wanted to tell them that she was filled with fear and that she would be their slave and do only their bidding. She wanted to tell them that she no longer felt her own desires and that her only desire was to serve, to be punished and suffer humiliation at their hands, but she could only say one thing.

"Slave! Slave! Slave! Slave!"

She kept shouting it at the top of her voice, but the hissing of the escaping steam, the roaring of the blazing furnace, and the barking of the wild mastiff stifled everything. Finally, her shouting faded away completely as she spun faster on the cords and became dizzy and disorientated. The images of the room got more and more confused, she could see the drooling fangs of the barking dog and thought of how she had seen Father Thomas like that and it made her feel so guilty. She saw Brother Arnold waving his arms and shouting and she wanted to crawl at his feet and serve him in any way he commanded. She saw two Brothers probing something inside the open door of the blazing furnace, and she wanted to beg to be their servant and carry their food and wash their feet. Then she saw them pulling something out of the furnace and she wanted them to plunge her into the sea and drown her.

Then the mastiff barked even louder and as he strained at his leash and snapped up at her feet her desire to serve and be humiliated overwhelmed her.

Then she felt her hips being grabbed and the spinning stopped. She could not see anything for a few seconds, everything was still spinning, but, as she became less dizzy and her eyes became less blurred, she saw that the two Brothers were holding two long rods of metal the ends of which were red from being held in the furnace. The mastiff barked uncontrollably and she felt fingernails digging into her hips, but she had no strength or desire to pull away. The hot rods came closer and she could see the Brothers leering at her as they approached.

The fingers around her hips dug even deeper and she shrieked in pain as she was spun around to face the group of Brothers. The mastiff jumped forward on his lead but the Brother just managed to restrain him and she hung in naked terror waiting to submit to their torture. Then she felt a searing pain against her bottom.

At first it just shocked her, but by the time she had realised the shock it turned into the most excruciating pain she had ever felt.

Maria yelled as her whole body tightened in agony and horror as the hot rods bit into her, branding her. She saw the open jaws of the mastiff and momentarily thought again of Father Thomas, then another hot iron burned into her skin and she could think of nothing but suffering. She yelled again and saw the jaws of wild beasts baiting and terrorising her, then another stab from a red-hot iron and another wave of pain, but this time she did not scream, she just opened her mouth and began to drool. She felt her spit dribbling out and she watched the mastiff as he snarled and growled before her, then another piercing stab in her buttocks and she began to growl and snarl back. She exposed her teeth and snarled again and, as she did, she felt a shudder of joy run through her limbs, she tried to ignore it, she tried to pretend it was not there, but she could not resist it.

Another burning stab from a red-hot iron sizzled in her skin and she snarled even more. She growled and dribbled and the shudder of joy began to run into a continuous wave of ecstasy. How could she have thought she could be saved? Then another stab and she felt her legs widening, and then another and the soft flesh of her labia swelled at her beautiful opening. Then another and she felt her clitoris probing at the front of her fleshy crack, and she snarled and dribbled and started howling even more.

Then the burning stopped and she waited, dropping her eyes and snarling like a rabid wolf. Why had they stopped? She did not know or care and she spit at the mastiff and wanted to get to him and wrestle him to the ground, she wanted to show him that she was his new master and when she spat again he growled back angrily. Then she fell to the ground as the cords were released.

The mastiff lurched forward and she smelt his breath. She turned her face and bared her teeth. He barked frantically as he was pulled back, the leash hardly seemed strong enough to hold him, but Maria did not care, she was an animal now and she wanted to take him on. Even the pain of the branding had not beaten her desires, and, as she crouched on her hands and knees and snarled at all the Brothers, her clitoris swelled even more and her cunt ran wetter than ever. Then she felt a lash across her back.

Crack!

Brother Arnold stood above her with a black leather bull whip. Its end curled in the air as he pulled it back again.

Crack!

Maria dipped her back as it landed hard across her.

Crack!

She dipped again and this time her legs opened a little.

Crack!

Another terrible lash and the tip of the bull whip cracked with heat as it singed her back. She felt her cunt getting hotter. Now she knew she could not be saved, there was nothing that could suppress her desire for pleasure. She wanted more lashing, more humiliation and more pain.

Crack! Crack!

Two more painful cracks across her back and she braced herself to take them. They stung her terribly but she bent up higher.

Crack! Crack! Crack!

Three more and with each one she raised her back up even more. The pain was terrible but the delight of it made her growl even louder. She did not want to scream any more and she dropped heavily to her elbows, lifted her back as high as she could and snarled and drooled.

Crack! Crack! Crack!

She took them all, rubbing her breasts against the rough stone floor and feeling her hard nipples scraping against the flagstones. She wanted them pinched and bitten, she wanted to offer them to the mastiff, she wanted him to bite them and suck them and feed from them. Her cunt swelled between the insides of her thighs and she opened her legs more. She could feel her outer labia beating with the engorging blood and massaging her hardened clitoris and as she opened her legs even more, her clitoris was inflamed with the massaging edges of her soft flesh.

Crack! Crack! Crack!

She opened her legs until they would spread no further, then suddenly dropped her hips to the floor and rolled onto her back. She splayed her legs wide and exposed the throbbing flesh of her widening, naked cunt. She forced her legs as wide as they could go and stared up at Brother Arnold as he stood above her with the bull whip in his hand. She was not submitting to him but, with her wide-eyed gaze, somehow commanding him, as she looked down at her cunt and then back up at him. She opened her mouth but could not form any words so just screamed.

Crack! Crack! Crack!

The tip of the bull whip snapped across the soft flesh of her cunt. She writhed with joy and screamed in an ecstasy of pain. She felt the spit foaming from her mouth and blew it from her lips in gaping screeches of exhilaration. She forced her hands down and pulled back her outer labia, they were hot and swollen and she peeled them back with her grasping fingers exposing the wet, pink entrance to her vagina. She wanted more pain, her desires were so great but so confused, she was so inflamed and she wanted to be fucked by the savage lashing of the whip.

Crack!

She opened them wider.

Crack!

She pulled them back some more and felt the burning crack of the whip stinging the insides of her cunt.

Crack! Crack! Crack! Crack!

She rose up and was seized with an overpowering orgasm, no scream could express it, no snarl could allow it to be released, she was consumed by it. She felt the inner edges of her cunt throbbing in between her fingers as pulses of wetness poured from her distended vagina and down the insides of her legs. She was completely dissipated and she pulled at her cunt roughly and poked her fingers deeply inside in a vain attempt to draw out her lust.

CHAPTER 12

Maria was only vaguely aware of being thrown into the back of the van. She lay cowering on the bare metal floor as it bounced along the road in darkness. As it came back into the city the street lights flashed intermittent streams of light in through the muddy windows in the back doors. She stretched on her back and, in the flickering light, saw the red stripes from the whip raised angrily on the insides of her thighs.

After a while the van stopped, she was dragged out roughly and pulled down into the muddy hole where she was chained to the iron grill. All night, Maria clung to the bars of the gate, her naked body shivering with cold as she stood up to her ankles in the sloppy mud, water dripping from the edges of the hole, running into her hair and down her face. She hung there, alone and fearful until the morning but, even when it became light, the hole stayed in the shadows and she moaned in desperation.

She thought of everything that had happened to her and began to sob. She hoped that someone would come to her rescue but, as it started to get dark again, she realised that her situation was hopeless. She tried to stretch her arms but she was too tightly bound and she bowed her head in painful and resigned misery.

In the darkness she felt herself dozing off and began to dream of captivity. She imagined she was bound to the back of a wild stallion as it galloped across open fields. She saw her naked body pulled down tight across its sweaty back, her legs were strained wide and a leather thong pulled her ankles tight beneath its girth. Her arms were drawn forward and bound with a leather leash beneath the animal's thick neck, her face was pressed hard against its

157

hot flesh and her reddened cheeks smacked against it as it leapt over fences and through muddy streams.

Every movement it made was transmitted into her bruised body, she felt its galloping hooves on the ground and the snorting from its flared nostrils. Her limbs were pulled roughly by the flexing of its mighty muscles as it took off over a hedge, and then by the shock in its flanks as it landed back down again. The movements spread through her flattened breasts and through the smooth skin of her tossed about face but mostly it came through her cunt that was splayed out across the broadness of the huge animal's back.

The soft folds of her outer labia squeezed down against the spiky hairs on the horse's back. When it jumped her cunt opened wider and the inner leaves felt the pressure from its shoulders and the stinging from its bristly hairs. As her cunt got wetter she felt her clitoris engorging under the sensation of roughness that the pounding caused and, as it grew and pressed down more, she felt the inside edges of her vagina opening and searching for the prickly ends of the coarse sweat smeared hair.

She waited anxiously for each new lunge and every time pulled herself tighter onto the heaving animal. She felt her face flushing with overbearing excitement and she felt the wetness from her cunt running warmly against the insides of her splayed out thighs and she started to bite the tousled mane of the galloping beast...

Then she started, opened her eyes wide and banged her head against the grill. Someone had their hand between her buttocks and was probing the edges of her cunt!

"Is this the one?"

Maria turned and saw that it was a tall, dark haired young man dressed in leather who was feeling her. Father Thomas stood in the shadows a little further back.

"Yes, that's her, Maria, I'm not sure whether she is ready, but she is wanted so I have got to send her. Make sure that you arrange for her to get the training we agreed on the way. Lay it on like I said and no mistakes now. Take her by the normal route and I will meet you at the docks as usual. I will take her on from there. I will be taking Caleb with me and that fool Kirk - the Mistress Lesley says he will make a 'useful addition' if nothing else."

"Nice cunt," said the young man pushing his fingers into Maria's vagina, "very nice, she must have been thinking of something good, she's very wet."

He pulled his fingers out of her vagina then thrust his hand further between her legs and felt her clitoris.

"I think she's ready for a fuck right now. What do you think Maria? Fancy a fuck before we set off?"

"There is not much time if we are to keep to schedule, so you had better get going."

The young man drew his hand away from Maria's cunt and slapped her playfully on the bottom.

"Come on boys, let's get going!"

Several men came down into the hole and started to untie Maria from the grill. They were all dressed in motorcycle leathers and, as they stretched up to undo her, the smooth leather pressed against her naked skin. Its coldness made her shiver and she gasped when some silver studs on one of the jackets stuck into her shoulder. When the ropes at her wrists were undone she slumped down exhausted. Two of the men caught her in their arms and held her until her ankles were released, one of them grasped her breasts and squeezed them hard. Then they dragged her out of the muddy hole and onto the pavement.

She looked up to see a group of large motorcycles with more men dressed in black leather standing around them. Some of the engines were ticking over and one of them

159

was being revved by a blonde haired man with a ring in his nose who called out over the noise of the engines.

"Come on you bastards, let's be off, we can make a night of it."

Maria was pulled over to a large black motorcycle that had an open sidecar fitted, she hung onto the men's arms and started to shake with fear.

"Stick her in, let's get going!"

They lifted her up and held her for a moment above the top of the side-car, there was no seat inside, only roughly painted metal and the tangled tubular steel of its chassis.

"Not that way you fucking idiots, head first!"

She gasped as they tipped her naked body upside down and thrust her headlong into the side-car, banging her head against the tubes of the chassis as it was forced down into the nose-cone. Two of them bent her legs and another held her waist up, she felt like a capture animal as her legs were squeezed inside and pressed down roughly until only her upturned buttocks stood up from the body of the side-car. She was terrified as her face was forced crookedly against the bodywork and she coughed as she inhaled the sickening smell of oil and leather. Then she felt some straps being pulled tight across her back and she was pressed down even further as they were secured to the sides.

"Nice arse!" one of them shouted and she felt another hard smack across her bottom as the engines began to rev loudly.

"And I see she's got a name, Maria!"

Then another smack, this time right across her still stinging brand, then, with a jerk, she felt the motorcycle pull away and roar off.

Maria could just see through a small hole in the front of the side-car. She watched the flashing street lamps and the headlights of traffic as the motorcycles careered at breakneck speed through the streets and out onto the main road. Her buttocks stuck up out of the side-car and she felt the cold air as it blew across her taut skin. She was trapped so tightly that she could not move her head and her arms were pushed up under her breasts. Sometimes the motorcycle went around corners so fast that the side-car lifted off the ground and she thought she was going to be killed. Then the road went dark as they drove on through the night in a noisy, frantic convoy. Every so often one of the motor cycles pulled in front and Maria could see its rider leaning back and gesturing, then it would drop back and pull alongside. Once, one of the motorcycles banged into the side of the side-car and she screamed in fear as her face was crushed against the tubular chassis. Then she saw some lights ahead and the convoy pulled off the main road and into a brightly lit cafe car park.

After revving loudly the engines stopped. Maria felt her heart pounding with fear as she waited in the darkness. She heard the riders propping up their bikes, shouting to each other and laughing. Above the sound of her pounding heart, she could hear lorries passing on the main road and as they went past the flash of their headlights threw some light across the car park and the motorcycles glistened against the black Tarmac.

Maria felt very frightened, she was terrified by what might happen to her and her skin tingled with fear and dread. She felt so captured and alone and her heart thumped even louder as she breathed rapidly against the inside of the side-car. Through her small spyhole she saw that all the motorcyclists were dressed in black leather and some had chains hanging from their waists or drooping from the padded shoulders of their jackets. They walked around their motorcycles, pushing and jostling each other,

161

some took their helmets off and hung them on the ends of their handlebars, then they congregated around the side-car and started laughing and joking about the position that she was in. She felt completely humiliated as they prodded her bottom and poked their fingers around the insides of her upturned thighs. She tried to twist herself away from their probing but it was impossible.

Then she felt the straps that held her down being eased. Though she was quaking with fear, she felt relieved as they slackened and she could move again. She pulled her face away from the bodywork of the side-car and tried to wriggle herself out but her antics made the men laugh and jeer and she felt overwhelmingly ashamed.

"Look at the bitch's arse wiggle!"

"See her cunt though, what a beauty!"

"Look how the bitch squirms, what a cunt!"

Maria felt like crying as they taunted and humiliated her, but even though she wanted to hide away, she pressed her hands against the front of the inside of the side-car and tried to force herself out.

"Hey Jacko, she's trying to get free!"

"Just get the bitch out, I need something to drink."

She felt hands pulling at her and she was lifted bodily out of the side-car. She cried out and tried to wriggle free but the men holding her only laughed. She felt their hands all over her naked body and her arms and legs being pulled all ways as they argued to gain control of her like beasts contesting their prey.

"Come on you fucking morons, just bring it inside," commanded Jacko.

"She's got no clothes on, the fucking bitch is naked, how can we take her in there?"

"Just bring the fucking bitch and if anybody wants to argue I think I can persuade them it's OK."

One of the men, tall with black hair and a silver chain hanging from the shoulder of his jacket, grabbed her breasts from behind and snatched her away from the others. He held her off the ground and began carrying her towards the cafe. As his hands gripped her breasts tightly, his fingernails dug into her soft skin and she thrashed her legs about to get free, but he was much too strong for her to even loosen his painful grasp.

"Fucking firm tits!" he kept saying as he squeezed them roughly and marched across the car park holding her up like a prize.

"OK, put the bitch down now, but keep hold of her, we don't want to lose her do we?"

The man carrying Maria let her down abruptly to the floor, her knees sagged as she felt her own weight again and she hung her head, but straight away Jacko grabbed her chin and turned her face towards his.

"This will make sure you don't get away from us."

He dangled a shiny chain in front of her and she pulled back, her eyes wide and filled with fear.

"Oh please, I can't stand any more. Please."

Jacko ignored her.

"Pretty? Pretty? Pretty little chain for a pretty little neck?" he taunted as he swung the chain from side to side and it glistened in the lights that came from the inside of the cafe. Then he turned around to the others, suddenly seeming to hear what she had said.

"Can't stand any more? What's that bitch? A pretty little bitch like you? Can't stand no more?"

He reached forward with the chain, pulled one end through a ring that was fixed to the other and, in one quick movement, dropped it as a noose over her head and around her neck. She gasped as she felt its coldness encircle her throat, then she cried out as he tugged it tight and it cut

163

into her skin. He snatched it tighter and pulled her face close to his own. She spluttered and choked and tried to reach up to ease the strain at her throat but he would not release her. Then he snatched it hard again as if to tell her to drop her hands. She saw the menace in his eyes, dropped her hands and stood limply, hardly able to breathe.

"Right, let's get something to drink."

Jacko pulled at the chain and dragged Maria behind him like a dog, the others followed, still laughing and pushing each other rowdily. The smoke filled cafe was filled with men at small tables covered in plates of food and mugs of tea. A blonde haired young woman wearing an apron stood behind the serving counter. Everyone turned and stared as the group entered, there was a moment's silence, then the men at the tables started pointing and laughing as they saw Maria being trailed behind Jacko on the chain.

"Got yourself a fine dog there."

"I think it's a bitch."

"Lovely little tits!"

Jacko walked straight between the tables and dropped his elbows on the counter, holding the chain up to his chin and tugging at it lazily. Maria stood closely behind him in an attempt to keep the chain slack, then she bent her face against the leather shoulder-pad of his jacket and shivered nervously. Jacko ordered some drinks and waited.

He ignored the stares and taunts of the men at the tables and casually twirled the end of the now slack chain between his fingers. Maria sniffed at the leather of his jacket and felt aroused by its animal smell, she bent her head closer, touched it with the tip of her nose and, as she inhaled deeply, she felt a surge of anticipation flow through her naked body.

Like an animal, she breathed in the scent again and

164

opened her mouth so that she could taste it on her tongue, then she drew closer and licked her tongue out slightly until it just glanced the surface of the shiny black leather. She felt her limbs tightening and the blood running fast through her excited veins as she laid her tongue flatly onto the leather and licked it with long slurping strokes. She felt her spit dribbling over her lower lip and licked it up keenly as she made longer, wetter strokes with her eager tongue.

The girl behind the counter brought the drinks and laid them down in front of Jacko. She stared quizzically at Maria licking the jacket but looked quickly away as Jacko caught her stare.

Maria stood back for a moment but then realised that Jacko was somehow protecting her, shielding her from the stare of the girl, and she bent forward again and carried on licking the jacket. She knew that she was going to be subjected to more torture and enslavement, but this time she was starting to feel the excitement before it even started.

She was waiting for Jacko to start things, she wanted to urge him to get on with it; she could hardly wait, she felt the animal inside her already demanding satisfaction. She licked harder at the jacket and worked her dripping tongue up onto the collar and then onto Jacko's tattooed neck. She tasted his skin, it was oily and sweet, and she lapped at it enthusiastically. He did not shy away and she felt him sensing her need to be both violated and fulfilled, she began to feel like his lover and wanted to whisper all her needs into his ear.

Then the room broke into a clamour of noise and activity. One of the motorcycle gang, a fat man with a wide leather belt, was arguing with one of the men at a table. Jacko turned and shouted.

"OK, you'd better get your bids in, we've a nice prize for you, and, if what I've been told is right, she will do anything, absolutely anything."

Maria's feeling of safety evaporated as the chain tugged tightly at her neck and Jacko led her into the centre of the cafe.

"What do you think of this? Firm tits, beautiful arse and look at that shaved cunt! She's a clean-shaven bitch to be sure!"

He spun her around on the end of the chain as if her was selling something in a market and the men ogled and pointed like excited purchasers.

"Anything! Yes, anything!"

The men started shouting what they would like to do and offered various amounts of money for the pleasure.

"Yes, yes," said Jacko trying to calm them. "Fucking, whipping, and she'll suck you until you die, but this is a special prize, she's going to want more pleasing than just that!"

He dragged a spare chair to the middle of the cafe and sat down on it. Maria stumbled as the chain pulled tightly at her throat, she choked and went to grab the noose to loosen it but Jacko snatched it hard to stop her. She had learnt the signal and dropped her hands obediently. Jacko put the end of the chain in his mouth and held it there while he undid the zip of his leather jeans. He lifted himself slightly off the chair and pulled them down together with his underpants until they curled up loosely onto the tops of his heavy leather boots. His cock fell onto the top of his left thigh, it was large and the glans was already swollen and probing out through the loose flesh of his foreskin.

"Lick it slave," he ordered as he tugged Maria's face towards it.

She lowered her face obediently and held out her tongue, its tip touched the swollen glans and she drooled spit onto it. As drips of spittle fell from the end of her tongue she licked them back carefully into her mouth, tasting the salty tang that lay on the hot flesh of his growing cock. She licked it more then slowly folded her lips around it and began to suck. It felt beautifully warm in her mouth and the glans swelled heavily onto her tongue as she sucked it hard and probed the tip of her tongue into the opening at its end. She wanted to hold it in her hands but did not dare unless she was ordered.

"Wetter! Wetter! Get sucking you bitch, it needs to be wetter than that!"

Immediately she sucked harder onto the now hard and throbbing cock and she pushed it from side to side inside her mouth. She massaged it with the spit that lay inside the edges of her cheeks and she drooled around the shaft as she drew her mouth up and down, closing her eyes and feeling its warmth probing towards the back of her throat.

"Enough!"

He snatched the chain and her face was pulled away violently. She wanted more and looked at him longingly as spit dribbled freely from her open mouth.

"Turn around and bend over bitch!"

His words caused a thrill of excitement to run through her thighs and hips and she felt her cunt moistening in anticipation. The words he used and the pulling of the chain were enough to make it wet but the thought of his cock made it drip. She turned obediently and waited for her orders, hoping she could suck his cock for longer and take it deeper into her throat, then some of the others grabbed her wrists roughly and her arms were pulled out wide. Jacko looked down at his cock, it was fully stiffened and the veins pulsated on its long, hard shaft as Maria's spit

167

ran freely down from the swollen glans.

"Sit on it slave!"

She did not hesitate and bent slightly forward against the strain of the chain and the pressure of the hands around her wrists. Her buttocks widened and she bent them towards the throbbing cock, the outer lips of her cunt parted and glistened as she lowered them down. She felt the heat from his cock as her cunt got closer and she pulled her neck forward against the chain and felt its gagging tightness at her throat.

"Your arse bitch! It's your arse I want!"

She stopped but did not hesitate. She widened her buttocks more and bent her anus towards the throbbing member, again she felt its heat but this time it was against the muscular ring of her arse. She let the tip of the hot cock touch the ring and it distended readily against the slight pressure, then she felt the wet end more fully and the growing heat and she pushed herself down hard onto it. The cock ran in easily and she gasped and dropped her head forward as she felt its length penetrate her.

"All the way! Get down on it bitch! All the way!"

She pushed herself down until she felt the widened base of his cock pressing against the tight, muscular ring of her anus; it was completely inside her. Jacko pushed her shoulders forward until her head hung between her knees and she gasped for breath. He pressed his cock into her arse as hard as she could while she lay forward, suffocating and gulping under the unrelenting pressure of his hands and the throttling of the chain around her throat. Then he yanked the chain hard and pulled her back until her head was drawn up against the side of his face. The chain cut into her neck and, as she fought to get her breath back, her tightening muscles and sense of desperation hardened her already prominent nipples until they ached.

168

"So, who's first?"

A tall and slender man stood up waving money in his hand.

"OK, let's see what you've got for my beautiful arse-fucked little slave shall we?"

One of the motorcyclists took the money, then the man came forward, stood in front of Maria and pulled his trousers down to his knees. His cock hung heavily between his thighs.

"Fancy a fuck with this bitch?"

Maria glanced at it and felt herself drooling, she felt so captive, so humiliated and so filled inside her arse, but it only gave her pleasure. She could feel the pain in her throat and the tightness in her anus and the terror of her humiliation, but they were all causing her cunt to run with ecstasy. She wanted to suck the man's cock, then she wanted to be fucked by it and all the time she wanted to feel Jacko's cock in her arse, the pressure of the chain at her neck, the straining of her outstretched arms and the men shouting and jeering at her.

She felt the chain slacken at her throat and she bent forward, straining eagerly towards the slowly stiffening cock. She wanted the chain to be loosened more quickly and yet she wanted it held more tightly so that it would cut even deeper into her throat. Her mouth reached the tip of the now hard cock and she sucked it straight in, it swelled inside her mouth as she dragged it down as far as she could. Then the chain pulled her back and she had to let it go. Her cunt was wet and as she opened her thighs expectantly, the pressure on her buttocks squeezed Jacko's cock tightly inside her arse and, as if suddenly reminded of it, she bore down on it to get some more.

The man lunged at her and drove his cock into her cunt. She felt it run in and fill her cunt completely and she

169

squeezed every bit of it as hard as she could, drawing herself tightly around it while at the same time squeezing Jacko's cock even deeper inside her arse. She drew up on them both then plunged down frantically, boiling over with excitement as she felt them both driving back inside. She lifted herself and plunged down again, then again and again until she was riding them both like a frenzied beast, sweating and tossing her face from side to side.

The man fucking her cunt grabbed her cheeks between his hands and squeezed them hard, then he thrust his fingers into her mouth and she sucked at them and bit down onto them until she felt a hot surge of spunk exploding in her cunt. She squeezed her vagina as hard as she could, and felt every drop being drawn out of his cock as she sucked it inside. Then she released the fingers and started screaming for more.

"Fuck me! Fuck me! Fuck me!"

She drove up and down but the cock in her cunt came out, dripping and used.

"Fuck me! Fuck me! Fuck me!"

She screamed at the top of her voice as she rode wildly on Jacko's cock but she was not satisfied, she felt her cunt open and empty and she wanted it filled again.

"Come on you bastards I can take the fucking lot of you. Fuck me you bastards!"

She heard her own disgusting words and knew that the captivity and humiliation had again overcome her, she wanted fucking and the more violently and painfully she got it the better.

"Fuck me! Fuck me! Fuck me!"

Another man came forward and drove his cock inside her cunt and she screeched with relief and joy and bore down on it in a frenzy. Then another man came forward, grabbed her hair and pulled her mouth wide with his fingers, she gasped and drooled as he pulled her face down and plugged her mouth with his cock. She sucked at it until it finished and filled her mouth to overflowing then she licked around it and drank it all until it was dry. Then another man came forward and she sucked his cock as well, and then another and her mouth ran with spunk as still she screamed for more.

"Fuck! Suck! Fuck! Suck!"

All the time Jacko's cock filled her arse and she rode him without restraint. Then another cock finished in her mouth and she drank it down and swallowed deeply, but she had so much in her mouth that, even though she gulped it down ravenously, spunk still dribbled down her chin and foamed in bubbles around her lips. Then she threw her head back, turned slightly and lifted her mouth towards Jacko's face, she smelled his sweat and tasted his breath, he felt like her lover.

"Release my hands," she whispered.

Then she pressed her face closer.

"Please, please, make them let go of my hands. Tie me up later, do whatever you want, you can do anything to me, but please, let my hands free for a few moments."

Suddenly her wrists were released and she reached forward and grabbed the next cock that came towards her open cunt and wanked it hard while she thrust it in. Then she took another and wanked it against her open nostrils, then let it finish all over her face before sucking the semen that shot from it. While she was waiting for another cock, she pushed her fingers inside her cunt and probed them deeply into her vagina, then she took them out and reached down and felt the base of Jacko's cock as it kept plunging deeply into her arse.

She ran her wet fingers around his heavy balls then back to his stiff cock and then she felt it starting to swell and throb as his semen began to run up its hardened length. She braced herself and threw her arms out wide, her wrists were grabbed immediately and she screamed like a beast as she felt an enormous flow of hot spunk squirting deeply inside her. Her whole body thrilled with it and she felt her skin burning all over as though it was being scorched by fire. She threw herself against the chain around her neck and choked herself as her face flushed red with the power of her enormous climax. Her fingers tightened into fists and she thrust her breasts out in a massive, inundating spasm of sexual pleasure. She roared and screamed as it ran through her and straight away she wanted more.

More hands grabbed her legs and she was dragged to the floor, spread-eagled and pinned down, semen ran freely from her distended labia, flowed to the rear of her open crack and dribbled stickily down between her buttocks. For a few moments, she pulled lazily against her captors' hands, languishing in the wetness of her cunt, then she felt the lash of a belt across her chest.

Whack!

It stung her as the edges cut into her flesh just above her breasts.

Whack!

Another hard blow, this time right across her firm breasts and she screamed in pain.

Whack! Whack! Whack!

She shrieked in agony as blow after blow rained down on her, lashing across her breasts and stomach and cutting across her thighs.

"Bitch! Bitch!"

The men shouted and brayed as they beat her, but they could not beat her enough to give her complete satisfaction and her frustration aroused her even more. She wriggled and fought but she was wriggling with pleasure

172

and fighting for more pain, more thrashing and more agony. Then she managed to break free, but before they could grab her she had turned over and crouched down with her face pressed against the floor and her buttocks held high.

"Whip me! Whip me you bastards!" she shouted as they took their belts to her and flogged her until they were exhausted.

Her buttocks were soon covered with red weals, but the men had not finished with her and she knew she had not finished with them. She wanted to start again and suck them all a second time, then she wanted to be fucked by every one of them until they finished. She wanted to be whipped harder and pinned down and tied up tightly and abused in every way and she wanted to wallow in their spunk and be beaten and punished for having so much pleasure. She screeched and raved at them and grabbed for cocks and sucked them and wanked them and shouted to them to do anything to her that they wanted. They dragged her into the car park, tied her to the wheel of a large lorry and whipped her mercilessly until she collapsed with exhaustion and fell into unconsciousness.

Jacko roused her by pulling the chain that still dangled from her neck and she looked around startled, she was still bound to the wheel of the lorry and her whole body stung with the beating she had taken.

"Come on," he said as two of the others began to untie her, "we've got to get you to the docks. What a fucking bitch you are! I've never seen anything like it!"

He wandered over to his bike, climbed on and started the engine and it roared as he turned the throttle eagerly. She slumped as she was released but she turned across to him and smiled, sensing inside herself a strange feeling of power that grew from knowing that she could still take more. She let herself be dragged over towards the side-car but then, as they bent her head to stuff her inside it, she pulled herself free.

"I'll ride," she said.

She strode over to Jacko's bike, lifted her leg across the seat, pressed her naked body against the back of his leather jacket and wrapped her arms tightly around his waist. She squirmed her wet cunt down onto the shiny, plastic seat that vibrated with the throbbing of the roaring engine, and squeezed her thighs tightly around his hips. He threw his head back against the side of her face and laughed, then he kicked his motorcycle into gear, leant forward towards the handlebars, and drove away into the darkness with the others following behind.

CHAPTER 13

Father Thomas was waiting at the door of a small hotel as the motorbikes roared up.

"Bring her in and quickly," he shouted as the engines were turned off.

Jacko grabbed the chain at Maria's neck and tugged it. She responded by bowing her head, lifting herself from the hot plastic saddle and following him obediently. Father Thomas led the way as they walked up some steep stairs to a small bedroom, he waved Jacko in first and Maria followed. He dropped the chain and it swung down between her breasts and she kept her head bowed as Father Thomas passed some money to Jacko. He turned to go, but stopped at the door and looked back at Maria. She lifted her head slightly and smiled but he just laughed and went out. Father Thomas closed the door and went up to Maria.

"Stand there, I want to look at you."

She stood before him and hung her head. She felt ashamed of her conduct in the cafe and wanted to admit it all to Father Thomas, she wanted to tell him about her wanton sinfulness and then she wanted to bend over and be whipped until she could stand no more. She looked at him and hoped he would ask her to confess. He pulled at his short, pointed beard then, as if preparing to share a secret with her, he bent his face forward and whispered in her ear.

"Are you ready to confess my child?"

For a moment she did not answer. Suddenly, she was no longer sure what she had to confess. She did not feel any remorse for her sinfulness, quite the opposite, she felt elated by her wrongdoing, indeed, the idea of her remorse had itself caused surges of pleasure as she had been driven back into the hands of Father Thomas. What she wanted to confess was her sexual desires, but not because she wanted them expunged, now she wanted to feel the thrill of admitting them. Of course! Her confession was just another thrill and she could feed it by making herself available for sex, for punishment, for humiliation and pain. Suddenly, she thought she understood it all and she looked up at him brightly.

"Oh yes Father, I am. Oh yes Father, I am desperately ready to confess. Please Father, hear my confession."

"Ah my child, I am so happy for you."

"Take my confession Father, please take my confession."

"Are you ready to serve? Are you capable of complete obedience? Are you prepared to confess all your sins and be purified?"

"Yes Father, I am. Oh yes, Father, I am. I have so much to tell you and I want you to hear every word."

"Caleb!"

The door to the bathroom opened and Caleb sprung out, he was not carrying his staff and looked a little lost without it.

"She is ready, at last she is ready, bring what we need then we can begin."

He pranced back into the bathroom and after a while came out holding a variety of things in his podgy hands.

"Ready! Ready! Ready!"

Father Thomas reached forward and slipped the chain from Maria's neck.

"You will not need this any more my child."

He handed it to Caleb who took it from him and passed him a very fine gold chain in return. Father Thomas held it up to the dim, yellow light and its delicate links glittered and sparkled.

"This will be your chain of obedience my child."

"Please Father, I need it. I need to be chained and I need to serve."

"I am so pleased you understand my child. Lie on the bed."

She moved to the bed and lay down on her front.

"Will you have to spank me first Father?"

"No my child, turn over on your back."

She rolled over slowly and her breasts tightened on her chest, her nipples were not hard but looked beautifully pink and receptive against the slightly darker ring that encircled them. She raised her knees then allowed them to drop to the sides fully exposing her naked cunt and its wet, glistening edges. She pressed her buttocks together and felt the tension of her muscles squeezing against the back edges of her crack, then she pressed them more and the soft petals of her cunt went wetter with anticipation and excitement. She felt relaxed and eager and she lolled her head to one side and looked at Father Thomas.

"What a beautiful cunt you have. Now I am going to make you its slave. I will have to tie you down though, you could not bear it without the help of some straps. Caleb!"

She did not understand what he meant but his words seemed ominous and her feelings of safety began to turn into anxious suspicion. She thought of drawing her legs together, but before she could do anything Caleb climbed up onto the bed and started winding leather straps around her thighs and ankles. He pulled them down the sides of the bed and tied them in knots around the frame, then jumped back up and hopped and bounced between her outstretched legs.

"Beautiful cunt! Beautiful cunt!"

"Get down Caleb and bring the spray! Now my child this is what is going to make you obedient to that beautiful cunt of yours."

Father Thomas held up a small golden ring.

"And of course this."

He held up the thin chain as well and she shivered with a fear she thought she had overcome.

"I am going to fit this little ring through your delectable clitoris my child. Yes, right through it and then I am going to feed this chain through it and every time it is pulled you will respond with pain and joy. That is what you like is it not, pain and joy? That is your problem, I know it, but this will cause you all the pain you want and reward you every time with instant pleasure. Caleb!"

"Father, please -"

"I thought you said you were ready, bitch!"

177

"I did Father, I am, but -"

"Well shut your fucking mouth. Caleb! Get me the spray!"

Caleb handed Father Thomas a small, blue and white can.

"This will numb the pain my child, but it will be cold."

He sprayed the contents of the canister onto her dilated cunt and she shrieked with shock as the cold spray covered her tender flesh. She squeezed her buttocks together but it did no good as her outer labia were drenched with the freezing liquid. He sprayed it all around her cunt, then, prizing between her outer labia with his fingers, he found her clitoris. He tugged at it and it hardened and protruded more keenly from between her soft lips. He massaged it some more and it grew between his fingers until he could hold it firmly, then he directed the cold spray at it and doused it.

Maria gasped and screamed. The cold shock on her sensitive flesh was terrible, and the feeling of him tugging at her clitoris was painful and almost more than she could bear.

"Please -"

Father Thomas reached up with his spare hand and slapped her across the face, the hard smack stung her cheek, her head was knocked sideways and she cried out in pain.

"Shut up you fucking bitch. There will soon be time for pleading."

He bent down between her legs and kept spraying the contents of the can all around her cunt but especially on her still swelling clitoris, which he gripped firmly and squeezed whenever it tried to retract between the soft edges of her frozen crack. Then he threw the can aside and, in one movement, punctured her hard clitoris with the sharp open point of the gold ring and threaded it straight through her engorged flesh. She did not know what he had done until she squeezed her thighs inwards a bit and felt it pressing sharply against the inside edges of her cunt.

"Oh Father, what have you done to me?"

"I have made you the slave of your cunt. You will see."

He reached across and took another thin chain from Caleb. He pulled it around her waist and clipped it together, then he took another and clasped it tightly around her neck. Then he took the loose end of the chain that was attached to the ring, fed it beneath the chain at her waist, clipped it to the chain at her throat and finally, attached a small gold cross to it.

"Caleb! Release her!"

Caleb jumped up and undid her bonds. Instinctively, she drew her legs together, but as she tried to lie back flat on the bed she realised that the tension in the chain meant that any movement in her neck caused the ring to pull in her clitoris. Because the cold spray was still numbing the flesh of her cunt she was not sure whether she felt pain or not.

"Stand up my child."

She rolled onto her side and stood up slowly, keeping her head bent down so that the tension was only slight.

"Look up you bitch!"

Maria raised her head slightly and immediately felt the arousing tug in her clitoris, then the piercing pain as it pulled hard into her flesh. Her eyes widened as she felt the full pleasure of her own slavery and she dropped her head back in response to the now searing pain of ecstasy. She moaned. It was agony but it was irresistible, and again she stretched her head back. The tension in the chain pulled at her throat and burned in her cunt. She had never experienced anything like it and she felt a primitive animalism forming inside that threatened to overtake any sense of self-control she might have. Every movement of her head brought a corresponding swell of pain, every time she lifted her head the ecstatic pain forced her to bow again. With her head held up she was in a depraved state of piercing pain which made her lower it again into the sweet ecstasy of bowed submission, slavery and penance.

"Good my child. Caleb! Stay with her, I need to make some final arrangements before we deliver her to the Mistress Lesley."

Father Thomas left the bedroom and went down to the reception. Caleb crouched like a gnome at the bottom of the bed and stared at Maria, but she was unaware of his gaze as she tantalised herself against the tension of the chain. She pulled her head back as far as she could, and the ring drew her clitoris clear of the folds of pink skin that opened at the front of her shaved crack. The chain pressed against her stomach and ran up between her breasts until it pulled tightly at her slender throat. She moaned as the pressure came on fully and, as she pulled more, she screwed up her eyes in ecstatic agony as the pain increased both her desires and suffering.

Caleb watched her eagerly then bent down and crawled slowly between her legs like a small dog stalking its prey, pressing his stumpy hands down quietly on the bed and creeping forward until his face was close to her cunt. He looked at it closely, turning his face this way and that, then bent his head forward and extended his tongue until it touched the delicate petals of her outer labia.

She felt its heat as his tongue slurped clumsily along the full length of her cunt, starting at the back near the opening of her anus and running up along her soft labia until finally, it curled around her hard, extended clitoris. The warmth of his wet tongue inflamed her even more

180

and she stretched back against the chain. Her clitoris reached out further under the pressure and, as soon as there was more to lick, Caleb slurped around it enthusiastically. She felt his spit dribbling between the lips of her crack and onto the small area of skin that lay behind it, then she felt it running around the ring of her anus and she opened her buttocks wider. She pressed down with her buttocks and encouraged her anus to dilate, and when it did, some drops of spit ran burningly inside its exposed inner edges.

Maria felt Caleb's shoulders pressing against the insides of her thighs and she widened them more to accommodate him, then she felt a sudden stabbing in her anus as his finger plunged in deeply. She gasped and threw her head back and the chain cut into her throat. The pain in her clitoris was masked by his lapping tongue but it still hurt and she let out a scream, but that made him plunge his finger even deeper and she responded by bending forward and bearing down on it. Her gaze followed the gold chain as it ran down between her breasts, across her flat stomach and pulled tightly at the golden ring that stretched her clitoris forward from the upper opening of her cunt. She saw his slobbering face looking up from between her legs, his eyes were wide and his tongue was licking her feverishly.

Caleb began thrusting his finger up and down her anus. She felt a flow of passion running inside her veins and she drove herself onto it and matched his movements. She squeezed her buttocks and held his finger tightly in her arse. She wanted more of it, she wanted it thicker and deeper and faster and more thrusting. He kept slavering at her cunt like a dog, but it was not enough, she wanted more and she reached forward and grasped his head tightly in her hands.

"Lick it you bastard!" she shouted at him and dragged

his head against her open cunt. "Lick it or I'll suffocate you in it!"

She pressed his face in deeper and his tongue went in like a hot cock, folding against the inside edges of her cunt and sending waves of exhilaration through her. Then it stretched forward and probed her vagina as deeply as it could and she pulled at the ring in her clitoris to match the pleasure with a commensurate amount of pain. As she rode his tongue, he kept plunging his finger in her arse and she drove down on it as hard as she could.

"Give me more! More you little bastard! I want more!"

She grasped his hair and pulled his head forward until he could not breathe.

"Keep licking it. I want it up there until I come! Keep licking!"

Maria felt ferocious and uncontrolled.

"Now your dick. Give me some dick!"

She released his head but grabbed his trousers before he could get away. She pulled them open at the front and took hold of his cock, it was stiff and hot and she squeezed it and pulled at it. Caleb cried out as her fingernails dug into the taut flesh of his throbbing member.

"Shut up you little bastard! Stick it in here!"

She opened her legs even wider and leaned forward to see her open cunt.

"In here!"

She forced the tip of his cock into her dilated cunt.

"Get fucking you little bastard! I want a good fucking so don't disappoint me. Fuck it!"

He started to fuck her but he was not vigorous enough and his cock was not big enough for her.

"Fuck it you little animal!"

He fucked as hard as he could, but her face grew angrier as her disappointment got greater. Suddenly, she pushed him back and, as his cock came out, she grabbed it again with both hands.

"Try it in here you little beast. Perhaps it will serve me better there."

She pushed the wet tip of his cock against the swollen ring of her anus, it opened to receive him and she fed it in until she felt his balls hanging against her outstretched buttocks.

"Now get to it!"

He yelped as she began fucking his cock hard with her arse, driving down on him and squeezing it so that she could feel every vein it had to offer.

"Fuck it you little cunt! Fuck it or I'll give you such a whipping you won't be able to walk for days!"

Caleb squealed again but Maria would not let him go. She felt wild and bestial as she fucked at his cock. She realised something had happened to her, something had changed, she was in control, she was making the demands and she was enslaving someone to fuck her. She felt as though she had captured him and taken him back to her lair and now he was doing her bidding. She was thrilled by the threats she made and overjoyed with the expression of fear and anxiety that strained across his contorted face. She had taken him as her slave and she could make him do anything she wanted.

Then she felt him starting to finish. She felt his cock swelling and the tip pressing harder against her insides, then she felt the flow of semen running through the stiff shaft as the veins stood out and forced against her innards. Then there was a burst of heat, then a long flow of hot spunk, and she tightened her anus onto him to draw up every drop. She sucked at him remorselessly but she did not finish, she felt in control of her orgasms and she was not prepared to release one yet.

"I hope you don't think I've finished with you?" she said tauntingly. "I have only just started!"

Caleb looked down in fear as he tried to pull away.

Maria dribbled spit from her mouth as she felt her pleasures elevated onto a new level of sexual debauchery and control, then the door opened and Father Thomas and Kirk came in. She looked up at Father Thomas and suddenly felt ashamed and afraid. She could not believe what was happening to her, she could not believe how her sinfulness had overtaken her so easily.

"Father, Father, help me! I am so sinful! Please Father help me!"

Father Thomas rushed forward with Kirk at his side and they both grabbed Caleb by the shoulders and pulled him away from Maria. Father Thomas scowled at Caleb as he shrunk back fearfully against the wall.

"Oh my child, what has happened to you?"

Maria could not answer.

"I think it must be time to take your confession my child."

Father Thomas sat on the edge of the bed and looked closely at Maria as she lay with her legs wide open and the gold chain stretched tightly from her throat to her engorged clitoris.

"Kneel down before me child."

She sat up and got onto her knees.

"Tell me your sins my child."

"Oh Father can you save me?"

"I think so my child."

He unbuttoned his trousers and pulled out his cock, it was still flaccid and hung heavily in his hands.

"Suck this, my child, and tell me your sins."

She leant forward and took the soft glans in her mouth, folding her tongue around it and licking the raised back

184

edge until she felt it begin to harden. As it swelled, she cradled it in her hands and drew her mouth away.

"Father I have sinned."

"Yes, my child, go on."

"I have desired such terrible things, I have wanted such terrible, terrible things, I have ached to have my cunt filled and I have yearned to be fucked."

"Now suck it my child, I will punish you as you suck it."

She took the cock back into her mouth, this time it was harder as she folded her lips around it. Then she felt a sudden sting on her bottom as Father Thomas's hand smacked down.

Smack!

She pulled back and his cock fell from her mouth.

"Suck it! That will mean more!"

Smack! Smack!

She wrapped her lips around it again and this time she sucked hard as she felt the painful smacks landing on her upturned bottom.

"Good, now what else?"

She drew her mouth away.

"I have enjoyed being bound and gagged Father."

Again, she encircled his still hardening cock with her mouth and waited for her punishment.

Smack!

This time she did not wait, she knew what was expected.

"I enjoyed being on the rack, I loved the feeling of exposure and torture."

She put his cock back in her mouth, sucked hard and waited.

Smack! Smack! Smack!

Three punishingly hard smacks fell across the taut skin

of her bottom, but she kept his cock in her mouth and sucked that much harder as they fell. When the spanking stopped, she drew her mouth away again, this time gasping for breath.

"And being shaved Father, I loved my cunt being shaved."

Her mouth went back around his cock, and this time she felt its full hardness as she drew the glans deep inside and circled her lips well down the throbbing shaft.

Smack! Smack! Smack!

"Yes, my child, what else?"

Maria gasped as the pain of the spanking stung deeply into her bottom.

"So many men Father, I wanted to be fucked by them all."

Smack! Smack! Smack!

"Yes, yes, what else?"

"I wanted to feel their spunk Father, all over my face, all over my cunt, in my arse, I wanted it lick it and drink it and wallow in it."

Smack! Smack! Smack! Smack!

The beating was hard and relentless. Every admission Maria made brought down a fresh rain of smacks and she had to take them all with Father Thomas's cock in her mouth, unable to scream out and unable to moan.

"Oh, but I wanted to be beaten Father. How I loved the cane and the whip, how I revelled in their cutting strokes, and I wanted the feel of it across my bottom and against my cunt and cutting my breasts, Oh Father."

Smack! Smack! Smack! Smack!

The beating was harder than anything she had known, her bottom stung with the heat of the frenzied smacks, but it was not enough, she wanted more and the only way to get them was to admit to all her desires. She broke her mouth away from the throbbing cock that she had forced right to the back of her throat.

"Oh Father, I need so much, I want to be humiliated and condemned to slavery, I want to be a drudge and a slut, I want to be beaten for my desires and I want to keep having them so that I can be beaten more. Thrash me Father, please thrash me for my wickedness, I need to be punished more and more!"

She gulped her mouth around his cock again and sucked at it wildly. She drew it in deeply and felt its tip pressing against the back of her throat. The smacking continued and she pulled it down more until it plugged her completely. Then she felt it expanding and she took it even deeper, she could not breathe but it did not matter, she did not care. She swallowed it and felt the stiff rod inserting itself right down inside her, then she felt the pulses and the run of fluid streaming along its length. She drew it in more and gulped and heaved and then it finished deeply down her throat and she broke free, choking and gasping and screaming and dribbling. She did not need to swallow it, it had come so deeply inside her that there was nothing around her mouth to drink.

"Beat me more Father. Please, more."

The smacking continued until she felt herself drifting into an unconscious oblivion. She did not admit any more though she knew there were still things to confess. She did not admit the new wave of sensation that had spread within her when she saw Caleb cowering as her slave and she did not admit the new feeling of control that she had sensed as she held her orgasm back until she had made him serve her enough.

As she bent before Father Thomas, and the blows of his hand continued on her buttocks. She glanced across the room and saw Caleb and Kirk both crouched down at the foot of the bed. Just before she gasped for the last time in pain, and fell into unconsciousness. She imagined them both as her servants and wondered what things she could do to force them to serve and satisfy her.

CHAPTER 14

The next thing Maria knew she was being hauled down the stairs of the hotel by Kirk and Father Thomas. Her mouth was gagged with wide tape and her wrists and ankles were tied tightly with thin rope. She was still naked and when she felt a stab in her side from Caleb's staff and pulled back in pain, she was reminded that her clitoral ring was still attached to the noose at her throat. They handled her roughly and as they pulled her through the door her face banged jarringly against the wall.

She was thrust into the boot of a car which was driven away at speed. After a while the car stopped, the boot was opened and she was dragged out. She looked around with bleary eyes and saw that she was in a large dock area. Father Thomas and Kirk carried her in through the door of a small brightly lit building on one of the piers and threw her down on the floor. Maria looked up and her eyes widened in horror.

A group of rough looking men dressed in overalls stood in a circle around her, several of them held snarling dogs that strained angrily on their leashes, two of them dangled chains from their hands and one was holding a wide leather strap.

"You do not have long," said Father Thomas. "The Mistress Lesley wants her ready in an hour."

"This won't take long," said the man with the leather

strap as he strode towards Maria. "You're a tidy little thing, aren't you? I hope you can run fast!"

He bent his head towards her and breathed hard into her face, then he pulled out a long knife and held it up in front of her eyes. Her nostrils flared and she fought for breath as he grabbed her hair and pulled her to her feet.

"Release her!"

"Yes, let's make the bitch run!"

The man with the knife bent down and slashed the blade through the rope which tied her ankles, and, as it sprung apart, she lost her balance and stumbled backwards.

"Run you little bitch! Run!"

Maria felt confused and frightened. The dogs strained forward on their leads and bared their dripping teeth. She shrunk back even more and fell over on her back. Her wrists twisted as she landed clumsily and she yelled out in pain as her naked shoulders scraped against the ground.

"Run you fucking bitch or do we have to give you a taste of the strap to get you going?"

The man with the strap came forward and without warning lashed her across her breasts. She wanted to yell as she felt it land heavily across her nipples but could only breathe harder through her wide open nostrils. Then another lash came down and she scrambled backwards in an effort to pull herself away, then another and she tried to get to her feet, then the strap landed across the front of her thighs and, in a terrible panic, finally she managed to stand.

"Run you fucking bitch!"

Maria shrunk further and further back towards the open door, then, overwhelmed and confused, she turned, dashed through the door and started to run away across the dark docks.

The men hung back for a while, holding onto the pulling dogs, as she disappeared into the darkness. As she ran, she heard the snarling and shouting fading into the distance and, when she came to a large container that stood on the edge of a pier, she dived behind it to hide and get her breath back. She could not hear the dogs at all now and she thought she might get away, so she ran on across the dockyards until her feet were cut and bleeding.

Then she heard the sound of the dogs getting closer and her panic returned. She ran as fast as she could but with her wrists tied so tightly behind her back, and the tape across her mouth, she knew they would catch her in the end. She knew that if she did not escape them she would be punished and raped and she would have to do whatever they wanted, and she ran on like a fox trying in vain to escape from the baying hounds.

She kept running until she could hardly move, then, as she turned to see how close they were behind her, she crashed into an empty oil drum, and fell over with the spinning drum clattering noisily across the ground beside her.

"There she is boys!"

She struggled to get up and dodged behind a stack of timber.

"Round here! She's round here somewhere!"

The dogs barked and yelped as she crouched, shivering and shaking, behind the timber stack, then a powerful hand grabbed her from behind.

"Got you bitch!"

Maria spun around in panic.

"Here boys, I've got her!"

She wriggled under his grip and fought frantically to escape but he grabbed her hair and held her back. She pulled as hard as she could but he gripped her hair so tightly that she could not get away no matter how much pain she endured.

The dogs appeared first, straining at their leashes, then the men came behind them and gathered around their victim. "They poked at her and taunted her, then one of them reached out and ripped the tape from her mouth. She let out a terrific scream, she howled and shrieked and the dogs barked louder as if inflamed by her bestial cries.

She was pulled to the ground and forced to bend over. She kept screeching and the dogs kept barking and straining towards her as she felt the lash of leather across her bottom as the strap came down.

Whack!

She screamed again and again but the beating did not stop, her buttocks felt raw from the flailing of the strap and she kept shouting for them to stop, then one of the lashes caught her tightly bound hands and she shrieked in terror.

Whack! Whack! Whack!

Then there was a pause, but it was only for a moment, the next thing she knew she felt the knife cutting through the rope that held her wrists. They sprung apart but were grabbed straight away as she was rolled over on her back. She felt stones and rubbish pressing into her back as they held her arms wide and forced her down and, as they splayed her legs wide, she felt the steaming, hot breath of the dogs as they pulled frantically on their leads.

Maria was terrified as she was held down, spread-eagled and totally exposed, but, as she writhed against the hands that held her, she felt the painful pull of the ring in her clitoris. The more she tried to break free the more the chain pulled at the ring and the more she felt the sensation of pleasure welling up inside her.

She felt the heat of a cock at the edges of her cunt. She threw her head back and the chain pulled violently at the ring in her clitoris, the pain was terrible but she felt it engorging and knew that her cunt was demanding more. She felt the lips of her cunt getting wetter and, as the cock thrust inside her in one forceful surge, she was silky and smooth and took it all.

She kept the pressure on her chain as the cock plunged deeply inside her then, as it started to fuck her, she began pulling rhythmically at the ring. She felt the fucking and its violent thrusts spread shivers of excitement throughout her, but the ring was giving her more pleasure. She felt a surge of energy and pushed her pelvis onto the cock as hard as she could. The ring kept pulling her clitoris and, as a heat boiled up in it and her body began to tingle with the surge of delight that ran from it. She fucked the cock like an animal until it shot its spunk deep into her vagina. She started screeching out again but this time she was screeching for more.

"Another! Another!"

Another cock plunged inside and she fucked it as hard as she could. All the time she kept bringing her clitoris to orgasm by pulling her neck against the chain, every painful pressure releasing a new climax, every tug on the ring causing her to run with a fresh, delightful spasm. She took another, and another finished in her mouth, then they turned her over.

"Yes," she cried, "yes, like a dog, fuck me like a dog."

A cock plunged into her cunt from behind and, as she was knocked forward by its onslaught. She kept pulling the chain and filling her body with orgasm after orgasm. She knew what was happening now, she realised that what was happening were her fantasies, all the things she had told Father Thomas were coming true. Of course, he was training her to live out her fantasies! Her body tightened into an enormous paroxysm, then she realised that she had not told him everything, there were still things she wanted that he did not know. He had taken her confession but there were still things to confess and she needed to tell him, she still had so many sins to be admitted.

Then she understood and she knew that she would never escape, her desires for pleasure and pain were ever increasing, she could be punished forever but it would never satisfy her need for forgiveness or the pleasure she got from being bad. She was overwhelmed with delight as the revelation struck her and she saw that what lay ahead was a life of punishment, pain and agonizing delight.

"Up my arse! Up my arse and fuck me like a dog!"

The sound of the dogs filled her ears, she wanted to run again and be caught, she wanted to be dragged down by the dogs and hauled over the ground and beaten and flogged and fucked like a dog. She realised that she wanted to be a dog and fuck like a dog, she realised that she wanted to be fucked like the animal she was and that meant only one thing.

"Like a dog!" she screamed. "Like a dog!"

CHAPTER 15

Maria was barely conscious as the men dragged her across the wide open area of the docks. She heard the sound of ships and the clanking of chains mixed with the barking of dogs and the sounds of a cracking whip. She was aware of being pulled into a metal building and made to stand, naked and alone in the dazzling light. As her eyes became used to the brightness, she looked up and shrunk back in surprise.

Lesley stood before her. She looked marvellous, be-decked in glittering chains and clothed in shiny leather, with a long, black whip hanging loosely in her hand. Still squinting, Maria looked at her closely. She wore a black leather waistcoat pulled tightly around her breasts with thin leather thongs and a black leather suspender belt was pulled tightly onto her well rounded hips. The suspenders held black stockings in their shiny metal clasps and disappeared into shiny leather boots that fitted tightly to halfway up her long thighs. She did not have any panties on and her black pubic hair curled tightly in a dense mat above the barely discernible pink edges of the front of her crack.

At her feet was Barbara. She was completely naked and crouched on all fours with her wrists and ankles manacled tightly to the floor in heavy silver rings. Around her neck a heavy leather collar was secured from one side to the floor and from the other to a ring which was attached to the ceiling. She did not seem to be able to move at all and her long, dark hair hung down over her face and trailed on the floor.

A naked man, with a leather mask and a silver chain pulled up tightly between his balls and his neck, straddled her back. He held a riding crop over her red striped buttocks and she looked exhausted and in pain.

There were a lot of other girls in the room. Some were shackled in chains, some were tethered to the wall with leather thongs, one was gagged and blindfolded, another, her bare bottom ribbed with angry red lines, was strapped naked and face down over a bench. A blonde haired girl hung suspended by her ankles from a chain attached to the ceiling and spun dizzily as a leather clad man thrashed her with a split cane. She seemed too tired to scream and just whimpered as her torturer thrashed her remorselessly. Then Maria realised that she recognised some of them, she could hardly believe it, one she remembered from work and several of them had been at her school. As she looked around, she saw Father Thomas and Kirk standing near to the door with Caleb squatting at their feet.

Lesley stepped towards her and Maria fell back in fear as she saw that look in Lesley's face that promised both reward and pain. Lesley pulled back her long arm and lifted her whip, it bent easily as its tip reached towards the ceiling. Maria felt a shiver of fear as she thought of it crashing down across her breasts or her bottom, and she shrunk back, afraid that at any moment Lesley would flare up into uncontrollable anger.

Then Lesley's expression began to change. It took on the look that promised only pain. Her smooth contoured face began to crinkle, and her eyes tightened and her lips curled upwards, as she flushed around the cheeks and took a deep breath. Maria fell back even more and she felt her heart beating frantically.

"You are a sorry sight, my dear. But why are you standing, surely you have been trained better than that? Don't you know how to be a slave yet? Surely you know how to beg and scrape by now? Get down on your knees you fucking slut!"

Maria dropped to her knees and bent her head.

"You don't remember me do you? Do you? No, of course you don't."

Maria did not understand. Of course she remembered her, it was Lesley, her boss at work, she knew her well, she had worked for her for ages.

"Lesley, what do you mean?"

"Address me properly! I am Mistress Lesley!"

Maria felt her heart pounding loudly.

"Please, Mistress Lesley, of course I know you."

"Hah! You may look up at me if you wish, yes, look closely and cast your mind back. Yes? Do you remember now? I think you do. I was one of the girls in that muddy

195

hole, yes? The day you walked past and saw me with my panties down having my young bottom smacked, remember? Yes? Well it doesn't matter a fuck if you don't. You missed a treat my dear Maria, oh yes, because that is how it all started. I went to Father Thomas, just like you, I went to beg for forgiveness. But I was different, braver than you. "Bend over my knee my child, a good spanking will save you." Oh, I can recall it so clearly. But I did not run away like you, I bent over his knee and let him pull my white panties down. I lay across his lap in that dark confession box and let him spank my bare bottom until I cried and sobbed for forgiveness. Oh, I still go wet at the thought, that beautiful punishment, that beautiful spanking. But things changed didn't they Father?"

Father Thomas smiled subserviently.

"His spanking was not enough for me, even the hard ones he gave me. I needed more than that and so, as time went on, though he spanked me so hard, oh so hard, poor Father Thomas had to find me more. A cane, a whip, a chain, but still it was not enough. It was not long before I was training him in the ways of punishment and humiliation. Father, how far we've come. Now, as you can see my dear, I have devoted my life to it. Sometimes I keep a slave for my own purposes, I am having this one, Barbara, but not you my dear, no, I am not going to keep you."

Maria felt her skin tingling with fear. How could Lesley say such things? She looked towards Father Thomas and saw his lips turning up at the corners in a wry smile and, as his teeth were exposed, she saw that wolflike grin spreading across his face and it caused a cold, wet shiver to run down her back.

"Ah Father Thomas, what a marvellous servant you have been. All those girls, how hard you've worked in finding them, how well you have prepared them. They have

196

all been across your knee and have all felt the whip that you have wielded so enthusiastically. We are all so grateful Father."

Lesley turned to Father Thomas and poked the tip of her whip against his face. He opened his mouth and his teeth shone wetly as Lesley ran the end of the whip slowly down the front of his chest until she reached his waist, then she stopped and turned away.

"So what of you, my dear Maria? Well, you will not be here very long, though long enough for a little entertainment I think. Father Thomas tells me you have a taste for being the master, a bit like me! How could you be like me? You are so small, your tits are puny and you are so snivelling and slutty. No, that will not do at all, but I think we can beat it out of you."

Lesley laughed as she stepped forward and stood over Maria who knelt submissively at her feet.

"We have some clients in South America. We have told them what a slut you are and they are eager to see you. You will be shipped out tomorrow. Caleb will be your escort, he will look after you well I'm sure. Perhaps he can help polish up some of your skills on the journey? But for now I need to see how you can perform. We shall soon see if Father Thomas has been doing his job properly!"

Maria was hardly taking it all in. Her eyes looked blackened and stared fearfully up at Lesley and the tape across her mouth caused her to breathe heavily through her nose. Her firm breasts were forced forward by the tightness of the ropes that bound her wrists at the back and her nipples stood out eagerly. Her slim body was smooth and radiant, her buttocks spread slightly as they were pressed outwards by her heels and her curvaceous hips accentuated her slender waist. The tiny, gold cross swung slowly from the thin chain that draped through the noose at her neck. The other end pulled down tightly across her belly and just disappeared into the soft edges of her shaved crack, before emerging again where it ran into the golden ring that pierced her clitoris. Her long hair fell back in a swirl around her neck and trailed loosely onto her shoulder blades.

Lesley bent down, took hold of the small cross at Maria's neck and twirled it slowly between her fingers. The chain pulled at her neck and this tugged at the chain that stretched down to her ring. As Lesley played with the cross, Maria felt the tugging of the ring in her clitoris and shivered as tingling waves of hot excitement flooded through her body.

She felt her clitoris swelling and demanding more and she bent her head slightly to increase the pressure. She looked down and, opening her thighs slightly, saw the ring emerging from the crack of her cunt as her clitoris engorged in response to the gentle pulling of the chain. She looked back up and smiled at Lesley as her clitoris became fully exposed and throbbed between the soft folds at the front of her shaved crack.

"Ah Maria, sometimes I feel so hard to please. I hope you will not disappoint me."

Maria shivered with fear as Lesley parted her legs and flexed the thin black whip between her hands. She thought of the whip and how it would soon be flailing across her buttocks, she thought of all she had been through in the last few days and wondered what else lay ahead. She looked up slightly and felt the tension of the ring in her clitoris, a wetness spread across the soft edges of her cunt and she looked up more.

"Yes, very hard to please,' said Lesley. "Now bend over Maria, and we will begin."

Then the whipping started and Maria strained with agony, delight and expectation.

Our book for next month is BARBARY SLAVEDRIVER by Allan Aldiss. This is the first Barbary book for some time, although the series goes back to our first book, Barbary Slavemaster. For old times' sake we introduce 'Slavedriver' with an extract from 'Slavemaster' - remember that this series can be enjoyed equally in any order, however:-

Barbary Slavemaster - AUTHOR'S NOTE

This novel is set in a time and place where harem women really were totally at the mercy of the rich men who owned them, and of the black eunuchs who supervised them. European women really were captured by the Corsairs and sold in the slave markets of the East. The Barbary States did have a reputation for treating Christian slaves unbelievably harshly, almost as animals, and there actually were slave breeding farms in the Ottoman Empire ... and although you won't find Marsa on the map, there are several places where it well could have been.

The story takes place during the long drawn out war between Britain and revolutionary and then Napoleonic France, which started in 1793 and only ended with the Battle of Waterloo twenty-two years later. Because the principal naval powers were busy fighting each other, the war gave a considerable stimulus to the Barbary Corsairs. It also saw the elimination of one of their main enemies: the Knights of Malta. Thus for much of this time, they had an almost free rein to plunder and kidnap along the coasts and islands of Southern Europe.

By this time the corsairs had replaced their sea-going galleys with fast sailing craft such as polacca-chebecs which carried a mixture of European type square sails and Arab style lanteen sails. The demand for large numbers of young male Christian galley slaves had therefore dwindled. Instead many of the Corsos, as the corsair raids were called, concentrated more on capturing young women.

In 1798, for instance, only a few years before the setting of this novel, Barbary Corsairs from Tunis carried off almost a thousand women and children from the island of San Pietro, off Sardinia. Some were ransomed a few years later, but many had disappeared, having been sold in the slave markets of North Africa and the Middle East.

Thus, although what follows is fiction, the background is realistic. However, those of a squeamish disposition are advised not to read the books of the Barbary series. For a more serious study of this fascinating period I would recommend books such as Stephen Clissold's 'The Barbary Slaves' (Elek Books), Noel Barber's 'Lords of the Golden Horn' (Macmillan), 'Harem, The World Behind the Veil' by Alev Lytle Croutier (Bloomsbury), and books about the Knights of Malta.

CHAPTER 1

THE PASHA MAKES A PURCHASE

It was in 1809 (by the Christian calendar) that the Pasha consulted me regarding the purchase of a woman - a matter which one would have thought to be a routine matter, and certainly not one in which it was either necessary or desirable to involve a renegade Englishman such as myself.

Hassan Pasha, the Governor of Marsa, was somewhat plump with a long grey beard and fierce eyes. He was much older and rather shorter than I. He wore an imposing red silk turban and a long robe, and had the commanding air of a man who had spent a lifetime in positions of authority, as indeed he had. His lips were the those of a sensuous man who enjoyed his pleasures, as again indeed he did.

Or perhaps this was accentuated that day, for we were in

the cool Arab style patio of the establishment of Achmed, one of the leading slave dealers in Marsa, and women were clearly on the Pasha's mind - or perhaps just this one particular woman. He was certainly a man who knew what he wanted, and - which made me somewhat apprehensive - not one to suffer fools gladly.

"The woman I wish you to inspect," he said, "is said to be English and of aristocratic stock."

I was struck dumb at the thought of any Englishwoman, let alone one of good family, being in the hands of a Marsa slave dealer. She would certainly be a very rare and valuable item!

"And you are also English of good stock, Colonel Hussein," he continued.

"Yes, Excellency, that is so," I replied. I was still not quite used to being Colonel Hussein of the Sultan of Turkey's Janissaries, instead of merely Captain Rory Fitzgerald of His Majesty King George III's foot guards and the son of a penniless Anglo-Irish Baronet. I collected my thoughts again after the Pasha's astonishing announcement. "But of course I am now a true believer."

"May Allah be praised!"

"Indeed, Excellency," I murmured, feeling rather a fraud, for my so-called conversion to the Moslem religion had been purely for practical reasons.

"You will, I presume, be able to tell whether this woman is what Achmet says she is? It is the thought of having a real English lady in my power that appeals to me - not some strumpet, not a mere servant girl."

His eyes lit up at the thought of it. A real English lady in his harem? Yes, I could certainly see how stimulating that would be! And since she would be a Christian, enslaving her would be all the more praiseworthy.

"Yes, Excellency," I replied. "I will be able to tell and it will be a great honour to advise Your Excellency." There could be promotion in this - I was second in command of the Turkish Janissaries in Marsa under Abdul Raman Bey at that time. Or there could be disgrace. I had learnt to be careful with this autocratic individual. Anything to do with a man's harem has to be treated very seriously and is a matter of considerable delicacy.

Moreover, I wondered how much he knew of the Bey's sloth and inefficiency. But my own position as an Englishman in the employ of the Sultan was also rather uncertain, for French influence on Constantinople was strong again.

"My chief eunuch has of course examined her." The Pasha's voice cut into my thoughts. "He says she is fit and well and he is confident he can train her satisfactorily ..."

I smiled at this. I knew well the impact such training would have on a white woman. Even in my own small harem the girls were kept well trained and submissive.

"So," the Pasha continued, "if the description is genuine I shall purchase her. Otherwise Achmed shall suffer ..."

He clapped his hands and Achmed himself appeared, all bows and greasy smiles. Eager as they both were to get down to business, we must first sip tiny cups of Turkish coffee and discuss the prospects for the current Corso, or raiding season, as well as the present state of the slave market: such is the way that business is conducted in the Orient.

We might have been merchants in a London coffee house, such as I had once been familiar with, discussing the state of the markets on 'Change' - except of course that I was in the uniform of an officer of the Janissaries, with a tall white felt hat, a short blue robe, baggy Turkish shalwar breeches and yellow boots, whilst the others wore Eastern robes. And, of course, we were all speaking Arabic, sitting cross legged on large ottomans and being waited on by pretty white eunuch page boys.

Presently the dealer's Negro overseer entered the room. He was carrying a long stiff whip with a little leash at the tip - it was the sort that was widely used to school horses and was also used by such Negroes as this to school the young women placed in their charge. He bowed to the Pasha and announced that the goods that the Pasha had returned to see were ready for his inspection in the display room.

Here, there were Eastern carpets on the floor and bright painted tiles on the walls, but the windows were barred.

"Speak to her," the Pasha said to me impatiently, indicating a heavily veiled figure standing on a low platform by one of the barred windows. What I saw was a shrinking figure on a dais, hidden behind a loose white caftan buttoned down the front. Her head was covered in an all enveloping white veil through which nothing could be seen of her features.

"Speak to her in English."

The Pasha, I thought, was getting increasingly impatient to get his hands on her. It would be tactless indeed to frustrate him now that he had the bit between his teeth, as it were. He was like a man buying a horse back in Ireland. Once a horse has taken your fancy, you want quick confirmation that it is sound and well bred, and then you want to get your hands on it, try it out, ride it hard ...

Actually, the chance of a well-bred English woman becoming a slave in Barbary must be remote indeed. It was almost certain that this would turn out to be some foreign tart who had picked up a few words of English from a client.

It would, however, be considerably more tactful to tell the Pasha what he wanted to hear, and that is what I intended to do, especially as Achmed had already taken me aside and shown me a very different young woman with a pale skin, sloe eyes, flowing black hair and a well curved figure.

"Do you like this one, Effendi?" he had asked. "She is from Sardinia."

"She's not bad," I conceded. She had already been depilated but obviously not yet trained.

"Then she is yours." He had looked round to be sure we were alone, and then up at me slyly - I am taller than most, out here - "She is a virgin, unsullied. I cannot afford such a gift if the Pasha is not well pleased with the other one."

He had obviously anticipated that the Pasha would not be able to check up on what he had been told, and was rightly fearful for his sweating skin.

"Let us hope that that is the will of Allah," I had replied with a wink, "for I would not wish to be impolite towards so generous an individual as yourself!"

So now we came to the moment of truth - or perhaps, since it would not affect my reply to the Pasha, I should say of revelation.

The wrists of the woman on the dais were fastened behind her neck to a ring high up in the wall, thus keeping her upright and helpless to intervene when the buttons of her caftan were undone to allow the inspection of her body - in this way she could be freely seen and felt without interference.

The pose would also bend her slightly backwards from the waist, raising her breasts and showing them to their best advantage, like on the carved figure head at the prow of a ship.

Slave dealers always displayed their wares in the most favourable positions - especially when they were asking the sort of price Achmed would be asking for this young woman, a price I myself could certainly not even dream of affording in those days.

I moved closer to her, ready to lie in the cause of prudence and politeness. The way she shrank back showed that she could see out through the veil.

"Who are you?" I asked, in English.

"Oh thank God!" The voice, though strained, was most attractive and definitely that of an educated English lady! "Oh thank God, thank God, you're English!"

205

"I am," I replied. "Or, rather, Irish."

"Have you come to rescue me?"

"Impossible!" I said. All the Barbary States had signed treaties with Britain exempting, in exchange for large subsidies, British ships and subjects from capture. These treaties were often ignored, but the existence of an English slave could not be admitted officially. "I am merely here to report upon you."

"Report? Oh God, what's happening?"

The girl was almost hysterical. She started to scream out in a most unseemly fashion. "You must save me! You must! You must!"

The Negro grew angry at this sudden outburst in a language he did not understand. This was far from the submissive and humble whisper she would surely have been taught to adopt in the display room.

He raised his whip menacingly, and the effect was dramatic. Brought back to her senses, she cowered from him.

"Oh no! Don't let that brute beat me again!"

Clearly she was absolutely terrified of the Negro and his whip. I waved him back and there was a little gulp from behind the veil.

I was fascinated. I admit it. I had not heard an Englishwoman's voice for years. I was quite taken by her lilting voice and intrigued by what might be behind the veil. And what did she make of me? She would see a tall young man of military bearing, strangely dressed. Would she be impressed by the long waxed Turkish moustache and short pointed beard? No wonder she had been surprised when I spoke English! But under it all I did look fairly European still. Though well burned by the sun I was still white and my hair and eyes are brown - I have been told I have humorous self-mocking eyes and a rather aristocratic Roman nose that adds to my distinguished looks.

"Tell me about yourself," I said.

"Are they going to sell me to that fat pig over there?"

It was extremely fortunate that the Pasha could not understand a word of English.

"You must be more respectful to him," I said. "Or it will be much the worse for you."

"You wouldn't abandon me to that horrible old man?"

"I have no choice," I said bitterly. "If I could buy you for myself, then I certainly would."

It was true. I had begun to wish she were mine without even seeing her face or body.

"Buy? Buy? But surely I will be ransomed?"

"Who would do that?"

"My husband!" she said. "My husband! If he can't rescue me! Wait till he hears about this!"

"I'm afraid he never will."

"Oh!" she gasped.

What did she look like? I was becoming increasingly interested - it was a long time since I had seen an English woman.

"She is indeed English, Excellency," I told the Pasha. "Beyond that, as to her breeding, it is hard to determine when I cannot read her face to know if she is lying."

I did not expect to be permitted to see the face of a woman who might be destined for the Pasha's harem. But I was wrong. The Pasha motioned to the Negro, who reached up and pulled the veil from her face.

I gave a gasp. Here was a beauty such as I had rarely seen before.

The shrewd slave dealer had had her blond hair carefully brushed straight down her back in the approved slave girl style. Blond, blue-eyed women were very much sought after in the Barbary States and sold for huge prices. This girl's hair was fine and honey coloured, like spun gold, and her eyes were a soft and alluring blue.

No wonder the Pasha was so taken by her - I myself was

utterly overcome.

Her elfin shaped face was young and beautiful, with a straight nose and full mouth made to please a man. But it was her brilliantly blue and carefully made up eyes that really caught my attention.

She seemed to be about to burst into tears, but then she shook her head and looked boldly at me.

That is when I became obsessed with her, with owning her, with having her in my own harem, to ... yes, my loins swelled mightily for her, but of course it was mad to think of even touching her. Only one of the richest man in Marsa, such as the Pasha himself, could ever afford to buy a creature like this.

Achmed the dealer was standing in a corner, watching in silence, sensing a sale. Apart from not wishing to offend the Pasha, he had doubtless invested a large sum in purchasing her from the Rais, or Captain, of the Corso ship that had captured her, and had then spent more in having her broken in thus far, and beautified.

"Tell me about yourself," I repeated.

This time she rushed breathlessly into rapid speech - hoping, I think, to convince us she should be ransomed. I began to translate into Arabic for the Pasha.

"I am Henrietta Hamilton, wife of Captain James Hamilton of the 56th. My father is the Reverend Hubert de Vere, a cousin of Lord de Vere." The Pasha's eyes lit up at this. "He is Vicar of a village in Hampshire, and we were always the poor relations" - this I did not translate - "I fell madly in love with James. We were married quickly for his Regiment was about to sail for Malta. I have never seen him since. I followed him to Malta but his Regiment had been sent to Sicily. I love him so much. I was on my way there in a local vessel when we were attacked by a Corsair ship - oh God, oh God, what is to become of me!"

When I had translated this, I bowed low and retreated

into the background. It had been an outburst that must have added considerably to the price that the Pasha was willing to pay. To enslave the wife of a Christian infidel is something that appeals greatly to the Turk. The fact that the woman still loves the husband she will never see again adds further spice to the situation, especially if she is the wife of an English officer.

I thought the Pasha would dismiss me now that the matter was resolved. He would not want me to speak any more with his future concubine now that her aristocratic background was established. But again I was wrong. Perhaps he was flustered, or perhaps he was pleased with my only too obvious admiration of his prize and wished to bask in it a little longer.

Achmed motioned to his Negro overseer, who came forward and started to unbutton the girl's caftan. She gasped as she tried to shake him off, but with her wrists secured to the ring bolt set in the wall behind her head she was unable to prevent those black hands remorselessly continuing down as he undid button after button.

The Negro pulled open the caftan to show off the girl's slender naked body. The Pasha's eyes were eager as he looked her up and down, then sat, leaning forward on a stool that Achmed pulled across the floor and set closely in front of her.

I too sucked in my breath, though being careful not to draw attention to myself. The body being displayed to us was indeed superb, and the twisting and writhing added to its attraction. As I had expected, she had been depilated.

At a gesture from the Pasha the Negro unfastened her chained hands from the ring bolt and turned her round so that he could admire her long slender back and soft buttocks, and then bent her forward to give him a different view of her intimacies. The girl squirmed away from every little touch despite whatever training she had had.

This was all quite normal, of course. I myself had had much less expensive girls displayed to me in a similar way before buying them. But it had been different, they had not been delicate English girls like this. My lust for this gorgeous Henrietta was rising too fast for comfort.

If only she were mine! But that could never be. It was obvious that the Pasha was about to purchase her.

Now for a surprise! Our Allan Aldiss is also Hilary James, who has written the astonishingly popular Emma series for Nexus. Many readers of the six Emma books will have been fascinated by the character of Ursula, Emma's tormentor. Allan (or is it Hilary?) has now offered us the unexpurgated version of a completely new EMMA novel featuring Ursula. It is called 'FETCH THE CANE, EMMA or Ursula's Revenge: The shocking story that could not be published'.

As many of you will know, this series deals with the domination of a young woman by an older woman, and consequently is against our policy of featuring dominant men and submissive women, and we wonder if we should include it in our list - we offer a short extract here in the hopes that readers will give us their opinions.

In this book Emma, literally, has puppies - by artificial insemination, we hasten to add! Your opinions, please?

Emma was standing silently at attention in front of Ursula's desk. As usual she wore nothing but a simple, short, blue satin tunic with her Mistress's crest and initials embroidered on the right breast.

Also as usual, Helga was standing behind her holding in one hand the dog lead attached to the ring at the back of Emma's collar and in her other her dog whip.

What was different this time, however, was that Samantha was standing alongside her, also wearing just a little tunic and standing silently at attention.

"Number 1233, make your report!" ordered Helga formerly in her strong German accent, giving Samantha a sharp little cut across her naked buttocks with the dog whip.

Instantly, like a well drilled soldier, Samantha held up her left hand and turned it palm upwards to display the mark of The Society and her own Registered Number.

"Miss de Vere's Registered Slave number 1233 reporting,Madam," she called out, her eyes still fixed on the wall behind her Mistress. Then she added the mandatory affirmation: "Number 1233 loves Miss de Vere, her Mistress. Her only pleasure in life is to give her Mistress pleasure, whenever she wants it, without any thought of pleasure for herself."

"Really?" commented Ursula.

Emma trembled at the anger in Ursula's voice, but before she could begin to wonder just what awful thing was about to happen she felt a tap on her buttocks and gave the same affirmation.

"Really?" came Ursula's icy tones again. She looked them both up and down for a minute. Then she pressed a button on her tape recorder. "Just listen to this you lying bitches!"

Both girls gasped as they recognised their own voices: giggling as they caressed each other, swearing undying love for each other, mocking their absent Mistress and confessing how they liked men and, for Emma, Henry in particular. It was a record of their conversation the previous day when Ursula was away and Helga asleep!

"So you thought you'd get away with deceiving me with each other, did you?" Ursula's voice was becoming increasingly shrill. "So you love each other and despise your Mistress, do you? So you want to run away together, do you? So you hanker after me, eh?"

There was another long pause and then Ursula went on in a now low and terrifying voice. "You pair of stupid bitches!

You'll never get away from me, never! Never, do you hear, never! You belong to me! If you think you love each other more than me, then let's see how long it takes for the cane to make you change your mind!"

She paused as they cowered before her, then suddenly barked: "Fetch a cane, each of you! Move!"

Terrified, the two young women, married women of independent means, and now just Ursula's slaves, scampered across the room to the cupboard and returned, each carrying a cane.

"Samantha, bend over the desk," ordered Ursula. "Reach across to grip the other side. Now, Emma, as just a little start, to warm up your beloved Samantha, you're going to give her five strokes - the first of twenty! ...yes, you're going to give each other twenty strokes. And if I don't think a stroke is hard enough, then it won't count, and so your precious little Samantha's torment will be prolonged."

"Oh, no! Please Madam!" cried Emma.

"Oh, no! Please Madam!" cried Samantha.

But Ursula ignored their pathetic pleadings.

And later:-

The two dark-skinned men, whom Helga now ushered into the room, were the most frightening either Emma or Celestia had ever seen. The very sight of them made the young women cringe back into the far corners of the playpen and clasp each other, as best they could with their mittened hands, for protection.

Both men were black, very black. One was huge and strong, completely bald. His face was scarred, as if with some tribal marking. His cruel-looking bloodshot eyes glittered as he looked at the two girls cowering in the playpen. He was wearing some sort of African robe over his gross body.

The other was equally frightening. He was a black

skinhead dressed in jeans with a face covered in Red Indian style was paint. His head was shaved except for a central man of spiky hair dyed green. He looked bad tempered and cruel.

Emma had often been attracted to handsome intelligent looking black men - but not ones like these. She could hardly bear to look at them

"My God, Ursula, where did you find these animals?" murmured one of her women friends admiringly.

Both the young women dressed as school girls were looking at these men with horror. Both were tightly holding the hands of their now standing Mistress, like little girls who were seeing something quite terrifying.

"Ladies!" said Ursula to the surrounding guests, "may I introduce you to Martok from Africa and Karl from Jamaica. And, gentlemen, may I introduce you to your little partners: Emma and Celestia. I'm sure you will both find these pretty little creatures sufficiently attractive to make it worth your while to earn the fees I have to offer you."

There was a long pause as both men looked lustfully at the two cringing and half-naked girls locked into the playpen, then Ursula spoke again.

"But first we must get them ready for you. I want them to offer themselves willingly to you. Helga, please take Emma out - take off her dress and put her on the couch to have her rompers taken off."

Helga unlocked the top of the playpen and reached down to pull out Emma. Holding her by her long blonde hair, she dragged the reluctant girl to the couch. Her big rubber dummy was still fastened behind her neck so that her screams of protest came out as little baby-like gurgling noises.

Helga laid Emma on the couch and strapped her wrists to the top behind her head. Another strap went over her neck, forcing her to keep her head back. The top of the couch was tilted back. Emma could not now see what was being done to her proffered belly.

Then Helga slid the plastic rompers and then the diapers down over Emma's thighs.

Ursula beckoned to the two men.

"Gentlemen, come and help Helga."

Eagerly the two men came over.

"Now, hold the lips well apart whilst Helga dries and powders her inside... wider, please..."

Emma felt utterly degraded a she endured those awful men's fingers pulling apart her most intimate lips. It was even worse that they were doing this in front of the fascinated eyes of Ursula's guests and their girls.

Suddenly Emma was appalled to feel that she was becoming aroused under the manipulations of these two repulsive men. She was shocked at her own uncontrollable sensuality. She could feel herself go moist and soft. She could smell her own shame-making arousal.

"Go on," said Ursula. "One of you fold the lips apart whilst the other feels up inside her."

All Emma could see were the repulsive faces of the two men bending over her loins as they probed and squeezed.

"Nice and tight, white girl," came the voice of the larger man in a strong African accent.

"That's because she's not normally allowed any men," said Ursula. "You're going to be a special treat."

"How old is this bitch?" asked the skinhead in a strong Caribbean accent.

"Oh, just a little girl," replied Ursula with a laugh. "That's why she has no body hair and why, when you remove her dummy, she'll lisp just like a baby girl, won't you Emma?"

Emma had found it exciting in the past to have to lisp to Ursula, but the idea of doing it in front of these awful men was horrible - but at least it would not be as bad as having to display her state of arousal in such a degrading way.

At last the ministrations of Helga and the two men were

over. Emma was unceremoniously lifted off the couch and told to kneel, now stark naked, on the floor, whilst the whole process was repeated with Celestia. The idea of the lovely body of her precious Celestia being mauled about and aroused by these two ghastly men made Emma feel dreadful. But she had to listen in silence whilst it was done.

As she knelt, she felt once again a growing need to spend a penny. Desperately she clamped her thighs together - a movement that was noticed by Ursula with with a smile.

Soon Celestia was kneeling alongside her, stark naked and also sobbing with the shame of her arousal.

"Before our little girls start pleasing you two fine gentlemen," they heard Ursula say, "I'm sure that you would like to give them the opportunity of relieving themselves - in front of you, of course. Helga, fetch their pots! But I don't want them to sit on them - our two guests want to see them performing from close up! Doubtless they'll both be very shy, so to encourage them I shall give the last one to start three strokes of the cane."

Two minutes later, Emma and Celestia were standing alongside each other right in front of the two now seated men. Their mittened hands were now on top of their heads. Each was looking at one of the men and blushing, for her legs were parted and her knees bent and a pot had been placed between her ankles.

Ursula stood behind them, tapping their buttocks with her cane, and whistling to encourage the two horrified girls, each torn between her acute embarrassment at having to perform in front of the Negroes, and her equally acute fear of being last.

Finally, after several false starts, a little tinkling noise announced that it was Emma who had won the little race, and Celestia who would get the three strokes of the cane from Ursula.

"I think it is time that we allowed our two pretty little

215

tarts to be allowed to kneel down and please you both," Ursula said. "Helga, take out their rubber dummies. Now remember girls, you are to lisp like little girls - or you'll get the cane. Now, Emma, let me hear you beg to be allowed to please Mr Martok. And do it properly!"

It was the first time that Emma had been allowed to speak ever since she had arrived in the house hours beforehand. She gathered her thoughts, Ursula's cane uppermost in her mind. In her aroused state, however, the most shame-making thing was not her natural revulsion at what she was going to have to do, but rather her excited longing to do it!

"This little girl," she heard herself lisp eagerly, "would like to please Mr Martok."

"And just what are you offering to do?" Ursula insisted.

Emma swallowed hard. She felt Ursula give her naked bottom a hard tap.

"This little girl would like to take Mr Martok's big manhood into her little mouth," Emma lisped with a sob of shame - or was it excitement?

"Then do it, you man-hungry little slut!"

Emma crawled on all fours between the seated Negro's knees. She raised her still gloved hands. Awkwardly, she raised and parted his robes. She gave a little cry of repulsion as she saw the flabby flesh of his huge belly, with below it the purple top of his half erect manhood. However, like a bitch on heat, she could not help responding as she smelt his male arousal. Oh how shameful!

Ursula gave her another hard tap with her cane.

"Go on!" she ordered harshly. "I heard you on the tape telling Celestia how you enjoyed pleasing a man. Well, go on and please this one!"

With a sob of despair, and trying not to be sick, Emma lowered her head and opened her mouth.

Now for our next instalment of ERICA REWRITTEN by Rex Saviour. The complete revision, with its added chapters, can be downloaded electronically (as can all our out-of-print titles) from our web sites.

3-4

Two weeks later Tom rang to say his apparatus was ready, and I arranged a time that afternoon for him to demonstrate it.

I decided to make the most of his visit. It was troubling me very much that, in spite of all my efforts at desensitization, Erica was just as shy as when I first got her, maybe more so. She still got quite distressed when I dressed her in certain ways - she didn't like a dog collar, for example, or even the rather pretty cat collar. And too short a skirt, that sort of thing - she never wore knickers of course, because we only had ones with snakes on them and she would not wear them however much I beat her.

So, I judged, it was high time to increase the exposure, the desensitization.

I went into the den and sat at the desk where I usually kept the bleeper. This is an example of modern technology I had purchased only a few days before, inspired by the model aeroplane club. It wasn't remote control, it fell far short of that, but it was a step in the right direction.

Each time I pushed my button the remote strapped to Erica's wrist bleeped. I could originate long or short bleeps, so she was busily learning the morse code. She could respond to several different messages already.

There was a time limit on the one I now sent. She had to

complete the instructions within twelve minutes, wherever she was, whatever the time, day or night.

Sure enough, she rushed breathlessly into the room less than ten minutes later, correctly dressed and groomed and carrying everything she needed. Correct dress was not difficult - suspender belt and stockings, ballet shoes, and, as always, the broad black leather belt at the waist. The belt was studded with metal, but I always used the smooth side on her, whatever she might be expecting. Face tastefully made up, but not too obviously so. I had started to paint her nipples and sex also, but discreetly, nothing too blatant. When wearing ballet shoes she stayed on points.

She didn't look at me. She just carried the small stool to the correct place and arranged the hood and other things on it. She took up her position with her legs astride the stool, pushed the special plugs into her ears and pulled the hood over her head. Then she folded her hands behind her back, pushing the wrist clips until they engaged with the rings attached to the opposite snake bands, the ones that decorated her upper arms. She braced herself like a soldier on parade and was ready in time, just.

I gave her a slap on the bottom, the signal to turn round and face the wall, which did did with alacrity. She knows I don't like a sluggard.

Tom was due in a couple of minutes.

I went out into the garden for a smoke, for it was quite a pleasant day, the birds were all busy and only a few small white clouds drifted by. A day to be lazy, but I had my duty to do...

"Sorry I'm so late," said Tom as he climbed out of his weasely little car. "Awful traffic!"

"Only half an hour. Doesn't matter a bit." He was carrying a big wing folded in two and another package.

I threw open the den door and ushered him in.

"Christ!" he said. The blasphemy confirmed my low opinion of him, but he was useful, still a useful little weasel of a man.

"Sorry," I said, "I forgot Erica was here. I was supposed to punish her. All part of the treatment, but it can wait, there's no hurry."

"My word!" he said, more than somewhat hot and bothered.

"Looks good, doesn't she?"

"Christ, yes." There he went again. It was mortifying to think that to an uniformed spectator his ungodly lasciviousness might seem not unsimilar to my own behaviour, which was of course governed by my mission.

"It's for her own good, remember," I said. "It is all part of the desensitisation treatment, you see."

"I see, yes," said Tom. "Is that right, dear? - why doesn't she answer?"

"She's wearing ear plugs," I said. "You have to slap her to get her attention."

"Oh!" He looked a bit sheepish. "May I do it, then, if it's really OK?"

"Sure," I said.

He slapped her bottom and she jumped. She turned round to face us, dropped to her knees - with arms folded behind the back that is quite a difficult thing to do with as much grace as she achieved - and raised her head.

"Remove the hood, Tom."

Her eyes widened when she saw him, but there was nothing she could do about it. I unbuckled her belt and pressed it to those succulent full red lips of hers and she kissed it, I had taught her to do this with real feeling, then she struggled to her feet again and bent over the stool straight legged, her arms secured high up behind her back. I use a low stool to emphasise this position. It is all routine, we use it several times a week, I suppose, occasionally she waits like that whilst

219

I go down to the pub, but to Tom it was something new.

I handed him the belt. "Ask her how many she thinks it should be, and, if you don't mind, get on with it. I'll be back in a few minutes, just something I have to do." I wrote a figure on a piece of paper, seven. "That's how many I reckon she's due. If she says anything less, give her three times what she says instead of this."

"I say," he said. "Good game, what?" He seemed to have forgotten all his reservations. "Then, before I start, do I tell her how many it's going to be?"

"Up to you."

"I say, this is fun."

"You really don't mind then?"

"Not at all, old boy, not at all. If it really is for her own good, well then I may as well do it."

"You don't need to leave her in that position," I said. "Just tell her what you want her to do. Over your lap, if you want."

"I say, really?"

I took her ear-plugs out as he patted his knee and licked his lips when Erica came over it. "Well miss, how many?"

"S-six please, Uncle Tom."

"Ah-ha!"

I decided to leave him to it and went in the garden to enjoy the sunshine and the flowers and have a smoke. I wanted him happy. He had some very useful expert knowledge. Weasels like him sometimes do.

Erica looked pretty good on the front lawn, wearing the wings. They went across her shoulders with a hole for her head, and she held them up with hand grips Tom had built into them. He had placed these perfectly, so that her arms were fully outstretched. A flying suit could be designed but at present nakedness was an advantage, good desensitization and we could see the fit exactly. Tom didn't seem to mind: he was becoming conditioned to Erica, I think.

He had brought two other things - a belt with batteries and an aerial at the back and four little valves, two at the front and two behind. These, I discovered later, are called servos. The battery was nickel cadmium, it seemed. The control unit, he boasted, could operate eight servos, if need be.

His hands were shaking as he strapped the belt round her slim waist.

Two of the servos were just below her breasts and little pins stuck out from them, ending in pads.

She had put her nipple rings in, and he fastened the back servos to them with thin cord that threaded over her shoulders, through the wings.

"Is that comfortable?" he asked.

She opened her mouth, the glanced at me. "Yes thank you, Uncle Tom."

"Do you really want to do this? You did say nipple guides were OK?"

She hesitated again, but not when I frowned. That usually suffices, these days. "Yes, Uncle Tom," she said, rather quietly but good as gold.

"Right then. These pads will press up against your breasts to tell you which way to turn, and the cords to your nipples will tighten to indicate bank - that is when you lean to that side, the harder the pull the more you lean." He turned to me. "We're ready, I think. Here, on the lawn, then? Is it smooth enough or should we take those ballet shoes off?"

"Let's try with them on," I said. "She'll go slower but look nicer. We could start like that and take them off for a zoom round later."

"Oh, I agree," said Tom. "Let's keep them on for now." He winked at me. "We can stay on grass in case she falls, it's quite soft I expect."

"Shouldn't we blindfold her?" I asked. "And put the earplugs in? Otherwise we won't know we're really steering her properly."

"Brilliant!" I put the ear-plugs back and he tied his disgusting handkerchief round her eyes, slapped her bottom and off she went.

"I see there's a charity show in the park next week," I said. "Shall we fly her then? A display of blindfold flying?"

"Well -"

"In a leotard, of course. And for engine noise, we could fit a microphone and a little loudspeaker, perhaps?"

"Brilliant!"

3-5

The night before the show, Erica and I spent a pleasant evening playing monopoly and watching television. She was wearing a tight jumper and jeans. She has a trim waist and looks good like that, and has a great wiggle when she walks, partly due to the cord I had her stitch inside the jeans, so that pulling them on tightens it under the crotch. They were a bit holey at the back, because if I thought her deportment was still not good enough I would cut a piece out of their bottoms, so now they made quite a pleasant change from short skirts or dresses.

At nine o'clock I reminded her of the big day tomorrow, pushed her ear-plugs firmly in, and, after a short prayer for success tomorrow, sent her off to bed. She had been frightened by hooting owls and other country noises when she first came, and ear-plugs save her from that.

It was a couple of hours before I followed. She was sleeping in the prescribed way: lying on her stomach, half under the bedclothes, head towards the foot of the bed. Before burrowing under she had put her arms behind her back and snapped the wrist bands to the opposite arm bands. The reason for making her secure her arms behind her back was to stop her playing with herself, as I had once caught her doing. I didn't want to have to punish her again for that, as I would have had to be very severe. Her bottom was exposed, the rest of her was under the covers, face down and in darkness. I had taken a lot of trouble in training her to do it right, to cure her of her fear of the dark.

She had taken off the broad belt when she undressed, and as always it lay invitingly to hand on the bedside table.

She was due for six strokes, according to my black book, and I thought it best to get that over with: if you don't keep up the punishment on a day to day basis it tends to mount up. She is never quite easy in her mind after a few days.

If she was asleep - and I know she tends not to sleep until after I come up myself - the first stroke woke her, for the bedclothes heaved and her exposed buttocks twitched in expectation. I gave her the rest at intervals, getting undressed and cleaning my teeth etcetera in between. She was still tense when I had finished, not knowing if there were more to come. Sometimes I add a few more than she is expecting, she wriggles so nicely.

I climbed into bed, and at once her tongue sort out my feet. She seems to think this makes it less likely I will get out to resume the punishment.

I wanted to read that night, so I pulled one of her legs over me. At once she wriggled into the position she knows I favour, sticking up her buttocks to make a book rest, her legs going beneath my arms, her head conveniently between my legs. Placed like this she is able to kiss, lick and suck, and lack of effort is easily cured by a pinch or two, or a slap. I had managed to overcome her childhood hang-ups sufficiently to allow her to suck me off - after, I have to say, some pretty prolonged beatings - but, however hard she tried not to, she always resisted the sex act. Her wriggling and squirming made it seem like rape every time, so I did it more often, because she struggled enough to make it really exciting but did not dare bite or anything like that.

223

Even just touching Erica is very enjoyable. When I caress her buttocks she shrinks away - she still tries to avoid my touch, although of course she doesn't dare take it further than that.

I had had a couple of glasses of wine and I must have dozed off, because when I woke it was morning and she was still there. Asleep of course, but a slap soon set her tongue going again.

It was a fine day. We should have a good crowd for our little display.

I sent her to draw the curtains. Standing by the window still causes Erica problems of embarrassment, although there is nobody out there, except maybe the gardener or two, and in any case I keep her naked so much you'd think she would have been over it years ago.

Then I had her come back to bed for a cosy little cuddle. I like the way she tries to lick me all the time.

We had a dressing tent in the park where the display was to be. It provided reasonable privacy, though some teenage lads had seen Erica go in and became quite a nuisance.

For this public display, we had to be very careful about her dress. The blindfold was no problem, of course, for that was our gimmick, that she could fly blindfold. For this we used a small black domino mask with no eye-holes. We decided not to use ear-plugs - it would be nice for her to hear the applause her display was sure to merit.

She wore a rather fetching little cap with the aerial discretely attached, and gym shoes and socks instead of the ballet shoes, which we thought it best to reserve for private performances. Her only other clothing was a leotard. Unfortunately it had become a couple of sizes too small for her, and, of course, had to stretch over the receiving belt with the servos and other stuff on it. We had tried this out, and found that a sash hid the bulge caused by these controls. The disadvantage of the leotard was that every time she banked it slipped a little, so that before long her buttocks would be rather exposed. However, we doubted if anyone would mind too much.

We had fitted a miniature microphone and amplification equipment to her. It wasn't very elegant but neither was it very obtrusive.

The tent was on a little rise in the ground, so we would fly her from there. I would make the announcement over her microphone and then she would be off.

At last it was time to fix her wings, and then to start.

"Ladies and gentlemen," I announced, "here is Miss Erica! She is about to do her world famous impression of a fighting aircraft! Please notice that she is blindfolded and will remain so throughout the performance!" There was some disbelieving jeering when they saw her mask. "See," I improvised, "I tie this handkerchief over her mask! Now do you all believe me? Well, she will come amongst you, close enough for you to see that she cannot use her eyes! She has psychic powers! It is the wonder of the age! She can even loop the loop!"

I gave her a push and heard her start humming, her imitation of an aircraft engine. The microphone picked it up nicely. Tom was at the controls. He thoroughly enjoyed himself, zooming her in and out amongst families sitting and picnicking. Applause increased as he put her into banking manoeuvres and the material of the leotard tightened back from her trim bottom. Is it trim or plump? I often wonder. It seems strange, but actually she has a rather special bottom, both trim and plump, and certainly it is eminently spankable.

The first loop-the-loop was a highlight. At practice, she had found it hard to somersault with the wings, but we had got it in the end. But this time, unfortunately, she ended up on her back, wings spread, legs kicking in the air. There was a roar of approval as some kind gentleman went to help her

225

to her feet. Exactly what he did I don't know, but when she set off again there was an even greater roar from the crowd.

The leotard had totally split and retreated towards her waist!

She may have felt a bit exposed, but the whistles from the crowd should have been reward enough. It was a pity we hadn't brought anything for her to change into, though. I found walking back through the crowds afterwards quite an ordeal, because of her squealing when the youths touched her up, and her inability to keep up with us. In the end I gagged her and we walked ahead, leaving her to follow at her leisure.

6

Noisy though the bar was that night - Susi was getting it harder and longer even than usual at that particular moment - there was almost a hush as I walked in, followed at a respectable distance by Erica. Erica and I were well known there by now, and were, I think, always welcome.

Erica always seems to shrink from exposure to the hot eyes and eager fingers of the customers, although, as I have explained to the other regulars, such exposure is good for her, and the main reason I dress her as I do, in so provocative a fashion.

The desensitisation was not working too well, but it was early days yet, and in any case I have every intention of persevering with the treatment until I succeed.

Anyway, I took a seat at one of the little tables in the middle of the floor and Erica, as I had bid her, walked to the bar. I say 'walked to the bar', but that is an extremely inadequate way of describing her extremely erotic and much appreciated progress, which drew whistles even from that almost satiated crowd.

In addition to the broad red leather belt with the snake clasp which she always wears - in case I wish to use it on her - she had nothing but her usual very high heeled shoes, from which the heels had been removed, and a short skirt and a very tight jersey which showed off her neat but adequate breasts to perfection, especially as there were holes in it for the nipples, from which little silver bells dangled from brass rings shaped like snakes with their tails in their mouths. Her head was held high, because a few strands of her long thick auburn hair were clipped at the back to a collar round her neck, shaped like a coiled golden snake - clipped in such a way as to keep her very straight all the time.

Yes, her posture was extremely upright, and she progressed like a soldier, hands rigidly at her sides. Her walk was not just upright, it was erotic in the way she seemed to sway and wriggle as she walked. The regulars knew from past experience that this would be due to a rough twine cord fastened inside the skirt in such a way as to cut tightly into the crotch, something that I like to do, always did for all they knew.

I was aware that there is speculation about our private life. Perhaps she had pyjamas like that? Or does she have a very shortie night-dress, down to the hips perhaps? If anything? Maybe, though, they wonder, a cord round the waist with an extension knotted between the legs, just to be consistent? Probably Rex really likes that wiggle it gave all her movements, they would be thinking - they themselves certainly appeared to!

They did know that when I sent her to our bed whilst I had a final cigar and a glass of brandy I made her burrow in head first, with the bed-clothes turned down to her waist, so that I could easily wake her up with the belt she would have taken off and left beside the big double bed.

Let them speculate. I am fortified by the knowledge that everything I do to this poor soul is done as part of my divine mission firstly to purge her of certain very grave sins she has committed and secondly to relieve her of her hang-ups by the well researched medical procedure known as systematic desensitization.

She was barefoot and had no stockings that night. Her lips were parted - as was the convention here - and they were full and very red, but not very much made up. Her eyes were blue, just a little eye shadow, and at that moment there were tears of embarrassment in them as hands reached out to stroke her beautiful smooth skin and pat her swaying bottom as she passed among the tightly set tables. She kept her own hands at her sides and did not try to do more than veer away from the many others that reached out to her, but her agitation was clear from the way her fists were tightly clenched, the knuckles white.

Her arms were bare and she had the usual snake upper arm and thigh ornamentation - golden snake jewellery twisting round them, that is - and ankle and wrist bangles also. These items are all very well done, very realistic, the snakes hissing with red eyes and their fangs and tongue showing, somewhat similar to her large ear rings. She thinks the tongue is a sting. It is all part of the therapy, fear of snakes being one of the most intractable outrages I am treating.

"Yes, my dear?" smirked Stephen, eyeing her up and down, as well he might. A raised slipper was in his beefy right hand and with his left he pinned poor Susi, his bar maid, to the top of the bar before him, face down, quietly sobbing, her pathetic little skirt turned up to expose her squirming plump bare bottom, quite red already, clenching and unclenching and quivering nicely as she waited for whatever she was about to receive. Now there is a bottom that really is plump, my friends, enticingly plump, one that Stephen cannot resist slapping, slippering, strapping or belting at every possible moment. He seldom whips her, he thinks too much of that would spoil the object of his adoration.

228

"A glass of white wine please," Erica said in that unintentionally sexy voice of hers, slightly husky.

"Just a moment, my dear, can't you see I'm busy?"

Stephen stroked Susi's flinching bottom for a while, and there came a couple more good slaps of slipper leather on squirming flesh before he turned back to Erica. "A glass of white wine is four pounds fifty."

All his prices are already somewhat exaggerated and keep going up, but the circumstances justify that. People who don't drink what he considers sufficient are not welcome.

"It's to go on Uncle Rex's account."

Stephen looked at her in a way that made her obviously very uneasy, all the time stroking Susi's rosy bottom with the slipper. Susi started to whimper, not that that was unusual. "I think you'd better go back and check that Mr Saviour accepts the price," Stephen said, tapping Susi's bottom, the signal that a big one was coming, and then raising the slipper.

Erica hesitated, shivering a little, her gaze travelling over the room. Then she set out back to my table, her hands still rigidly at her sides, fists clenched, going as fast as she was allowed, dead slow.

Stephen lowered the slipper, caressed Susi's flinching bottom with it, then changed it for a heavier one from the shelf behind him, something she always listened for, and brought it down hard. Susi squealed pitifully. As usual she was begging for mercy, but of course nobody ever took any notice of that. Her hands were over her face, hiding her eyes, but perhaps she could anticipate the blows, for her cringing bottom seemed to shrink away just before they arrived. Perhaps the wind of the slipper just preceded its arrival. Anyway, she was to receive several more blows before Erica returned, and she made the usual fuss about it, which only encouraged further abuse. Stephen was in full flow that night, having already absorbed a whisky or two, which always stimulated him to greater efforts in regard to Susi.

At last Erica swayed and squeezed her way back through the men lining the bar, her cute little face red and flushed, tears almost overflowing, hands still clenched at her sides.

"Well, my dear?"

"Uncle Rex says that's rather a lot."

"Does he indeed?" Stephen changed to an even heavier slipper and Susi began to howl under his heavier blows. She knew that tone of voice.

"But he says OK, but it must be properly chilled, he said, he said I was to say properly chilled."

"PROPERLY" - slap - "CHILLED" - slap - "INDEED!"

The slipper came down on Susi's bare flesh again and again with resounding thwacks. There was absolute silence in the room when he paused, apart from Susi's heaving sobs and useless pleas, show me mercy just this once, just this once, oh please please please ...

"Yes, he said properly chilled or he'll be angry with me."

"DO" - slap - "YOU" - slap "DARE" - slap - "TO" - slap "INSULT" - slap - ME?"

"No, no, but Uncle Rex said it must b-be - p-properly ch-chilled - THIS TIME, he said."

"THIS TIME?"

Stephen was thoroughly outraged now, and Susi shrieked and wriggled, clutched at her bottom in agony and falling off the bar at last as her contortions became extreme. No wonder. He had vented his fury in a sustained assault of the hardest possible blows.

She sprawled on the floor in front of the bar, obviously scared out of her wits as he glared down at her, almost snarling. Then he leant over and seized her by the hair, hauled her up and stood her like a doll on the bar, still holding her by the hair.

"Did you see that?" he called out to his clients in genuine amazement. "She rolled away! Deliberately! She used her hands! What the hell are things coming to? That means a strapping!"

"Oh no, oh no, oh no!" shrieked Susi.

"Right now," shouted Stephen, outrage in his voice. He shook her. "You've got it coming to you, my girl, my God you have!"

"Oh no -"

"You know what that means, don't you?"

"Oh yes yes, the whipping frame, but please not, I can't stand it, not again ..."

Susi was crying as we had never seen her before, absolutely sobbing her heart out. Evidently whatever had happened before had been pretty unpleasant.

"FETCH IT!" he said.

"Oh no ..."

"FETCH IT! NOW!"

"Oh no ... not in public ... not in front of all these people ..."

Stephen just glared at her, and then as she slunk despairingly away, her head in her hands, he turned back to Erica.

"All my white wine is properly chilled," he said, his good humour restored. He poured a glass and held it out to her, swirling the yellow liquid round in it lovingly. "Tell him that!"

"Thank you, Uncle Stephen." She stood there like a statue, rooted to the ground, her eyes on the glass, her hand still rigidly at her side. Then, slowly, she lifted them to take the glass and a gasp went round the bar - the hem of her skirt was attached to them.

Stephen pulled back his hand and grinned. "I'll put it on a tray for you," he said.

Her passage back to serve me with the wine and then stand behind my chair can well be imagined, and she wasn't neglected as she stood there - everyone wanted a closer look, maybe to feel how smooth she was as I sipped my wine. But then came an even greater distraction - the emergence of

231

Susi from some back room, a heavy short handled strap in her teeth, naked now, dragging a whipping frame.

"On the stage," said Stephen - there is a small stage at one end of the room, once used for bands, now sometimes for more interesting events.

Susi, encouraged all the way by the patrons, managed to get the frame close to the stage, but, try as she might, she could not raise it the two feet or so required to finish the job.

"Never mind," said Stephen from behind the bar. "Push it aside -" He waited until it was in a position that gave a clear view of the stage. "Now, up with you."

Susi climbed onto the stage. She too is kept shaven, and she stood with her drooping shoulders and head bowed, half covered by the abundant golden hair that fell forward over it, and her hands clasped at her crotch, legs tightly together, sobbing freely.

"Enough of that!" shouted Stephen from the bar. "Get on the drum." That was a little raised bit in the middle of the stage, and after she had scrambled up onto it she was maybe another eighteen inches higher, now fully visible from all over the room, and a pitiful sight she made.

"Now," shouted Stephen, "wait the way I taught you last time!"

Immediately she took a new position, shaking her head to send those golden tresses down her back then standing very straight with legs astride and toes turned slightly in. Then she clasped her hands behind her neck and pushed her chest out. The strap was still in her nice even white teeth. It was a wicked looking appliance, with its decorated handle. Judging by Susi's expression she knew exactly how it felt as well as how it looked. Doubtless her present obedience to Stephen resulted from the frequent application of it after closing time. And the idea of them in bed together didn't bear thinking about - he was at least twice her size.

She shut her eyes and tears came trickling from their

corners.

"Eyes open!" shouted Stephen.

Susi opened her eyes and looked round the room. Then she started to scream and the strap fell to the floor at her feet.

"Stop that noise," shouted Stephen, "or I'll double the punishment!"

The screams stopped, to be replaced by that familiar whimpering sound, but this time loud enough for everyone to hear.

Stephen walked over to the stage and twitched the curtains, adjusting them to his satisfaction. He is quite artistic, as the original show of photographs prove. Then he switched on some spot lights and adjusted Susi's position slightly before dimming the lights in the rest of the room.

He picked up the heavy leather strap and swished it into the palm of his other hand a couple of times, then stroked her with it. We saw Susi flinch, but although her flesh seemed to shrink away from its touch she held her pose.

"Hands out," he said. Everyone thought she was about to receive a strapping on the palms of the hands, but what he actually did was place the strap into her hands.

"Hold this above your head ... higher ... brace up, girl ... hold the strap taut, that's it, arms as wide as you can, well back over your head, that's good. Legs a bit wider. Now - TIPTOES! If you move a muscle the punishment is doubled, OK?"

She was like a statue now, blatantly displayed, hands up in the air pulling the strap taut, breasts thrust out one way, plump little buttocks the other, tears streaming down her face although no one had touched her yet.

Satisfied at last, he turned to us. "Anyone like to use the strap on her?" he asked.

There was an eager chorus of acceptance.

He held up a protesting hand. "You can't all," he said,

"not tonight, that wouldn't be fair. Why don't I sell tickets? Yes, let's say three tickets, each good for five strokes. Fifteen strokes, Susi, do you hear? Unless you move, of course, you better not move, my dear, because twice fifteen is thirty!"

She trembled but said nothing, concentrating on keeping her balance.

"I'll auction the tickets," said Stephen, after a moment's contemplation, "then we can draw for precedence."

It was a popular decision, as the applause showed.

"Tell her to turn round," someone shouted. "Let's see her bum."

"Yes," shouted another, "don't hide the target area. Make her keep turning round."

"But she mustn't move," Stephen responded. "If I tell her to move I lose the chance of selling more tickets. Oh no! I can do better than that. Watch this."

He pressed a button behind the bar, and the little drum upon the stage started to revolve slowly. It wasn't long before the target was nicely presented, seeming to shiver and flinch all the time, no doubt finding it harder to stay still as she was carried round and round before us.

There was spontaneous applause.

"There!" said Stephen. "A tempting sight, is it not? Should be a good spectacle, five strokes gives one a good chance to warm up and three fresh arms should really get her singing! The bidding better be good! But first, anyone need more drinks?"

There was quite a rush. It must have kept him busy for several minutes whilst Susi, neglected, revolved under the spotlights, strained and stretched and taut and still, and entertained us with her rather appealing little whimpers.

When things settled down a little, Stephen conducted his auction. Each of the tickets went for over a hundred pounds.

"We must do this more often!" he grinned, rubbing his hands as he thought of his bank balance. He knows when he is on a winner, does our Stephen.

Next the tickets were to go into a hat, and Erica was called over to draw them out. The tickets didn't actually go in a hat, as Erica didn't have one - she had to take her skirt off to make a bag for them. Erica's skirts are all the same - a single piece of thin material wrapped round her waist and fastened by press studs onto a piece of webbing that holds the under-crutch cord. I always keep the webbing in place, so undressing is just a matter of unsnapping the studs, or a change in colour or length is only a matter of tearing off one piece of material and substituting another. The material overlapped, or perhaps met is a more accurate term, in the middle of the back. On a windy day it is more interesting to walk behind Erica, so I usually send her ahead of me. It is not only the cheeky views but also her very upright walk and unusual squirming sort of sway.

She drew the tickets out in the order two one three. This led to an argument between the lucky holders of one and two, in the course of which the skirt she had used as a bag got somewhat torn apart.

It boded well for the spectacle that was to come that one of the ticket holders was a particularly big and burly fellow and one a woman known to be extremely vicious in her treatment of any unfortunate in her power, specially other women, specially luscious ones like Susi. The burly man, holding the winning ticket, was particularly outstanding, as could be seen when he took off his jacket and gleefully rolled up his shirt sleeve.

Stephen led them over towards their victim, who by some miracle had managed to keep absolutely still all this time.

They must have been quite a fearsome sight, specially the first man's huge shoulders and bulging muscles as he flexed them and grinned at evilly.

That is when she cracked.

She jumped off her little pedestal, screaming, and ran

the for door, her long blonde hair streaming behind her.

The door was locked, of course, to stop strangers coming in.

Stephen took the key out of his pocket and waved it in her face as she beat her fists on the unyielding wood, then seized her by the hair and dragged her towards the stage, where the others helped him to secure her frantically struggling figure, slippery in its nakedness, to the frame.

In an instant the frame was hoisted onto the stage with her in it, and fixed in the place formerly occupied by the little revolving drum, so that it too could revolve to display its contents, Susi bound there, naked and ashamed.

Her wrists were tied to the two ends of the upper bar and her ankles to the uprights, so that she was beautifully spread-eagle, spread-eagle upright that is, and absolutely helpless as well as blatantly displayed in all her curvy lushness. There was just enough play in her bonds to allow her body to thresh about wildly, and she continued to scream until Stephen thrust a gag into her mouth, after which nothing but little bubbles came from her mouth.

"Well," said Stephen, "she didn't keep still, did she?"

"No!" came the replies.

"Another three tickets?" asked Stephen.

"Yes, yes, yes!" came the eager response.

So, standing beside the still uselessly struggling girl in the frame, Stephen auctioned another three tickets, and Erica was called forward once again to volunteer the tatters of her skirt to hold the tickets. The draw was successful, but in the process the skirt somehow vanished. I am sometimes asked how I got a bare-arsed Erica home, but that is another story. Although it is quite nippy outside, sleet and all that, what you might call unseasonable, she certainly didn't have a coat, I don't permit her such a thing. I once took her into town when it was snowing and she didn't have one then, just the same tight sleeveless jersey and thin skirt as she was wearing at the pub that night, so why bother with one at all? It isn't as if I take her to football matches. At least I haven't done so far, but it's a thought.

Stephen was obviously gloating over his bank balance once more, and inspiration glowed in his greedy eyes.

"In future," he announced, "the first Friday in every month will be Susi's flogging evening, and a minimum of six five-stroke tickets will be auctioned. That'll teach the wretched girl to run like that! I'll not be having it!" He turned and stared into her horror struck blue eyes. "Yes, it's you I'm talking about, my girl! I'll not tolerate disobedience like that, do you understand? And if there's any more trouble the number of tickets will be doubled again, doubled again do you hear?"

"Wouldn't she look nice if we oiled her body?" some genius suggested.

"And rouged her nipples," another added.

"And gilded her cunt lips!"

"You'll be wanting to paint her finger nails next!" next Stephen. But he was not displeased. He found some oil and rouge and Erica was deputed to get on with the job. There wasn't any gold paint, so Erica had to use a little lipstick there too. She, Erica that is, looked really cute in just that tight jumper, but unfortunately a couple of young fellows took over the job before we had had a really good sight of her. Still, the way Susi's wriggles increased made up for it.

"Shall I leave her gag in or take it out before we start?" asked Stephen. "Tell you what, I'll take it out for now and we'll see how we go. Erica dear, if you would oblige?"

Erica climbed onto the stage again and stretched up to reach Susi's mouth, walking round as the drum revolved. Not an easy job. It became obvious that the cord between her legs was doubled up and very tight, though it did slide around a little. I received quite a few compliments later, and it became quite the thing to twang it.

Susi began pleading for mercy as soon as the gag was out of her mouth. She is pretty good at this, having had so much practice, though you'd think she'd have learnt to save her breath by now. Mercy was not ever to be had, and she must have known that perfectly well. Maybe it was to stop herself from whimpering, because Stephen often increases her punishment on account of that, but doesn't seem to mind the pleading so much.

"Well," said Stephen, "I'll take orders for a few minutes, then the first contestant can get cracking."

"Contestant?" someone queried.

"I thought we'd vote," said Stephen, "on vigour and style and so forth, who can get the best response out of her, what?"

"I suppose you'll be giving a prize then?" someone laughed.

Stephen was somewhat taken aback, but quickly rallied. "Certainly," he said. "An extra five strokes for the winner - the winner to be judged by volume and duration of applause. Judged by me, that is. I'll say how many points I've awarded out of ten. Ten minute interval between contestants, I think, to allow her bottom to cool off a little. We don't want to make it too easy for the later contestants."

That would encourage more drinking as well. He was a good Landlord, Stephen, always with an eye to business.

A few minutes later, after everyone had recharged their glass and pulled their chairs up to the stage, Stephen heaved himself onto it and held up a hand for hush.

"Will the first contestant step up?" he said.

The very burly man with rolled up sleeves and the muscles came forward. We now saw that he also had tattoos on his arms and hairy chest, your typical docker one would have thought. Or maybe an all-in wrestler. As soon as she saw him coming, Susi, broke into a despairing wail.

Sorry folks, that's all we have room for. Continues from here next month

OUT OF PRINT TITLES

All titles (including above) are available plain text on
floppy disc
£5 or $8.50 postage inclusive
(PC format unless Mac requested)

All our in-print titles (listed overleaf) can be ordered from
any bookshop in the UK and an increasing number in the
USA and Australia by quoting the title and ISBN, or directly
from us by post. Credit cards show as EBS (Electronic Book
Services - £ converted to $ and back!): Price of book (see
over) plus postage and packing UK £2 first book then £1.30
each; Europe £3.50 then £2; USA $6 then $4. Please make
US cheques payable to Silver Moon Books Inc.

DON'T MISS OUR WEB SITES
http://www.silvermoon.co.uk
http://www.silvermoonbooks.com
http://www.thebookshops.com/silver

All the news we don't have room for here

Contact other readers

Free extracts to download - and an electronic bookshop

Silver Moon

Silver Mink

UK £4.99 except *£5.99 --USA $8.95 except *$9.95